THE RETURN

The Eternity Road book 2

LANA MELYAN

Copyright © 2018 Lana Melyan
All rights reserved. No part of this book may be used or reproduced in any manner whatsoever without written permission except in the case of brief quotations embodied in critical articles and reviews.
This is a work of fiction. Names, characters, places, and incidents are products of the author's imagination or are used fictitiously and are not to be construed as real. Any resemblance to actual locales, events, or persons living or dead is entirely coincidental.

Lana Melyan

www.lanamelyan.com

Chapter One

"OH GOD, CRAIG," she whispered into his ear, hugging him tighter.

"Eleanor." Craig breathed out. "It's you . . . it's . . ." His voice broke. It was her, his Eleanor. He was holding her in his arms, feeling the warmth of her body, and it wasn't just one of those dreams he'd been having for the past century and a half. It was real. "Are you all right? Do you remember?"

"I do." She let go of him. "It's coming back." Her eyes teared up as she said it.

Craig wanted to comfort her. He tried to remember all he had thought he would say to her. Things that were supposed to sustain her, help her through this surreal transformation. But he couldn't remember any of them now.

The reason for his sudden muteness was probably imprinted on his face, because Eleanor smiled weakly and said, "Craig, I'm fine."

"Are you sure?" he asked, wiping a single tear from her cheek with his thumb.

"Yeah." Eleanor nodded, then looked away. She walked to the

open balcony door, pushed aside the swaying lace curtain, and stepped out.

Craig waited for a moment before following her. He had spent so many years trying to imagine what she'd feel the moment she realized she was back, the moment she saw him. Suddenly, this one thought blocked all the others. It was a question, which had never occurred to him before––would he be the same Craig to her?

The orange glow radiating from the tip of the rising sun looked like a beacon fire behind the foaming waves.

"We are in the castle," she said.

She was in shock, he could tell.

"Yes."

"How long was I asleep?"

Her voice grew distant with every word.

"Only a night."

"Only a night? Why?"

"Samson said that it wouldn't take long. The Book recognized you, so you didn't have to go through all this . . . I mean, it recognized your soul, it just needed to restore your immortality and give your powers back."

"Samson," she muttered. "Is he here too?"

"Yes. They're all here. Can I let them know?"

She considered for a moment, then nodded.

"Samson," Craig said into nowhere. But wherever Samson was at the moment, he would hear Craig. As the Keeper of the Book, Samson had the special power to speak to Hunters at a distance. He could speak to each of them individually or to all at once.

"Yes," replied Samson, and only Craig could hear his voice.

"She is awake."

There was a moment of silence.

"If she is ready . . . we'll be in the great living room," said Samson.

"They are waiting," Craig said to Eleanor, "Whenever you are . . ." but he stopped. All of them supposed that she'd be confused, and Samson had warned him that it wouldn't be easy, but he couldn't bear her not looking at him. "Eleanor," he called. She turned around. "Eleanor, I missed you so much."

She stepped closer and took his hand.

"I missed you too," she said, but her brown eyes didn't express anything. She closed them and kissed him, a short kiss. "Let's go. I want to see them."

But when she opened the door, she stopped. Her lower lip trembled as she looked back at Craig.

Before he could say anything, she ran out of the room. He ran after her, but when Craig saw her silhouette flash into the hallway, down the stairs, and slip out of the castle door, he didn't follow. He felt stupid and selfish; he shouldn't have tried to discern if she still cared for him before she even knew who she was. The fact that he had finally gotten her back had fogged his mind, and for a second he forgot she was the one with millions of questions.

Craig went to the hall and sat on the stairs facing the castle's front door. She needed some space, and he'd give her as much time as she needed, wait as long as it took, but he wanted to be there for her when she came back.

∼

SHE KNEELED on the grass under one of the trees behind the castle.

When she woke up in the bedroom, she realized that she was Eleanor from one flash in her memory. She remembered the church. She remembered running down the altar stairs with the Book in her hands, Fray's wild scream, the last, desperate look at Craig's face, and the iron teeth, like arrows, coming out from the Book's clasps, piercing her hands.

Now, the recollections of her previous life rushed in, flooding her with emotions. Her mind gave her a tour into her past, and scenes, one after another, flickered like a movie put in quick reverse. Her last kiss with Craig in the barn. Her conversation with Samson, when he told her that she was the one who had to close the Book. Gabriella's funeral. Hanna's wide eyes fixed upon Gabriella's body, lying on the floor covered in broken glass, and the ball in Paris. The hunts. Her whole happy life with Craig. And then further and deeper into her past, or rather--the beginning. Waking up in the castle as a Hunter. Giving birth to Margaret. The lodge and her first kiss with Craig. The day she met Craig and watched him fight the werewolf. Her husband, Richard. Her previous mother and father.

This last memory abruptly snapped her back to reality. Lindsey. She shook her head. How was she going to explain to him that she was not the daughter he raised, that another person lived inside her? She felt the warmth of the blood rushing through her veins, the strength filling up her body. She couldn't hide it from him. Sooner or later he'd realize something wasn't right. Not because she'd never get sick, but because one day he'd notice she was not aging. She'd always look like the Amanda that turned eighteen a week ago.

She remembered her birthday cake and the wish she'd made when she blew out the candles. She'd wished that Craig would finally notice her. No, she'd never be that careless girl, whose biggest problem was her unrequited love, again. Empty houses in her dreams wouldn't scare her anymore.

She remembered the old, dilapidated house, the fountain with the statue of a baby cherub, and her eyes prickled. That had been her house! Eleanor couldn't believe it was still there. And the Book. It was there, too, in the library. Why?

She looked up at the clear sky, then at the grass, covered with morning dew. She turned her gaze to the small wooden bridge leading to Gabriella's garden. Everything was so well maintained that it looked almost the same, except for the trees, which were much taller now.

Pain cramped her chest. More than a hundred and sixty years

stood between Eleanor and Amanda. Those years were a big sacrifice, not just for her, but for all of them. Had it worked? She was certain that the vampires Fray turned hadn't woken up. But now, with the Book open, they sure would. Had Samson found a way to prevent it? She stood up, brushed off the pieces of grass from her dew-soaked jeans, and headed back to the castle.

~

THE SUN WAS RISING, and the yellow light from the lamp on Samson's desk faded more and more with each minute. The rays of sunshine hadn't reached the window yet, and as he turned the lamp off, the room dimmed.

Samson had spent the night writing down the latest events in his journal—how the Book was opened, Melinda's death, Eleanor's return. He had never kept a journal before. But after they started looking for those turned by Fray and now transitioning vampires, looking for the Book and the daggers Fray had stolen all those years ago, it seemed important to Samson to keep a record of all their efforts.

He heard footsteps in the hallway. The door opened, and Hanna walked in.

"Eleanor... she ran out," said Hanna, worried.

"I know," said Samson. He glanced at her slumped shoulders, at her weary face after the restless night, and stood up. "Come here," he said, pulling her into his arms.

"Do you think she'll be okay?" asked Hanna, resting her head on his chest.

"I am sure of it. She just needs some time." Samson stroked her dark blonde curls collected in a low ponytail. "You waited so long for this day. You should be glowing now."

"I am happy." She pulled back and looked up at Samson. "But ... it was her, Eleanor, next to me for three years. And now, when I think back . . ." There was a note of horror in her low voice as she said, "I almost lost her. Twice."

Samson knew what Hanna meant. A few days ago, vampires had grabbed her and Amanda right in front of their house. They were saved by Riley, who showed up at the last minute. The second time was the previous night, when Amanda ran away with Alec. Alec spared Amanda, but if the Hunters hadn't found her in time, Fray would have killed her himself.

"Your panic attack is a little belated," Samson smiled. "Besides, it wasn't an easy task, and you did a great job. She is here, isn't she?"

"Right." Hanna sighed. "You know what? Now that I've said it to you, I feel better." She stood on her toes to reach his face and kissed him on the cheek. "Thank you."

"Hanna," Samson called as she headed to the door. Hanna turned around. "I wanted to ask you about Kimberly. What do you think we should do about her?"

"Nothing. She's my friend, and I trust her." Hanna grinned. "And I think you're asking the wrong person. You should ask Ruben."

"I'm asking you because Ruben was always . . ." Samson hesitated. "He never brought anyone to the castle before. Do you think this might be serious?"

"I think it is," said Hanna softly. "I think he is in love."

Ruben had been alone for such a long time. Samson hoped it was true, that he'd found the one he was looking for.

As Hanna walked out, Samson went back to his desk and sat down. He picked up a picture in a small wooden frame. Behind its glass, Gabriella looked at him with her black eyes full of love. From the moment he'd met her, he couldn't imagine a day without that look.

He wasn't the only one who'd lost the love of his life. He'd watched Craig endure his pain all those years, and all those years

Samson had to live with the fact that he was the one who signed Eleanor's death sentence.

Today was a big day. Eleanor had returned, and the Book was open. This meant that it was time to get back everything Samson had lost.

Everything, except her. He'd never be able to bring back Gabriella. She was gone forever. She was the light of his life, and nothing could live without light. All he could do was make sure no one in his family ever suffered such loss. His plan was ready, and he had to make it work, no matter what.

Chapter Two

ELEANOR WALKED into the living room holding Craig's hand. Everybody stood up. Seven pairs of eyes were fixed on her. She didn't look at anyone but Samson.

"Hello, Eleanor," said Samson.

She knew that Samson couldn't change, that it would be the same Samson only with different, modern clothes. But she didn't expect that the pain she left him with would still be there, too. After all those years, even in this very significant moment, which he had been waiting for more than one and a half centuries, his eyes were still extinguished. It made him look older.

"I am sorry," he said, "Your return took much longer than I anticipated."

"You don't have to apologize," said Eleanor. "You never said that it'd be quick and harmless. I remember what I signed up for." The sound of her voice surprised her. It wasn't Amanda speaking. Her voice was firm. It didn't belong to that easily blushing girl she was yesterday. Eleanor's strong, confident consciousness was taking over. "I suppose it was a lot worse for you all. Waiting is much more difficult. I hope that my death, and what you had to go through, wasn't for nothing. Is the Book safe?"

There was a profound silence.

"No," Samson said finally.

"What?" She turned to Craig. "But it was there, in the library. And you had your powers back." She looked at Riley, then at Ruben, then at Hanna and Ned. "What happened?" Something drew her attention back to Ruben, something that seemed to be out of place. "Kimberly, what are you doing here?"

Taken aback, Kimberly shrugged childishly and looked up at Ruben, standing beside her.

"She knows," said Ruben, "She was there when everything happened. When you opened the Book, remember? After that, Fray showed up with his bloodsuckers..."

At those words, Kimberly's face changed. She looked back at Eleanor like a wounded dog.

"Oh, God, Kimberly," Eleanor rushed to her. "Are you all right?" she asked, pulling her into a hug.

"I don't know yet," Kimberly whispered into her ear. "So much happened."

"Did you get hurt?" Eleanor asked, pulling back.

"No, no. I was in that room with you. Those vampires, they couldn't get in there."

"Wait. Alec, he was there, too. Where is he? Is he okay?" She turned

to Hanna.

Hanna glanced at Samson, then at Craig, then at Eleanor again.

"He is okay," she said.

"For now," said Riley. "He got out in time, or I would have killed him myself."

"What?" Eleanor said, snapping her gaze back to him.

"Melinda sealed the library so that vampires couldn't get inside," said Riley. "We left him and Kimberly there with you and the Book, to keep all of you safe, then we kicked Fray and his leeches out of the house."

"So they didn't take the Book. Then who . . . you mean . . . Alec? Why would he do that?"

But then it hit her. She remembered the picture of the house, and she realised that Alec having it wasn't a coincidence. A moment ago, she was feeling guilty for dragging him to that place. But now it was clear she didn't bring him to that house—*he* brought her there. Everything had been planned. She'd done exactly what Fray expected her to do.

"It's all because of me," she murmured. "It's my fault the Book is gone."

"Eleanor, nobody blames you," said Samson.

"You had no idea what was going on," said Craig. "You were just trying to protect us."

She took a deep breath. "So, what are we going to do? What's the plan?"

"There's something we need to do this afternoon. Then, Craig and I are leaving tonight," said Samson.

"Tonight?" She turned to Craig with a disconcerted look.

Craig nodded. "We have to."

"I'm sorry for taking him away, Eleanor, but it has to be Craig," said Samson.

"This sounds too familiar." She stared at him. "Just promise you'll bring him back alive."

"I promise. You have nothing to worry about," said Samson. "Now, you better rest. You need some time to get back to reality."

Eleanor nodded. Samson was right, she was still so confused.

She looked at Kimberly, the only reminder of Amanda's life, the connection to the mortal world which seemed so different now. The castle was her home, but there was another home in Green Hill, which she loved, too. The thought of Lindsey filled her with longing. She loved him, and she didn't want to hurt him. She would have to go back and pretend to be a normal teenager, at least for a while, for her father's sake.

She glanced around, and her eyes stopped at Hanna. Eleanor

suddenly remembered the first time she saw her, the look on her face when, as Amanda, she held out her hand to her at school. Hanna's look lingered on her like she was expecting some sign of recognition.

"You were with me for three years, and I never noticed. . . How did you do that?" she asked.

"It wasn't that difficult, since I didn't have my powers," said Hanna softly. "Now we have to be more careful."

Eleanor looked at Ruben. And then at Craig. "I am so sorry. All I put you two through. . ." She laid her hand on Craig's chest. Now she knew why his shirt was ripped and covered with blood. He had been stabbed in the heart.

"It was nothing," he said, putting his arms around her. "You're back; that's all that matters."

"And Melinda." She turned around. "She must be so angry with me for running away like that." She smiled guiltily.

But nobody smiled back.

"Judging by the looks on your faces, she really is. Where is she? Did she go home?"

Nobody answered.

A shiver ran down Eleanor's spine. "Where is Melinda?"

"Melinda is dead," said Samson.

"What? How did this happen?"

"Alec killed her," said Riley.

"What have I done?" Eleanor's voice broke. She pressed her hand to her mouth.

"It wasn't your fault," said Samson. "One way or another, you had to come to that place to open the Book. Fray planned to kill you after that. We are lucky he used Alec, who has feelings for you. Otherwise, you would be dead too." Samson's cellphone rang. He walked out to the hallway to answer it.

Hanna stepped to Eleanor, and they hugged. "This time it would ruin me forever if you died," she whispered. "And imagine what would happen to Craig."

Eleanor turned to Craig and looked into his glittering blue eyes.

"Eleanor, you're back, and you are alive," said Hanna.

"Samson is right, I need some time to process everything that happened," she said, wiping away the tears from her cheeks.

"That was Amelia," said Samson as he returned to the room. "The casket is ready. We'll bury Melinda as soon as it's here."

"Where is she?" asked Eleanor.

"Upstairs," Craig replied.

"Take me to her."

They climbed to the third floor and entered one of the rooms. As they passed the threshold, Eleanor stopped. The draft from the open windows pulled aside the silky white cover from the body on the long, wooden table. Melinda was dressed in a black gown, her hands crossed on her chest.

"How did he kill her?" Eleanor asked.

"He stabbed her," said Craig. "Kimberly saw it happen."

"Poor Kimberly. Her eyes . . . she's still in shock." Eleanor moved toward the table but stopped again. "Fray sent Alec to get the Book. It means he trusts him."

"Fray trusted him. He wanted him to kill you. But he underestimated Alec's feelings," said Craig.

"Alec thought . . . I gave him hope. I gave him a reason to think it might work between us," said Eleanor, remembering her last few days with Alec. "Craig, I am sorry, I was—"

"I am glad you did. It saved your life." He walked back to the door. "I'll be in our room."

He closed the door behind him, and she stepped to the table to look at Melinda's peaceful face. In Eleanor's memory, it seemed like only yesterday she stood beside Gabriella's body. How ironic was that? To come back after all this time to face another loss, another sacrifice. For nine years Melinda looked after Amanda. Made sure that she was well fed, neatly dressed, took care of her when she was sick, smiled at her little pranks, teared up at her small achievements. She kept her promise to Amanda's dying mother to stay with her until she turned eighteen. All this time Melinda was probably also hoping that one day Amanda would become Eleanor and had been looking forward to meeting her.

Eleanor put her hand on Melinda's.

"I'm sorry you didn't get to know me as Eleanor," she whispered. "I know I wasn't just an assignment. I know you loved me. I'll miss you so much."

She stood in silence for a long moment, then she kissed Melinda on her forehead and left the room.

When she reached her and Craig's bedroom, she stopped before the open door. Craig was standing in front of the balcony door with his hands folded on his back. He turned around, and they started toward each other. Her body quivered the moment his lips touched hers.

"We don't have much time," whispered Craig.

"Then let's not waste it," she murmured.

His hand closed around Eleanor's waist. Craig lifted her a few inches, and, in a flash, they were laying on the bed. Eleanor's boiling blood pulsed even faster. The heavy thoughts, the room, the castle, the whole world melted away, and there was nothing else but the two of them.

"If your lips had kissed me only once when I was Amanda, I would have recognized them in a second," said Eleanor an hour later. They were still in bed. She kept her eyes closed, lying on her back while Craig's lips wandered around her neck. "Why didn't you kiss me?" she asked, running her fingers through his hair.

"You wouldn't," said Craig. "I mean, you probably would, but you wouldn't know why. I was afraid if my kiss made you feel something like that, the inexplicable sensation would only torment you. Besides, what if it wasn't you? What if it was just one of your great grand-grand-et-cetera granddaughters," Craig grinned before he continued, "who just looked like you?"

"Didn't you know that it was me? Couldn't you feel it?" Eleanor made a serious face and poked him in the ribs.

"I was nearly sure. I felt it the moment I saw you." He took her hand and kissed the poking finger. "That's why I asked Hanna to give you the bracelet. I thought that it might work as a trigger, that if I was right, you'd react to it somehow. And a little while later, you did."

She recalled how she had reached for the bracelet every time she met one of the Hunters.

"But the bracelet... what if it wasn't me?"

"The bracelet would remain in your family and would one day be yours anyway. I was afraid that I might be confused by the familial resemblance. That's why I avoided you until you turned eighteen." He looked into her eyes. "Even then, I missed your eyes so much. But every time you looked into mine, I turned away. I could see I was hurting you. That was the worst part."

Craig's blue irises were glossed with tears. Eleanor rolled him onto his back, and as he closed his eyes, she kissed them.

"Will you ever be able to forgive me?" she whispered, sitting up.

"I was angry," said Craig quietly, "if angry is the right word for what I felt. But not with you. I was angry with Samson." He pulled up, too, and leaned against the headboard. "I hated him. I wished I could kill him for taking you away from me. But it didn't last long because I knew I was wrong." Craig sighed. "I knew he didn't have a choice. We always think our pain is worse than anybody else's. He was in so much pain. He started drinking. Losing Gabriella, asking you to die for the mission, losing the Book, the daggers, the powers. It was unbearable to look at him. Besides, he lost Gabriella forever, and I still had hope." He paused.

Eleanor moved closer, "Then?"

"Then, I shut down. Isolated myself from everyone. I spent weeks at the lodge, visiting your parents' house, waiting for

Margaret to show up. Only then did I notice how much she looked like you.

"Riley and Ruben were trying to convince me to come home, that they needed me, but every time I pushed them away. Ned was going crazy because Hanna had shut down too. She would disappear for days. The castle was like an empty ghost house. Everything was falling apart, because the others were in pain, as well.

"Then one day I looked around and realized I was wrong. It couldn't continue like that. So I went to Samson. I told him I was sorry for his loss, for our loss. We got drunk together, had a good cry." A bitter smile crossed Craig's face. "We decided that it was time to get back to work. Fray was powerless, but not his vampires. They were still out there and stronger than us." Craig kissed Eleanor's hand, clenching his fingers.

"What did you do?" she asked, wiping her wet cheeks. "How did you fight them?"

"I know you have questions. But we don't have much time. Eleanor, I know this isn't the right moment. With everything going on . . . and you are still confused. But I am leaving tonight. I waited so long, and I need to know. . ."

"I am not going to lie to you, my coming back–it's intense. But I want to stay here, with you, for the time we have, and you can ask me anything."

"Tell me you love me. That's all I want to hear."

"You know that I—"

"No, I don't. That was then. It's different now. Amanda was a teenager who grew up in a different time, where guys like Alec—"

"You mean killers?"

"You know what I mean. Amanda is still a part of you."

"Yes, she is." Eleanor smiled. "And we are both madly in love with you."

Craig pulled her closer. "I love you so much. Once again, you've made me the happiest man in the world."

∼

"COME WITH ME," said Samson to Riley and Ruben, as Craig and Eleanor left the living room.

He led them to the library. It was illuminated by the rays of sunlight, penetrating through the stained, arched window. The three of them sat down in the velvet armchairs around a low oval table.

"Do you think she's all right?" asked Riley.

"She is absolutely fine," said Samson. "And I need you to keep her safe while Craig and I are gone."

"That won't be easy," said Ruben. "It was a hell of a job when she was Amanda, and now that she is Eleanor, who just got her powers back . . ."

"She already died once," said Samson. "I don't think she wants to do it again, especially now that she knows there'll be no coming back this time."

"And you think that'll stop her?" Ruben chuckled. "Last thing she remembers as Eleanor is her walking to the scaffold and Gabriella's funeral, and the moment she comes back, she's about to attend another funeral. She's a Hunter, and right now her blood is boiling."

"What I've prepared for Craig, it's a gift," said Samson, leaning forward. "But if something happens to Eleanor, that gift will become a curse. They deserve to be happy after what they've been through." He looked at Ruben, then turned his glance to Riley. "I know that you both agreed to what is about to happen, but Craig and I are leaving today, and I need to be sure that you are certain about your decisions. Riley, it should have been you, not Craig. You are the oldest."

"I'm absolutely certain. I don't want it. Besides, as you said, we owe them that much."

Samson turned to Ruben.

"Maybe I have more years on me than Craig, so what," Ruben

said with a shrug. "He's like my older brother. Craig is the one you need for this."

"Samson." Riley pierced him with his gaze. "I want to ask you the same. Are you sure you want to do this?"

"Riley, we've been through this a hundred times," said Samson in a tired voice. "I'm sorry if I let you down."

"No. I know it's killing you being here without her," said Riley quietly,

On the word *killing*, Samson took a deep breath. There were so many days he'd wished he could die.

"You know what I mean," Riley rushed on. "And I know what you're thinking. I'm glad you can't, because we need you to win this war." He leaned forward. "I just thought that now, since you got your powers back . . . I thought, maybe . . ."

"It doesn't change how I feel. Getting the powers back was the only thing that gave meaning to my existence. Fray betrayed us." Samson's voice remained even, but the muscles on his face stretched. "He ruined our lives, and I needed my powers so I could finish him."

Riley hesitated for a moment, then said, "I still think we should tell the others."

"Samson," said Ruben, "you can't do this to Hanna. She can't find out what you're up to at the last moment. If we tell her now, she'll have time to—"

"No," Samson interrupted. "This is a secret mission. If I tell her now, it'll be all she thinks about, and I need her to concentrate on the job. The same goes for Eleanor."

"Eleanor is a part of your plan," said Riley. "She needs time to make a decision. You and Craig, you can't drop it on her at the last minute."

"Now isn't the best time either," said Samson. "She just got back. To make this decision, she has to have a Hunter's spirit. Eleanor needs to get back on track. She's not ready yet."

Those weren't the only reasons that kept Samson from telling the others the truth. His plan was based on information from the golden pages, and he was afraid that knowing what he was up to might put them in danger. He blamed himself for Gabriella's death. If he hadn't told her the secret of Fray's power, she would still be alive. He wouldn't make the same mistake twice. The less the others knew, the safer they were. He told Riley and Ruben only because this journey, and its result was a tremendous privilege. The right to it belonged to the oldest Hunter, and Samson couldn't just hand it over to Craig without asking their permission.

"Right now, we have nothing," said Ruben. He stood up and walked back and forth. "We don't know where the Book, or the daggers, are. We checked every suspicious place for the transitioning vampires. We went after him," Ruben rotated the big globe beside him, "everywhere, and we still have no idea where he hides their bodies."

"They are close by, I am certain of it," said Samson. "He let us follow him all over the world, but never around here. Here, his vampires watched us constantly. He needs those bodies close because he plans to attack us right after they wake up."

"He did outrun us before," said Ruben. "And I am sure he is well prepared."

"Agreed," said Samson. "Still, he knows I won't come to this point empty-handed, that there's a reason I never told him what's on the golden pages. He fears them. Just like us, he doesn't know what to expect."

"Yeah, but the difference is that, in this game of hide and seek, we are the ones who are seeking, so we don't have as many options as they do," said Riley.

"Right now, I want you to look for the bodies. They are not far, and the vampires are no threat to us anymore. It's different now. With our powers back, we have a chance," said Samson, "There is always a loophole. You'll find it. Check the places we marked. We know that he keeps some coffins there. Find out what's in them. And be careful; you know he likes to set up traps."

Riley looked up at Ruben. "Let's start with that gas station at Mountain Road."

Ruben nodded. "Man, I hope there are vampires there." His fingers clenched into fists. "I'm starting to feel itchy."

Chapter Three

THE PLANE DOVE into the clouds, and white mist covered the view behind the small window through which Alec had been staring the whole flight.

He'd just killed Melinda. Amanda would never forgive him for that.

He had never killed anybody before. Animals, yes, but never humans. The sensation of a blade sinking into human flesh was new to him. Now, it kept coming back, no matter how hard he tried to get rid of it. His hand clenched into a fist like he was still holding the dagger. Subconsciously, his lips curled up in the same nervous smile, and Kimberly's short, horrified holler pierced his ears again and again.

I'll get over it, he thought.

There was another unpleasant moment ahead of him. Alec was about to meet Fray, who had given him very clear instructions-- kill Amanda as soon as she opens the Book. He never planned to do it, but he had been afraid Fray would pass the task to someone else. Alec convinced him that he was never in love with Amanda, that he got close to her only because Fray asked him to. Alec assured him his feelings were for Debra Gordon, that he only broke up with her because he had to.

The view cleared up. The ground grew closer and the roofs of the small houses bigger.

Alec had never meant to let Fray down. Even though they didn't live together, Fray was the only parent he had ever had, and Fray was the one who made Alec the strong, confident, determined man he was now. Whenever he thought about his biological parents, he felt disgusted. He wasn't sorry for what happened to them.

When he was six, his drunken father and mother forgot him in a grocery store. When he looked around and realized they were gone, Alec went outside. He ran up and down the street looking for their car, then after a while he returned to the store, hoping they'd come back for him. When he asked the grocer if he had seen his mom and dad, the grocer called the police. That evening the policeman showed him pictures of a man and a woman and asked Alec if he recognized them.

A car crash had happened only two blocks away. They didn't get too far, but Alec always wondered if they would've come back for him. He never got over this awful feeling that they left him in the store on purpose. That feeling, mixed with anger at them for being so stupid and careless, made his hatred toward them even stronger.

Alec ended up in foster care with 7 other children. It didn't take long before he isolated himself from the other kids. He got sick of hearing their pity stories. Unlike the others, he never wanted to be adopted. If his own parents didn't love him enough to stop being so careless, how could strangers love and care about him? And even if they could, what if they died, too?

It was a two-story house that sat on an open land. The owners had a few greenhouses where children worked to grow plants and flowers for sale. Alec mostly spent his free time drawing in a corner.

The place greatly reminded him of his life with his parents: grown-ups didn't care what he did, as long as he didn't bother them. There were only two differences, one good and one bad. The good one was that the owners didn't drink. The bad one was that where at home he was the only child, here his solitude annoyed the older boys. First, they stole his drawings and ripped them to pieces. Then came the name calling. Eventually they became more aggressive, and when their grudge got physical, Alec gritted his teeth and fought back.

Freedom was all Alec dreamed about. He wanted so badly to run away. But where would he go?

He was ten years old when he decided to make a few rounds on a bike one night after dinner. There were two bikes in the house, one big and one small. Alec knew that nobody dared to take the big bike without asking Kris. Kris was fifteen. He was the oldest, he had his rules, and he hated Alec more than anybody else. Alec felt the same way about Kris, and to show him that he was not afraid of him, he jumped on the bike and took off.

While he was passing one of the greenhouses on his way back, something struck him in the head out of nowhere. He fell from the bike. Squinting from the pain, he glanced back. In the dim greenhouse light, he saw three figures walking toward him. Alec forced himself up, got on the bike, and pedaled for the main road. They ran after him. His bike slid onto the sleek asphalt from the dirt road. At the same moment, the headlights of an oncoming car blinded him. Alec lost his balance and collapsed. The braking Jeep hissed and stopped sharply beside him. The passenger door opened and the light inside came on.

"What the hell do you think you're doing?" said the man sitting at the wheel. He didn't sound angry, just annoyed.

With his sleeve, Alec wiped the blood coming down his forehead, then looked back into the darkness at the approaching figures.

"Running away, huh?" said the man, following his gaze, "Get in."

Alec hesitated. He glanced at the man, at his neatly combed, short hair, at his expensive-looking suit. He'd never been around people like this man before. And when would he get a chance to ride in a Jeep again?

Alec pulled himself up. He chanced a look behind him to find Kris standing at the edge of the road. He glared at Kris, showed him the middle finger, and jumped onto the shiny, leather seat.

"So where do you live?" the man asked as he drove.

Alec looked at the house, getting smaller in the distance. "Are you taking me to the police?"

"Should I?"

"No. I didn't do anything wrong."

"Nothing?"

Alec shook his head.

"Ever?"

Alec shook his head again, then shrugged.

"That must be boring," said the man. "I do wrong things all the time."

Alec grinned.

The man smiled back. "I think you do, too. You just don't realize it," he said. "I've known you for only a few minutes, and I already witnessed one wrong thing. You got into a car with some man you've never seen before, and I'm sure your parents taught you to stay away from strangers."

"I don't have parents."

The man eyed the road, then after a moment, said, "My name is Fray."

Fray took him to his mansion in Williamsburg. Alec's jaw dropped as they walked into the hallway.

"Is this your house?" he asked, looking at the marble floor and the columns.

"Do you like it?" asked Fray, leading him up the stairs.

Alec looked up at him and nodded slowly.

They entered a grand room with a large fireplace, leather couches, and armchairs. Walking on the soft carpet, Alec stared at the paintings on the walls, at the big statue of a black horse in the corner, then at the small sculptures, placed on the dark wooden and marble stands. Axes and swords hung from the wall on both sides of the fireplace. Alec stopped and looked at them with wide eyes, wishing he could touch them.

"I'll let you look closer tomorrow," said Fray. "It's late now and you need to go to bed. I'll show you your room."

Lying on the comfortable, king-sized bed, Alec spent half of the night with his eyes open. He stared at the gypsum cells of the ceiling, thinking about everything that had happened in the last few hours. He liked every moment of it: the last desperate look on Kris's face, the road trip, the house. Most of all he liked Fray, the way Fray talked to him. There was no pity in his voice, and he was real; he didn't pretend like other grown-ups did.

But Alec also had many questions. What was going to happen now? Were the police looking for him? Why would Fray help him? Maybe he was a murderer, or a cannibal and was planning to eat Alec for dinner tomorrow.

In the morning, as Fray came in and told him about his plan, all Alec's fears and worries vanished. First, Fray kept his word and let Alec hold the weapons and even try them out. But they were too big and cumbersome for the ten-year-old boy, and Fray promised that he'd get a suitable size for him. Alec's heart leapt at those words. Did it mean he was allowed to stay? He didn't dare ask.

The second part of Fray's plan was to have breakfast in town and then drive to Richmond.

"We'll do some shopping," said Fray.

"Shopping?" asked Alec. "What are we going to buy?"

"You name it. But first, we'll buy some clothes for you. You can't walk around in this," said Fray, pointing at Alec's faded shirt and the old jeans, ripped at the knees. "No one would let you into the restaurant like that."

"Restaurant?" asked Alec again, like he was learning new words and looking for

approval that he was pronouncing them right.

"Yes." Fray nodded once. "Have you never been in a restaurant?"

Alec shrugged. "Not that I can remember."

At the store, Fray asked him if there was anything he needed besides clothes, shoes, candy, comic books, and games—which they had already purchased. Alec asked if Fray could buy him a sketchbook and a pencil. Fifteen minutes later, he was carrying a fat shopping bag full of big and small sketchbooks, paints and brushes, a palette, and dozens of pencils and erasers.

Alec was grateful to Fray for his generosity, and to thank him, he decided to draw Fray's portrait. After they returned to the mansion, Alec went to his room. He pulled the big sketchbook and a pencil from his bag and sat on the bed.

Sometime later Fray entered the room. "I need to talk to you," he said.

Alec's stomach clenched. "Did I do something wrong?" he asked carefully.

"No," said Fray, "It's not about you, it's about us. Let's go to my study."

Alec slid down from the bed and followed Fray into the hallway.

In the study, as they sat across from each other at the mahogany desk, Fray smiled slightly and asked, "Do you like it here, Alec?"

"Yes, sir," said Alec quietly.

"And you would like to stay?"

Alec nodded.

"I would like it too," said Fray. The second Alec smiled, he raised his finger. "But," he said, "before making the final decision, I need to tell you something. I need you to know who I am."

He couldn't tell how long Fray spoke. He started with some legend about hunters, and Alec found it interesting. But when Fray said that it wasn't just a legend and that he was one of them, an immortal, Alec started to fall out of the monologue. After catching the words, *all my friends are vampires*, he spaced out completely.

Alec sat paralyzed, his eyes fixed on the big ring on Fray's finger. He blinked at the sound of his name.

"Alec," Fray said again, "are you listening?"

Alec stared at him, his insides vibrating. "Vampires don't exist. You're just trying to scare me."

"Are you scared?" asked Fray calmly.

"No," said Alec, putting his hands on the armrests of the tall chair and pushing himself deeper into the seat.

"Good. Because you don't have to be. You're safe with me," said Fray. "A couple of them will arrive the day after tomorrow. You have until then to decide what you want. If you want to stay, you'll have to keep this a secret for the rest of your life."

"What if I decide to go? Will you kill me?"

"No. I don't kill children."

"You'll just let me go?"

"Why not?" Fray shrugged. "I'll take you back myself. Those guys, the ones who were chasing you," he narrowed his eyes, "what do you think they would do if you told them everything you just heard? Would they believe you?"

Fray was right. Alec had no one to whom he could tell the truth, and he also couldn't bear the thought of returning to that place.

"You said you can't die," said Alec after a minute of silence.

"I did."

"Never?"

"Never."

"I am staying."

Fray didn't live in the mansion himself, just visited from time to time. One day, he brought a man and a woman who he paid to live in the house as its owners. Matilda and Clark Mayson, which were their false names, were hired to play the role of Alec's parents at school and satisfy his needs at home.

Alec loved spending time with Fray and looked forward to his visits. Fray took him on rides and taught him how to fight. Once, when he came from school, Fray drove him to a farm. The backyard had a big stable. When they walked in, Fray said he could choose any horse he wanted. Soon after that, he was given a present —a bow and arrows. They hunted often so Fray could teach him how to use them. Before their trip to Europe, Fray bought Alec his first Nikon.

One day when they were hunting at the lake, Alec, who was aiming at a duck, suddenly turned to Fray and shot him in the shoulder. Fray, whose eyes were looking pointedly at the duck as it flew away, chuckled even before the arrow pierced him. "I was wondering if you'd have the guts to do it."

Clutching the bow in his hand, Alec took a few steps back.

"I have to say, I'm impressed," said Fray, stepping toward him. He pulled out the arrow and took off his shirt.

Alec stared at the shoulder. The wound vanished in seconds, leaving behind a couple of dry blood stains. Fray brushed them off with his shirt.

"Sorry," said Alec, "but I had to check."

"Then you should have shot at the heart."

"No. I would never do that to you."

"I know why you did it," said Fray softly. "Don't worry, boy, nothing is going to happen to me."

Alec was happy. He was rich, he was free, and he had Fray, who would never die on him.

The more he learned about Fray, the more he wondered why Fray wanted him. Once, when Alec was thirteen and Fray said that he had to leave after only staying two days, Alec asked, "Why? Why can't you live here?"

"I told you I have enemies."

"And?"

"And they watch me. This is the only safe house I have. I come here only when I'm sure nobody follows me. That's why you are not Alec Wald. You are Alec Mayson, and this is *your* house. Nobody can know the truth."

"So I'm your cover story. Is that why you took me?"

"Yes. That was the plan. But you're not just that. Not anymore. Now you are one of us."

"I'm not one of you. You're all immortal, and I . . . I can die at any moment."

"You are part of the team. And, if you're lucky, one day you can become immortal, too."

"How?" Alec stared at Fray.

"You're too young for that." When Alec opened his mouth to protest, Fray raised his hand, stopping him. "One day I'll tell you how. I promise."

Over the years they became close. Alec was twenty now, and for the last decade Fray had taken care of him, showed him the world, shared with him his secrets and desires. But he couldn't say that Fray loved him. Alec wasn't sure that Fray had ever loved anybody, or that he knew what love was.

Two years ago, when Alec was eighteen, he got his first assignment.

The fact that Craig arrived at Green Hill and stayed there more than a year seemed suspicious to Fray. That's when he decided to change Alec's age and last name and send him to L.A.

"Back to sophomore year," exploded Alec, when Fray told him he would be going back to high school, which he had just graduated. "You're joking."

"No, I'm not," said Fray angrily. "This is a small price to pay for your immortality. If Craig is there, it means that this girl might be the one we've been waiting for. She even looks like Eleanor."

"She does? But she's in Green Hill."

"I want you close to that place so you can step in anytime I need."

When Fray explained to Alec how much depended on him, going back to school didn't seem that bad anymore. It was his first serious task, and he wanted to prove to Fray that everything he had done for Alec, wasn't for nothing, that Alec was worthy of becoming immortal; to become Fray's only human partner. Besides, one of Alec's biggest desires was to meet Eleanor. What if it really was her?

Years ago, when Fray finally told Alec everything about the Book of Power and how it was closed, Fray also showed him the Hunters' pictures, so that Alec would know who the enemies were. All photographs were modern, except one. Eleanor's was a painting, and she wore old-fashioned clothes. When Alec questioned why, Fray explained that she was the one who died a century and a half ago when she closed the Book and turned his life into misery.

But Alec never shared Fray's hatred towards her. To him, Eleanor was the biggest mystery of them all. She wasn't just one of the Hunters, but a beautiful, brave, young woman, who sacrificed herself for her family's mission. And he might actually witness her return.

∽

ALEC WALKED DOWN THE RAMP. He didn't have any luggage, so he sped forward. As he came out from the gate, he quickly crossed the waiting area and stepped out of the airport. It took him a few minutes to find the car left for him in the parking lot by one of the vampires. He pulled out the spare key from his pocket, got in the car and opened the glove box, where a piece of paper with a new address lay. He knew he hadn't been followed, but he kept looking into the rear view mirror until he was entirely sure that he could hit the road. This short flight was only an extra precaution, and now he had to get back, to the house on the outskirts of Green Hill, where he would meet Fray.

Fray trusted him, but Alec hadn't killed Amanda, and now it would be obvious that he lied when he said he would. He had to come up with an explanation.

Chapter Four

THEY BURIED Melinda at midday in the castle's garden. Her grave was only a few feet away from the white, marble gravestone with Gabriella's name. Eleanor wiped her wet cheeks, then took from under the tree a small vase of violets she'd picked earlier and put it on Gabriella's grave.

"Gabriella loved them," she said to Craig.

"Yes," said Craig, "she did."

Eleanor's eyes searched deeper into the garden. "I don't see my grave. Where did you bury me?"

"You already had one, remember?" said Craig. "Where your husband, Richard, buried you when he thought you were dead."

"Oh. Right," she said quietly.

"We knew you'd come back, and we didn't want you to live the rest of your life next to your grave." A sad smile crossed Craig's face. "We buried you there."

"Did Margaret ever visit it?"

"You know she did."

"No, after . . ."

"You mean after she got married. You think she forgot about you?"

"She . . . she never knew me. Why should she. . . ?"

Craig hugged her. "She visited your grave regularly. Your family loved you very much. Your parents and your brothers were the connection between you and your daughter. She didn't just put flowers on your grave, she talked to you."

Eleanor pulled back to look at him. "Really? It might sound ridiculous, but it's good that my grave wasn't empty anymore." She smiled. "What did she say?"

"I don't know. I didn't want to eavesdrop."

Eleanor thought for a moment. If Margaret came to talk, she probably needed comfort. "Was she unhappy?"

"No." Craig took her by her arms and looked into her eyes. "Eleanor, she had a good, long life. She had a good husband. Believe me, I know. I was there, watching her entire life."

"Thank you." Eleanor stretched up to his face and kissed him. Craig hugged her.

She pulled back again. "Kids? What about kids?"

"She had two sons. Which, to be honest, scared the hell out of me."

Eleanor laughed. "You were afraid that I'd come back as a man?"

Craig grinned. "It kept happening. There weren't many girls in your bloodline. But when I asked Samson, he assured me that you'd be the same Eleanor."

Eleanor's eyes unfocused. "Hmm. I just remembered." She looked toward Melinda's grave. Hanna and Kimberly were planting flowers into the freshly dug earth at the head of it. The others were still there, too. Eleanor walked to Samson, who was talking to the witch who lived in the castle and managed the household, Amelia Cox.

"Can I talk to you?" Eleanor asked as Samson turned to her.

"Of course," said Samson, and together they walked to the small wooden bridge, heading to the castle.

"You were sure that when I came back, I'd be the same Eleanor."

"Yes, I was sure. The Book was absolutely clear about your coming back exactly the same person you were."

"When I told my dream, or whatever it was, to my father, Lindsay, he said that he had the same dream when he was my age. He was in that house, and he tried to open the Book."

"Did he?" Samson looked like he was about to laugh.

"Why is that funny?" asked Eleanor, perplexed.

"Fray never knew the details. He needed your bloodline safe as much as we did," said Samson, becoming serious again. "We were too few to look after every one of your family members, and I was glad he was watching them, too. I think he assumed that if we were looking after one of your descendants, that was the candidate."

"So one of you had been looking after my father?"

"Yes. We took turns. Ned was the last one. He and Lindsey were friends. That's why he couldn't come back here with Hanna. Your father, or somebody else who went to college with them, could have recognized Ned. Besides, Craig was too sure you were Eleanor, and he wanted to be here himself."

They walked in silence for a moment, then Eleanor spoke again.

"There is one more thing," she said, looking far ahead. "Melinda . . . I remember her talking to my mother in the hospital. Do you know what she was saying to her, how she convinced my mom to hire her?"

"You want to know if she used magic," guessed Samson. "She did. She was trying to save your mother, and when she failed, she used it to ease her pain. Your mother knew she was dying and was worried about you. I don't know exactly what Melinda said to her, but I know she promised to keep you safe and look after you until you turned eighteen."

Eleanor's heart sank. She'd never be able to thank Melinda for everything she did for her. For dedicating nine years of her life to Eleanor, someone she never knew. Her eyes teared up.

They neared the stable. Eleanor looked into its open gate and saw Gabriella's horse.

"Yes, she is still here," said Samson in a low voice, following Eleanor's gaze.

"It seems strange even to me," said Eleanor, stopping. "Did anybody ride her?"

"Amelia. It was safe, since the horses lost their speed, too. I don't think she'll be able to do it now."

"Gabriella sacrificed her life as well," said Eleanor. "She didn't have children to continue her bloodline, but she died for the mission, too. Couldn't the Higher Powers find some way to bring her back?"

"No." Samson sighed and looked at the sky, like he hoped to see her up there. "She was killed with the dagger." They resumed walking. "The dagger breaks the enchantment, which means Gabriella died as a human. It's different in your case. You were killed by the Book. You died as a Hunter."

The rest followed them back to the castle.

The food was served in the great dining room. Next to each plate stood a small glass of whiskey. As they lifted their glasses, Samson raised his and said, "To Melinda."

"To Melinda," they echoed.

They ate and talked, and after a short moment, Samson stood up once again and raised his wine glass. "Eleanor," he said in a deep voice, and silence fell in the room. "I am sorry we didn't get to celebrate your return. You lost someone today. We all did." He looked down at his glass for a moment, then back at Eleanor. "It wasn't how I imagined you to come back. And I know I'm not making it any better by taking Craig away. But we'll have to postpone the celebration until the fight is over. For now, I want to say—welcome home."

"Thank you," said Eleanor. "Where are you going?" she asked as Samson sat down. "For how long?"

"First, Norway. Then we'll fly to Egypt. It might take eight, ten days, max. During that time, the rest of you will need to find the transitioning vampires."

"Find the transitioning vampires?" asked Eleanor . "You're saying you don't know where they are?"

"No, we don't." Samson cleared his throat.

"Through the years, we've seen Fray move some coffins from place to place," said Ruben, putting his hand on the back of Kimberly's chair next to him. "But we never got a chance to get near them."

"It might be a distraction," said Riley, "but we still have to check those places."

"You need to be careful. Double check everything," said Samson. "I'm sure he's thought of many different ways to confuse us, to put us on the wrong trail. We have two weeks, at most, until their awakening. This is our chance to defeat Fray. If they wake up, we could lose."

The silence in the room deepened. Eleanor and Hanna exchanged a grave look.

"One more thing," Samson added, "If Fray shows up—keep an eye on him. Please don't fight him. Keep your tempers under control."

"Why?" asked Eleanor.

"Because he still has the daggers."

"No. What?" Eleanor couldn't believe what she had just heard.

"We were powerless. We were weak against the vampires," said Ned. "And Fray had too many of them."

"Then what's the difference?" Eleanor couldn't hide her disappointment. She gazed at Samson. "It means I died for nothing. You suffered all those years for nothing. Nothing has changed."

Ruben and Riley exchanged a glance.

"I wouldn't say so," said Samson calmly. "We didn't have a chance then. Now, we can defeat him."

"How?"

Staring at Eleanor like she was seeing her for the first time, Kimberly blinked, and her eyes darted to Samson.

"There is a way," said Samson.

Eleanor spread her hands. "If there was a way, why haven't you done it all those years ago?"

"Because back then a trip to Norway and then to Egypt used to take months, and by the time I'd get back, Fray would have an army, and it would be impossible to stop him," said Samson. "The others will fill you in on the information we have."

Eleanor felt bad for her outburst. She had no idea what had happened after her death, or what they'd been through during this long time of her absence. "I'm sorry. I shouldn't—"

"You don't have to apologize," said Samson. "You have a right to be disappointed."

Craig chuckled. "Actually, your reaction was much better than he expected."

It was late afternoon when they all went down to the front yard.

"I miss you already," whispered Eleanor as she kissed Craig goodbye.

"See you soon," said Hanna, hugging Samson.

They all waved after Samson's car as it pulled out of the drive. When it vanished behind the trees, Riley turned to the others. "Who wants a drink?"

"Me," said Ned, following Riley back inside.

Ruben put his hand around Kimberly's waist and led her down to the beach.

Eleanor and Hanna headed to Gabriella's garden. They walked up the trail, past the big oaks, and reached the small, wooden bridge. Crossing it, Eleanor looked down at the creek, sparkling under the rays of the setting sun.

She stopped as she walked into the garden. "What happened?" she asked, looking around.

"What do you mean?" asked Hanna.

"It's the end of spring. The bushes are green, but nothing is blooming. Not even the lilac. Why?"

"Yeah," Hanna sighed. "It's been like this since her death. We haven't seen a single flower in this garden for a hundred and sixty-two years. We tried everything. Riley asked Samson's permission to change the bushes. Samson said we were wasting our time, that nothing would help. But Riley did it anyway. He planted the new bushes in the exact same order, so it'd look the same. But Samson was right. The new ones didn't bloom, either."

"Riley did that?" Eleanor looked blankly at the water shooting up from the fountain urn.

Hanna sat down on the bench. "Are you surprised?"

"No. Actually, I'm not." Eleanor sat beside her.

"You know, I always had this feeling. . . ." Hanna hesitated.

"What feeling?" asked Eleanor, now looking at the dandelions growing around the pool wall.

"I always thought . . . Just, please don't laugh . . ."

"That Riley was in love with Gabriella?" Eleanor turned to Hanna. "I don't think it's funny."

"Yeah." Hanna nodded, gazing at her. "So you felt that, too?"

"No. I didn't feel it. I knew it."

"You knew it? How? Did Craig tell you?"

"No. Gabriella did," said Eleanor. Hanna's eyes widened and her eyebrows moved up. Eleanor took her hand. "Hanna, breath. Nothing happened."

"Then how . . . how did she know?" Hanna asked, stammering.

"When Samson turned Ned, Gabriella told Riley that she hoped one day he and Ruben would find someone, too. Someone they would want to be with forever. That's when Riley confessed his feelings, saying he had already found his someone. That maybe she wasn't his, but he was happy because he got to see her every day, to hear her voice, her laughter." Eleanor sighed. "And he got to live with her under the same roof forever."

"Oh no. How could I be so blind?" A tear dropped from Hanna's eye. "He lost his love, too, he was in pain, and nobody was there to comfort him." She glanced at the bushes and shook her head.

"Maybe Samson did. Because I think he knew," said Eleanor quietly. "After Gabriella told me, I started remembering things. The way Riley looked at her. That he didn't travel with us if Gabriella wasn't coming. I noticed that he stayed close to home so he could be there for her if she needed something done. Only then did Gabriella realize why he was always the first one—after Samson, of course—to wish her good morning. I think Samson noticed these things long before we did."

"I wish she had told me," said Hanna, looking down at her lap.

"She didn't mean to tell me either. It just happened, it was one of those moments. We were talking. Word after word . . . it just came out. Besides, she was afraid of your 'jealous daughter' reaction."

"No. He didn't do anything wrong."

"You say that now. But if you knew then, who knows." Eleanor stood up.

"Eleanor." Hanna sobbed suddenly. She dashed to Eleanor and hugged her tightly around the neck.

Eleanor put her arms around her, not surprised by the outburst.

"You're back. It's you," Hanna muttered into her ear. "We were friends for three years and I thought. . . ." She sobbed again.

"You thought that you could handle this without emotions?" Eleanor smiled sadly.

"I missed you so much. I lost you both, and I had no one to talk to. The boys, they were so good to me, but it's not the same."

"I know," whispered Eleanor, tears running down her cheeks. "And I was so sorry that I had to leave you in that mess."

"I kept repeating to myself the last words you said to me, that you needed me to be strong," sniffed Hanna.

They stood like that for a long moment.

"Do you wanna go for a ride?" said Eleanor, pulling back.

A few minutes later, the shadows of two horses flashed across the yard and disappeared into the woods.

∼

KIMBERLY, who saw the two horses vanish in two seconds, glanced at Ruben.

"I still can't believe this is real," she muttered. "I expect to wake up any minute now."

"You'll get used to it," Ruben said, taking her hand.

"Should I?" She looked at the ocean. "Then what?"

"Kimberly..."

"It's not that I don't want to. It's just . . ." She pulled her hand away and walked closer to the beach. "Everything is so different now."

"Kimberly, I know you're confused."

"I don't think that's the right word to describe what I feel," she said, her eyes fixed on the wet sand. "I feel like I lost something. I thought I knew the difference between possible and impossible. Not all of it, of course, but there was some kind of line, and now it's gone. Vampires are real, and I went to a party with them. My whole life I knew that this story about immortal Hunters was just a beautiful legend, and now here you are, killing vampires on your porch."

The sun was still glittering above the hill, but to Ruben, the view became much darker. "Do I scare you?"

She looked at him. "No," she said quietly. She stepped to him and put her hands on his chest. "I thought we were getting closer, and now there is this abyss between us."

"Kimberly, nothing has changed. I am the same Ruben." He took her face in his hands and kissed her. "You don't mind that I am almost five hundred years old, do you?" Ruben forced a smile.

But Kimberly's face remained despondent. She hugged him. Gently, like she was a thin crystal glass, he put his hands around her. With his powers back, he had to be careful. While he adjusted to them again, he'd have to control his every move not to hurt her.

Her head slid down onto his shoulder. Through the thin fabric of his shirt, he felt the touch of her warm lips.

Chapter Five

ALEC STOPPED the car in front of a large iron gate connecting the ends of the tall stone fencing that surrounded the two-story house. It was around midnight. Through the bars of the gate, the headlights illuminated the wide front yard, the only light in the total darkness.

The gate swung open. He drove in, stopped the car before the low stairs, and got out. When he reached the front door, the vampire on guard opened it for him.

"He is waiting for you," said the vampire.

The plan had worked, and now the house was full of vampires, waiting with anticipation for their turn to fall into the long sleep that would make them even more invincible and allow them to walk in daylight. Alec wasn't sure how he felt about that. He had witnessed their violence for ten years, but he couldn't say he had gotten used to it. They were monsters about to get even more power. But if that was what Fray wanted, what Fray needed to stand up to Samson, then so be it.

He climbed up the polished wooden stairs to the second floor, where Fray waited in the spacious study, sitting behind a mahogany desk.

"Everything is clear," said Alec, walking into the room. "They were too busy to follow any of us."

"That's not the only reason," said Fray. "They didn't follow us because they have other plans, which we know nothing about. We need to find out as much as possible."

Fray stood up and opened the old wooden case lying on his desk. The Book was open to the essential page. Alec stepped closer. He'd been the one to place the Book on the stand at Eleanor's old house. He hadn't had time to look at it after Eleanor opened it. Fray and the vampires had caught up with him before he'd reached the cars hidden between the trees at the edge of the woods. He'd handed the Book to Fray, and from there, they'd all driven in different directions.

It was on his fifteenth birthday that Fray showed him the Book for the first time. That day he told Alec the rest of his secrets. About how he took it from Samson and how to use it, about Joanne—how he chased her, that the idea to turn vampires came to him after he met her, and how she became his first companion. When Fray said that Joanne was transitioning at the moment The Book was closed, Alec asked if it meant she was dead. But Fray explained the transitioning would resume as soon as The Book was opened, that Joanna and fifty-two other transitioning vampires would wake up when the process was finished.

The more questions Alec asked about Joanne, the more he understood what she meant to Fray, and the more he wished that she would never wake up. Fray was his, and he didn't want to share him with anyone. Especially with someone as old and powerful as Joanne, with whom Fray had such a deep history.

Fray's voice pulled him out of his thoughts.

"Those golden texts are a big mystery," said Fray, flipping the pages. "And they can be very dangerous. We have to find out what Samson is up to and, more importantly, we need to keep them occupied until the transitioning vampires wake up."

"Well, I'm glad you have an army of vampires to help you

during my absence," said Alec with irony. He gazed at The Book, then at Fray. "Let's not waste time."

Fray stepped out from behind the desk. "You lied to me." He glared at Alec.

"I killed the witch and I got The Book, didn't I?"

"But you didn't kill *her*. You said that you could do it."

On his way back, Alec had rehearsed different reasons to convince Fray that he never got a chance to kill Amanda. But they would just be more lies. "I lied," he said without blinking. "I was never going to do it."

Fray didn't seem surprised. "Why? Because you love her?"

"Yes. If you know what that means."

Fray bowed his head. "I know what it means," he said. Alec heard a tension in his voice, and when Fray looked at him again, his eyes burned with rage. "It means weakness, and you've just proven it one more time. That woman—she isn't Amanda anymore, she isn't the girl you fell in love with. She is a different person now."

"And I will be, too," said Alec, piercing him with a glare. He stepped to the table and put his hand on the Book. "Do it."

Chapter Six

THEY HEADED BACK to Green Hill. Riley drove Craig's Jeep with Ruben next to him and Eleanor and Kimberly in the back seat.

"I can't see it. The Wall," said Kimberly as the car slid into the woods.

"It only works one way," said Eleanor. "Look back."

Kimberly turned around and peered into the semi-darkness of the woods. Seconds later the air rippled, and from behind it emerged Hanna's car, blinding Kimberly with its headlights.

"Unbelievable," said Kimberly with perceptible excitement in her voice.

Ruben glanced back at Eleanor. They exchanged a tiny smile.

After driving several miles down the main road, they heard sirens.

"Do you think it's the police?" asked Ruben.

"They found the bodies," said Riley. "That was quick."

"What bodies?" asked Eleanor. "Where?"

"The vampires we killed at your house," said Ruben.

Eleanor knew there had been a fight, but since she hadn't seen the vampires, she'd forgotten all about them.

"It's not the police," said Riley. "Look." He pointed at the piece of sky above the woods, where clouds of black smoke rose up from between the trees.

The sound of sirens got closer. A short moment later, they saw them: with flashing lights, three fire trucks took the exit from the highway and sped up the narrow road leading to Eleanor's old house.

"They're getting rid of evidence," said Ruben grimly. "Fire is good. Fire trucks can't reach that place, and by the time the firemen get their hands on the bodies, they'll look like barbecued human bones."

Kimberly's hand fidgeted at those words, and Eleanor took it.

"We'll be home soon," Eleanor said softly.

"I'm fine," said Kimberly.

But her quick glance and artificial smile told Eleanor she was far from fine. That everything, including Eleanor herself, was new and frightening. To Eleanor, Kimberly seemed different, too, now that her mind was flooded with memories from her past. Kimberly had been her best friend for nine years and their friendship was still very dear to her, but it felt like it had happened a million years ago in some other life. They both needed time to adjust to these abrupt changes.

The road sign WELCOME TO GREEN HILL shone golden in the darkness.

Eleanor felt nervous when the car turned to the familiar street. As it stopped in front of her house, she looked at its dark windows and her heart sank.

"Are you sure you'll be okay?" she turned to Kimberly. Kimberly nodded, and Eleanor opened the door. "Call me if you need anything."

As Eleanor got out of the Jeep, she glanced at Hanna's car behind it.

"I can stay with you if you want," Hanna said.

"No. Don't worry, I'll be okay," said Eleanor.

"You don't have to come tomorrow. You should get some rest," said Riley.

"We don't have time for that." Eleanor's face darkened. "See you in the morning. And don't go anywhere without me."

Eleanor stood on the dark porch for a moment after everyone left. Everything seemed different to her, new, but Amanda's feelings pushed themselves forward. The memories began to swirl, warming her heart. She looked at the bench where her mother used to sit with her cup of coffee while Amanda played outside. She looked at the tree where her swing once hung, and at the place where the sandbox used to be, now occupied by her car.

The front door wasn't locked. She stepped in, walked into the kitchen and turned on the light. The kitchen was clean and neat as always, but the unusual silence was unbearable. Eleanor ran her hand over the countertop and clenched her teeth. Only a couple of days ago Alec was here. They were having dinner and he was complimenting Melinda's special, delicious raviolis. Did he know then? Did he know that he would have to kill? Of course he did. And Fray knew that he could do it, otherwise he wouldn't have given him the dagger. She closed her eyes. In her mind, she promised Melinda that Alec would pay for what he'd done. She couldn't kill Alec—he was a human—but she'd find a way to punish him.

When she was a little girl she liked to spend time in Melinda's room, but now she couldn't remember when she'd been there last. She pushed the door open. Nothing much had changed since her last visit. It was light and modern, except the chest. It was an old, hand-carved African chest, with a depiction of people working on the plantations on its sides and a palm tree on its lid. That mysterious chest always attracted little Amanda, but it was locked, which increased her childish curiosity and imagination even more. When begging Melinda to open it didn't work, one day, during her absence, Amanda snuck into the room with a screwdriver, which ended with a few scratches around the keyhole and Melinda's angry shouts.

That memory brought a smile to Eleanor's face. She stroked the scratches on the old wood, then tried the lid. The chest opened. Melinda had been in a hurry and there was no need to hide its contents any more. Eleanor knelt before it. She eyed a big stock of candles, the small jars with some kind of powder, a wooden box with tied bundles of sage, and a big, old book-- Melinda's Grimoire. As she pulled it up, she saw another, smaller book lying under it, with a supple leather cover and two leather clasps like a journal. Eleanor picked it up, undid the buckles, and pulled aside the cover.

On the first page with big letters was written *ELEANOR,* and beneath it, with smaller letters, *the seventh generation.*

A cold shiver ran through Eleanor's whole body, covering her arms with goosebumps. She opened the next page.

Today, May 17th 1997, Amanda Shane was born, daughter of Lindsey and Claire Shane, who represents the seventh generation of Eleanor's bloodline . . .

Eleanor released a soft gasp. "She has been watching me my whole life." She flipped a few pages.

I renew the protective enchantment around the house every month. But I can't do as much outside since I can't follow them everywhere . . .

    Sometimes I can sense their presence and it alarms me, though I know that they need her too, and they are not going to harm her . . .

Some pages were a little bulky. She opened one of them and saw a photograph attached to the page. Baby Amanda looked back with a toothless grin. There was another photo of a slightly older

Amanda playing in the front yard with a kitten. The next picture was taken on her first day of school, with her young mom and dad watching her from a distance. She had never seen these pictures. They had probably been taken by Melinda herself.

Eleanor's phone vibrated, and she saw Craig's name on the screen.

"Hi. Where are you?" she asked.

"We're in New York, and we have several hours until our next flight."

"I just found Melinda's journal, and I'm a bit . . ." Eleanor sank down on the bed. "She has been watching over me my whole life."

"I'm sorry you have to find things out this way. I wish I was there with you." Craig sighed. "Then I would do more than just tell you everything in my mind like I have for the last hundred and sixty-two years."

"It's okay," said Eleanor quietly. "It's only for a few days. And don't worry," she said in a more cheerful tone, "you're the only one who can tell me the stories I really want to hear."

"How about a date? When I come back we can have a date. In the garden, on our bench, at the place where everything started."

Eleanor took a deep breath. "I don't think we'll be able to, Craig."

"Why? Because of the bodies? It's his house now. I'm sure he'll want to get rid of them before the police find out."

"That's the thing. He did. He burned it down." Eleanor heard Craig's heavy breathing. "Is the lodge still . . ."

"No," muttered Craig. "It burned decades ago. All these years I thought it was an accident."

She knew what it meant to him. All this time she'd been away, those pieces of their past were all he had. They helped him get through his pain, to hold onto this life during those years of waiting.

"Craig, I know it upsets you, and right now things are not how you expected them to be, but it's impossible to plan things a century ahead and expect them to work."

"I know. Those memories—they kept me moving, they were all I had then," said Craig, his voice slightly unsteady. "It's time to make new ones."

After Eleanor hung up, she sat looking at the phone for a long while. She could still hear Craig's sad voice, echoing the pain he had suffered. Eleanor put the journal back in the chest, went upstairs to her room and, without turning on the light, lay down on the bed. The last events of her old life and the first moments of her new one were full of loss and grief. She had tried to be strong all day and push the thoughts away. Now that she was alone, she let it sink in, and the moment she did, it engulfed her. The sorrow surged through her chest, and she let out deep, suffocating sobs.

Chapter Seven

RUBEN SAT in the armchair reading the morning newspaper.

"Anything about the fire?" Riley asked, sitting across from him on the couch.

"They think it was an accident. That it was a bunch of hikers intruding on private property," said Ruben. He folded the paper and threw it on the coffee table.

"These places seem so dull," said Ned, looking at the list of locations where they knew Fray had hidden coffins.

"That's what Samson kept saying," said Ruben. "It wouldn't take long to check them, now that we have our powers back."

"And now that we don't have to babysit anymore," added Riley.

"What the hell is wrong with you?" said Hanna, coming out from the kitchen. She held an empty box of chocolate cookies in her hand. "What's that supposed to mean?"

"It means we are finally free." Riley picked up the newspaper from the coffee table. "And we can finally act."

"You make it sound like it was Eleanor's fault," said Hanna sharply.

Riley threw the newspaper back and stood up. "No. I

remember whose fault it is, Hanna, and I can't wait to crush his vampire nest."

"And we are right there with you," said Eleanor, walking in.

They all turned their heads. Hanna's jaw dropped as she looked at her. Eleanor's outfit had dramatically changed. It was absolutely dissimilar to Amanda's. She wore tight black pants with a wide brown belt, black satin shirt, and dark brown boots. Her long brown hair was curled and looked exactly like Eleanor's. Golden coins of her Hunter bracelet shone around her wrist.

"Sorry I'm a bit late. I had to do some shopping," she said, moving forward.

"Shouldn't you be at school?" chuckled Ruben, looking at her from top to toe.

"No," she said without breaking a smile. "But you should."

"Been there. I drove Kimberly. I couldn't convince her to stay at home."

"So she's there alone. It's not safe."

"What? Now we have to babysit Kimberly?" barked Riley.

"Excuse me?" Hanna jumped up from her spot on the armrest of Ned's chair. "We are the ones who put her in danger. It's not her fault the bloodsuckers are here."

Ned grabbed Hanna's hand and pulled her back.

"No," said Eleanor, "it's mine." She dropped on the couch. "How much did you find out?"

Ned nodded toward the sheet of paper. She picked it up and scanned the list.

"You're joking, right?" She gazed at Riley.

"We've seen them carrying coffins into the gas station, the crypt, and the warehouse. The rest are just suggestions."

"Riley," she sneered, "a gas station?"

"It belongs to him."

"Fray? He couldn't be that obvious."

"Of course not. It's not under his name. There are nine coffins there and we have to check them. He keeps changing their locations, knowing we can't follow him everywhere." Riley sighed. "We don't know what's in them. During those years, we lost him several times. In the beginning of the nineteenth century, your bloodline was in danger of dying out. First, one of your grandsons refused to get married. Then your great-granddaughter's..."

"Stop." Eleanor shook her hands. "Could you do it backward? You make me feel . . ."

"Old?" Riley shrugged. "In our case, it's an honor and privilege."

"Still."

"Fine. Your great-great-great-grandmother's seven-year-old daughter died of leukemia. Her fifteen-year-old cousin drowned—"

"On your watch," Hanna cut in.

"It wasn't my fault," thundered Riley. "The boy jumped from a seven-foot high dock and crushed his skull against a stone."

"Guys," Ruben rolled his eyes, "it doesn't matter now."

"What's going on?" asked Eleanor, moving her narrowed eyes from Hanna to Riley and back. "Why are you all edgy?"

"Riley ate her last chocolate cookie," Ruben said.

"The point is," continued Riley, annoyed, "keeping a closer eye on your ancestors became more important."

"What are we doing now? What's the plan?" asked Eleanor.

"Ruben, Ned, and I are going to that gas station. You and Hanna might want to check Alec's house. Obviously he isn't there, but maybe you could fish something out from his parents. Something that would help us find him."

"Two girls asking about a boy. Bad idea." Eleanor waved her hand dismissively. "Hanna will go with Ned and I'll come with you."

"Me?" Ned poked his forefinger into his chest. "What do you expect me to do? I'm sure his parents know what his friends look like. Besides, what am I going to ask? I don't know him or anything about him."

"That's what Hanna's for." Eleanor stood up. "Riley, you didn't drink the last coffee, did you?" she smirked. "You don't want *me* to get cranky."

Passing Ruben, she shot him a glance and inclined her head toward the kitchen. Ruben followed her.

"What's going on?" she asked him, pouring herself a coffee. "They're acting like pissed off teenagers."

Ruben stepped closer and leaned on the countertop. "It's the powers. The energy is kicking in."

"Really? That's the reaction?" She leaned on the countertop next to him. "You and Ned seem okay."

"Yeah. It's because I've been kicking the punching bag in the cellar the whole night. And Ned—" He chortled. "First he and Hanna went to the bedroom, but after a moment they realized this wasn't the castle and the earthquake they created might bring down the whole house. So Ned spent some time climbing up and down the trees in the backyard, calling it training."

Eleanor released a short laugh.

Ruben looked at her sideways. "And you? Eleanor, how are you doing?"

She used her finger to wipe off the drop of coffee sliding down her cup. "I'm fine," she said, keeping her eyes on the spot. "No side effects."

"Are you sure?" Ruben's eyes moved from Eleanor's boots up to her chest, taking in her unbuttoned shirt-collar. He beamed.

"This is my new fighting outfit. What? You don't like it?" She ran her hand down her waist.

She looked up when she heard a click. Riley stood in the doorway with his cellphone in his hand.

"Did you just take a picture of us?" Eleanor squinted.

"Yeah. It's a Snapchat for Craig. I think he needs to hurry." Riley smiled broadly. "Let's go."

Ruben turned to Hanna as they walked out. "Could you pick up Kimberly? We might be late."

"Don't worry, I'll get to the school as soon as we're done," said Hanna.

～

HANNA STOOD IN THE HALLWAY, listening. The moment the car was gone, she dashed to Ned and punched him in the chest with both hands. He flew back and flopped onto the carpet.

"Are you crazy?" he growled, lifting his head.

She landed on top of him. "We are alone," she whispered with a seductive smile.

"Then why are you whispering?" Ned grinned. "Let it all out."

～

HANNA PARKED the car opposite Alec's house. Behind the neatly trimmed, low fence bushes, a BMW was parked on the left side of the porch.

"What do I say?" asked Ned.

"Just ask if Alec's home. I'll take over from there."

"What if he's home?"

"Then I'll stick this stake right up his ass," grumbled Hanna.

She looked up and down the street. A woman with two plastic bags in her hands came out from the house next to Alec's, heading for the trash can.

"Wait," she said as Ned reached for the door handle. "We don't need witnesses."

They watched the woman until she returned to the house. Then they got out of the car and walked up to the front door. Ned knocked. After waiting for about a minute, he knocked again. They waited for another minute, and when nobody opened the door, Hanna peered through the patterned glass.

"The car is here, someone has to be home," said Ned.

"Someone is," muttered Hanna. She tried the door. It was unlocked, as she suspected.

"Do you smell that?" asked Ned the moment they stepped inside.

"Yes," said Hanna grimly.

They crossed the threshold and stopped under the wide arch leading to the living room. There, on the polished oak floor, lay Mrs. Stafford, her face pale and her neck covered with blood. A pair of legs stuck out from behind the couch. Hanna drew closer. Mr. Stafford lay on his side between the couch and the coffee table. His mouth was slightly open, and there was a puddle of blood around his head, already thickened. It was formed not just from two small holes on his neck, but also from the cut on his temple.

"It happened recently. The smell isn't that strong yet," said Hanna.

Ned walked around the couch and moved toward the kitchen. "They're dead because they knew," he said, stopping in the kitchen doorway. "Look."

On the kitchen floor lay a dead vampire with a stake in his heart.

"They fought back," said Hanna, astonished. "They actually had a stake in their house, and they fought back."

"You think the vampires killed Alec, too?"

"No, I don't think so. Fray trusted Alec. I'm sure he's with them now. But let's check, just in case. You go upstairs."

Hanna checked the first floor, then went to the basement. The light from the hallway fell on the stairs. It illuminated a piece of flooring covered with cigarette butts and the corner of a pool table with empty bottles on it.

The same sickening smell stopped her right in the doorway. She muffled the scent, burying her nose in her sleeve, then slowly moved forward.

At the end of the room something or, evidently, someone lay on the couch. Keeping her eyes on it, Hanna stepped to the table and pulled the chain of the lamp hanging above. As light filled the room, Hanna gasped.

That someone was Nicole Price. Her blond hair was messed up, and her bluish face frozen in horror. *What did they do to her? Did they torture her?* The thought stopped Hanna's breath.

"What the hell were you doing here?" she yelled desperately. But then she remembered the party and Nicole's new boyfriend, the one who had looked suspicious to her. Alec had introduced them.

"Hanna," Ned called from the top of the stairs. "What is it?" He ran down and stopped next to her, his nose wrinkling. "Who is this? Did you know her?"

Hanna nodded. "She's from school."

"You think she knew something, too?"

"No. They probably used her to watch us." An unwitting deep breath of the putrid air choked her. "Did you find something?" she asked, coughing.

"No. He isn't here."

She threw one last glance at the thin, lifeless body, then said, "We have to go," and hurried away.

Chapter Eight

THE GAS STATION was about a forty minute drive from Green Hill. Sitting in the back seat, Eleanor didn't say a single word while they drove through the town. She was looking at the streets, at its houses, at its shops and cafes, and as she saw a woman pushing a stroller before her, Eleanor's thoughts drifted away.

She was a mother once. Maybe a mother who never got a chance to hold her child. A mother who had to watch her daughter grow up from a distance and who died right before her daughter's wedding. But a mother nonetheless, full of love toward that girl, her flesh and blood.

And she would never be a mother again. It was long, long ago for others. But not for her. To her it was like she had fallen asleep, and when she woke up, she was right where she left it. The past eighteen years of her life were like one thin, young branch on a big tree.

"Eleanor," Ruben said.

"Huh?" She turned her head to him, a little startled.

"Are you all right?"

"I'm fine." She looked at the cap in his hand. "What's that?"

"Extra precaution. Last time we checked, the gas station was closed. It had an alarm and cameras."

She took the cap and threw it on the seat. "I'm not a criminal. I'm a Hunter."

"Eleanor..."

"But Fray is. He's a killer. So I don't think that alarm is connected to the police station, and those cameras are just to watch for us. What kind of criminal would want the police on his tail? You said there are nine coffins in there. If the alarm goes off, the police will be here in minutes. What do you think would happen if they found the coffins?"

"We're not sure if there are transitioning vampires in those coffins. They could be empty," said Riley.

"Even if they are empty. Nine coffins at the gas station? Does it sound normal?"

"You're right," said Ruben. "Fray doesn't need police. He can set up traps all by himself."

The place looked abandoned. Riley parked the car a good distance away. As they got out, he opened the trunk. They all grabbed the stakes lying at the bottom. There was also a crowbar. Riley took it, and the three of them headed toward the entrance.

The next town was only ten minutes away, but this wasn't a main road, and only a few cars passed by.

They walked into the shadow of the concrete overlap above the entrance and looked through the glass doors. All lights inside were off.

"This looks too easy," said Ruben. "It's like a huge 'welcome' sign."

"Maybe there's nothing here," said Eleanor.

"Or maybe that's what he wants us to think," said Riley, and swiped the crowbar into the glass. The glass didn't break. "Bulletproof," he said, and sent another blow.

"Don't bother," said Ruben. "There has to be another way in."

They rounded the building. Behind looked as neglected as the rest of the place. There was one small covered trailer, a few pallets stacked on top of each other under the wall, and a dumpster.

There was also a big garage. Using the crowbar, Riley pulled off the combination lock hanging on its wide, newly painted wooden flaps. A gray van was parked inside, its back doors open. The concrete floor looked new, as well. The shelves were almost empty, except for a few cans of different sizes. An open plastic toolbox sat on a working table in the corner. Riley bent down to check the floor under the van.

"No hatches, no suspicious doors," said Ruben.

The lock on the thin, metal backdoor of the gas station seemed a little complicated. Riley wedged the crowbar between the lock and the door-frame. The second he pushed it, something on the other side of the door exploded with such power that the three of them flew back twenty feet in different directions. Pieces of pallets and shards of concrete showered down on them.

"What the hell was that?" wheezed Eleanor, sitting up and shaking the dust from her hair.

"Sorry, honey, did it ruin your new outfit?" said Ruben, looking at the tear on his hip and the blood on his jeans. "Look at the bright side," he groaned, pulling himself up and rubbing his back. "The door is open."

The lock was still in its place, but the other side of the door was crooked, the blow having uprooted the hinges from the metal frame.

"He knows it's not gonna stop us," said Eleanor, irritated.

Riley picked up the end of a wire running to the trailer. He stepped to the trailer and threw aside the synthetic blue cover. "But this could, for a while," he said, gazing at eight ten-gallon gas cans sitting in it, with something bulky wrapped around them. He bent down and looked under the trailer. "There is a detonator."

"Yeah, I suppose this firecracker was his idea of an alarm. Except his pyrotechnics sucked," said Ruben.

"He could have just put it next to the door," said Riley with a shrug.

"No," said Ruben, staring at the gas cans. "He wanted to knock us out first. That way we'd burn longer."

"We have to get rid of it, before someone gets hurt."

"Not yet," said Ruben. "This cloud of dust will settle down. But if we set off those cans, the next car that passes will see the fire and call the police, and all we'll be able to do is scrape ourselves from the ground and run before they arrive."

"Right. We'll do it after we search the building."

Riley dragged aside the crooked metal door, and the three of them walked through the small entrance. They passed the toilet and the broom cupboard. Stepping on the scattered pieces of concrete, they moved into the shop area. Chunks of plaster were on the floor, a few chip bags and chocolate bars had fallen from the shelves, but altogether it looked undamaged. At the other end of the shop, in the passage next to the counter, were the office and storage room.

The location wasn't big and searching didn't take long.

"There's nothing here," said Ruben.

"Empty or not, the coffins are here, hidden somewhere," said Riley. "Look behind the shelves. Eleanor, you check the office, I'll take the storage. Ruben, you search the store."

Eleanor walked into the office. Nothing seemed big enough to cover some secret passage. She moved the table to look at the piece of floor behind its solid sides, then pushed aside the metal filing cabinets. She also made sure there was nothing behind the jackets hanging on the wide clothes hanger before approaching a wooden cabinet. She pulled it, but it didn't budge. She peered around it. There was no gap between its back and the wall, and when she opened the doors, it was empty. The back panel of the cabinet wasn't wooden but a thin, shiny, gray metal. Eleanor looked at the wall and in the cabinet again. The piece of metal wasn't leveled with the wall; it sat visibly deeper.

"Guys," she shouted over the rattle coming from the other rooms, "I think I found something."

"It looks like a port," said Ruben, joining her. "But there's nothing to get a grip on."

Riley swung the crowbar, and with two blows he crushed the cabinet. Now that the light fell on the metal, Eleanor could look at it closer.

"Step aside in case it explodes again," said Riley, ready to thrust the crowbar between the wall and the metal.

"Wait," said Eleanor. "If this is an entrance, there has to be some way to open it." She bent down and placed her hands on the slick surface. First she tried to pull it up, then aside, but it didn't move. She examined the metal and saw that on its top, beneath the piece of broken wood still sticking out from the wall, was a dark, horizontal stripe. Eleanor pushed it, and the metal door slid up.

Crouching, they passed through the opening. On the other side of the wall was a staircase.

"This is the back side of the building," said Riley, walking down the stairs. Seeing a turn to the right once he reached the bottom, he added, "And this way leads us—"

"Under the garage," finished Ruben.

They rounded the corner. At the end of the passageway was a room with nine open coffins placed on stands along the walls. They gazed at the pale bodies, illuminated by the weak, yellow light coming from the ceiling lamps. Three women and six men.

"How long have they been here?" asked Eleanor, walking from one coffin to another.

"A couple of years," said Riley.

"Why are they open?" She stopped beside the last coffin of the row and ran her hand along its side. "This is odd."

Riley and Ruben walked up to her. Rubbing her fingers together, Eleanor crushed a piece of dry dirt between them.

"Look at their clothes," she said. "And look at this." She pointed at the Nike shoes and at the white silk covered with dirt.

"Those are just--" Ruben thrust the stake into the chest of the body lying in the coffin, "--vampires."

The vampire winced in pain. His eyes flew open, but after a short moan they closed again, and the body began shriveling.

They heard a noise behind them. Riley swung around. The tip of a massive knife was only inches away from his chest. He clutched the hand holding it and punched the vampire in the face. Staggering back, the vampire hit the casket behind him. Riley pulled out the stake and thrust it into his heart. In the same second he was attacked by two others.

The woman standing in her coffin jumped down at Eleanor, but Eleanor bounced back to the wall. Clinging to Eleanor's legs, the woman stopped herself from falling flat. Eleanor grabbed her by her long hair, pulled her up and hit her face on the corner of the casket.

Two vampires ran toward the exit.

"Eleanor, the van," yelled Ruben.

"I got this," she said, dashing after them.

In a few seconds Eleanor was upstairs. She reached the vampires at the back door, but the moment they stepped outside, she stopped. The garage was only thirty feet away and the gates were open. The vampires were moving forward, but they had no sunglasses, no jackets. She watched them cover their squinted eyes with their searing hands, writhing under the burning sun. She could have staked them right there. But she didn't. She looked at the gas cans in the trailer.

∼

RILEY AND RUBEN looked at the deep and already healing knife cuts on their chests and arms.

"What the hell was this?" said Riley. "Why would they sleep in coffins?"

"They were probably—"

Before Ruben could say another word, a loud bang came from above. They exchanged a quick, worried glance and darted to the exit.

"What happened? Are you all right?" asked Ruben, rushing to Eleanor.

"I am fine," she said dryly.

Riley and Ruben looked at her face, covered with a thin layer of soot, and then at the garage. Everything was in flames, and a huge black cloud stretched up to the sky. Screams came from the burning van.

"Did you do this?" asked Riley.

Eleanor nodded. "Didn't you say we had to get rid of it?"

"Yeah. But... Couldn't you kill them first and wait for us?"

"No. They were already in the van. I had to stop them." She looked at the lighter in her hand and tossed it away.

Without moving his head, Riley's eyes turned to Ruben, who was gazing at her.

"Okay," Riley said quietly. "Let's get out of here."

Chapter Nine

HANNA SAT on the bench facing the school building. She looked around with longing. It was over. Not only because it was the last day of school; it was the end of a time when she was just a normal girl--a girl who had fun at parties, who got nervous before exams, who went to school dances, who hung out with friends, who sent applications to colleges she'd probably never attend.

She thought of Kimberly. She must have been feeling lonely today without her best friends.

To Hanna's surprise, Kimberly came out of the school building with Debra Gordon. As Debra took off, Hanna started toward Kimberly.

"Hi," said Hanna, approaching her from behind.

Kimberly stopped her scan of the parking lot and turned around. "Hanna, hi."

"He's out of town, but he'll be back soon," said Hanna. They started toward the parking lot. "He asked if you could wait for him at our place."

Kimberly nodded, but her look remained absent.

"Did Debra want something?"

"She was asking about Alec. Alec and Aman..." Kimberly pressed her lips together, looking annoyed.

"Kimberly, it's okay, you can call her Amanda."

Kimberly threw her a quick glance. "Neither of them have been to school in two days. She asked if I knew where he was."

"What did you say?"

"The truth." Kimberly shrugged.

Hanna stopped, but Kimberly kept walking.

"What truth?" asked Hanna as she caught up to Kimberly

"That I don't know where he is, but I am absolutely sure he isn't with Amanda because Amanda's with her boyfriend, Craig. That all of us were at a big party outside of town, where we spent the night, and even though I am still battling my hangover, I had to come to school to avoid my mom's judgmental glare."

Hanna chuckled. "Well done."

Kimberly shook her head. "I'm not an idiot, Hanna."

"What? I never said . . . Kimberly, I've been lying to you for three years, and what I am saying is, I know how difficult it is to slip out from unexpected questions."

"I have one of those for you right now. Let's see if you can slip out of this one. Hanna," said Kimberly, and the note of sarcasm in her voice changed into perceptible anger. "Where is Nicole?"

Hanna wasn't going to hide from Kimberly what had happened to Nicole, but the tone of accusation in Kimberly's voice paralyzed her. "What do you mean?"

"She's missing. The police were here. They've been questioning us all day."

"Kimberly," Hanna sighed. "Ned and I, we went to . . . we just found out . . ."

"Oh God, she's dead, isn't she?" asked Kimberly, her lips shaking.

"Yes. We found her at Alec's house. In the basement."

"I knew it had something to do with yo... I mean with those..." She resisted saying the word. "Or maybe it was Alec?"

"No." Hanna shook her head. "She was bitten."

"Did you call the police?"

"No."

"Hanna, everybody is looking for her, and you know where she is." Kimberly stared at her with wide eyes. "You can't just leave her there." She stopped. "What about Alec's parents? If there is a dead girl in their house, why didn't they call the police?"

Hanna averted her eyes.

"No." Kimberly gasped. "Both of them?"

Hanna nodded.

"Hanna, three people are dead. You have to inform the police."

"I can't. If I call. . . . It's not just them. There is a dead vampire there. We think Alec's parents killed him."

"You mean they knew?" said Kimberly, looking at her in disbelief. "That's crazy."

"I don't know how the vampires are planning to clean up their mess. We couldn't do anything during the day, but we'll return to the house tonight, see if we're able to get Nicole's body out of there before they take her. We'll put her some place where she can be found."

They reached Hanna's car in silence.

"You know what," said Kimberly as she opened the car door, "I changed my mind. I want to go home."

"Kimberly, I'm not letting you leave my side. I promised Ruben—"

"Tell him we can meet later." Kimberly threw her satchel in the back seat.

"Are you sure? It'd be safer if you stayed with us."

"You have more important things to do than babysit me," said Kimberly coldly. "Find those monsters."

"We will," said Hanna.

They drove in silence, and only when Hanna stopped the car in front of Kimberly's house did she say, "Please, stay at home, don't go anywhere without us."

"Where would I go without you?" said Kimberly, averting her eyes from Hanna. "I don't go anywhere without my friends." She got out and slammed the door behind her.

∽

HANNA SAT at the kitchen table. The window in front of her was open. Outside was quiet and all she could hear were birds. While Ned was in the basement, burning his energy by kicking the punching bag, she stared into the open laptop, checking the local newspapers to see if anyone else was killed or missing. From what she had read so far, Nicole was the only one the police were searching for. Hanna thought of Nicole's parents, what they were going through, and she felt guilty. The only thing she could do for them now was make sure their daughter's body was found. Kimberly was right to be angry with her. The Hunters were the reason vampires came to Green Hill, making Nicole's death their fault.

Hanna heard a car, and the next moment the Jeep showed up in the driveway.

"I can see you had your first hunt," she said as Ruben, Riley, and Eleanor walked into the hallway. "What happened?" she asked, eying the bloodstains on their torn, dusty clothes.

Riley headed to the living room. "First there was an explosion."

"At the gas station?"

"Yep, in the backyard. Then there were vampires with big knives,"

"And the coffins?" asked Ned, coming out from the basement door, "Did you find the coffins?"

"That's exactly where we found the vampires--in the coffins. They used them as beds."

"Yeah, it was just one of Fray's traps," said Ruben. "Where is Kimberly?" he asked, looking around.

"I drove her home," said Hanna. "She was sad and wanted some time alone."

"Sad? Why?" asked Ruben, wary.

Hanna looked at Eleanor. "Nicole Price is dead."

"What?" Eleanor gasped. "How did it happen?"

"Vampires. We found her at Alec's, in the basement."

"Nicole?" Ruben sat on the couch. "Isn't that the girl from the party?"

Hanna nodded. "It's not just Nicole. Alec's parents are dead, too."

"They killed Alec's parents?" Eleanor sat down next to Ruben, looking perplexed. "I was sure he did what he did for a reward, that Fray promised to turn him. Instead, he got punished. It doesn't make sense."

"Maybe they found out about their son's extracurricular activities and became a problem?" suggested Ruben.

"They knew," said Ned. "There was a staked vampire in their kitchen."

"Riley, what do we do?" asked Hanna. "We need to find those vampires. We can't just let them run around killing people."

"Well, we just killed nine of them," said Riley. "But it's obvious there are more." He looked at Ruben. "We'll do as we planned—we'll check the other locations."

"Right," said Ruben. "That's the quickest way to find those bloodsuckers. They'll be, if not in the coffins, then somewhere around, guarding them."

"Which place do you think we should check next?" asked Ned. "The crypt or the warehouse?"

"Let me know what you decide," said Eleanor, getting up. "I have to go. I need to get out of these clothes and take a shower."

"Sure," said Hanna. As Eleanor closed the door behind her, Hanna turned to Ruben. "How is she? Is she all right?"

"She seems okay." Ruben shrugged. "But who knows how she really feels."

"You're right. It's Eleanor. No matter what, she'll pretend she's fine," said Hanna.

Riley dropped down across from Ruben. "She's not fine. She just fried two vampires. If she had time to find a lighter and position the trailer, I'm sure she had enough time to stake them. But she chose to burn them."

"I know," sighed Ruben. "That's what I've been thinking."

"She's angry," said Hanna, nodding slowly.

"She's not just angry," said Riley. "She's in pain. She doesn't just want them dead, she wants them to suffer."

"Maybe if Craig were here—"

"Well, he's not. So we have to keep an eye on her, help her control her emotions. Her rage can get her into trouble. And not just her."

"Now that we've sorted that out," said Ned, "which place first––crypt or warehouse?"

Hanna, Ruben, and Riley stared at him.

"What?" shrugged Ned. "You had your fight, I want some, too. I'm exploding here."

∼

THEY DECIDED to check the crypt first, but they couldn't break into it before dark. The graveyard was located in a populated area and acted as a park during the day. People came just to sit on a bench, read a book, walk their dog, or cut across its walkway with tall, arched trees as a shortcut from one street to another.

At night, the darkness scared the people away. And if there were vampires in those coffins, that would be the time for them to get out. The four of them agreed it would be better to go before sunset to keep an eye on the crypt and wait until dark.

Ruben pulled out his cellphone and went to the backyard. He sent a message to Eleanor letting her know about their plan, then he called Kimberly and asked her to meet him. After their conversation at the castle's beach, he couldn't help thinking he was losing her. When he drove her to school that morning, she'd barely said a word, giving curt answers to his questions and excusing them with lack of sleep.

Of course, there was a lot for her to take in. She needed time for that, and he hoped she'd let him help her instead of pushing him away. He wanted to be there for her, and not only because he cared about her. He felt responsible for turning her world upside down. She became friends with Amanda when she was nine years old. Nobody knew then that Amanda would become Eleanor, not even the Hunters. But if it weren't for Ruben, she might never have found out who Amanda was, that the Hunters were not just a legend, and that monsters were real. It was his fault she witnessed the murder of somebody she knew, that she got in the middle of this fight. And now that Fray had seen Kimberly with him, she had become a target.

~

IT WAS HOT. They walked down by the canal until Ruben noticed a bench in between the trees.

"I can't stay long," said Kimberly as they sat down. "Mom and David are meeting friends tonight. They want me to look after my brother."

"Be careful. You know how it works. Don't invite anyone you don't know into your house."

"I won't. Don't worry, I'll be okay."

Ruben took her hand. "Kimberly, I can't apologize enough for getting you into this mess. I shouldn't have let you come with me that day."

"You didn't do this. You wanted me to go back to Green Hill, but I was too stubborn."

"I should have forced you," said Ruben, looking at her. "I'm sorry."

Kimberly didn't meet his eyes. "I'm not," she said quietly, her gaze fixed on the motionless shadow of leaves from the branch hanging above them. "After everything that happened that day, the only thing I'm sorry about is that Melinda got killed and I saw it happen. I'm not sorry for knowing the truth about you."

"But you're angry with us. We're the reason they're here. Hanna said—"

"I was. When I heard about Nicole, I couldn't think straight. I needed time alone, to put my thoughts together. So much has happened in the last two days. You're not the bad guys––they are, and because of them, everybody in this town is in danger."

"I know you're scared," said Ruben. "We can't guarantee there will be no more deaths––there are too many vampires out there, and we still don't know where they are. But I'll never let anything happen to you. We'll all look after you."

"I know." Kimberly nodded. "I know my superhero friends will do everything they can to keep me safe. I'm a lucky girl," she said with irony. "I know I'm in danger, too, but that's not what scares me. What I'm really afraid of is one day waking up and you're gone, and so are my friends, and I'll have no memories of any of you." She pushed back her long ginger hair. "I'll be lonely, but I'll never understand why I have a big hole in my chest, and why I feel so empty."

"Kimberly, what are you talking about?"

"Isn't that what happens when you erase someone's memory?"

"What? Nobody is going to erase your memory."

"It's not up to you to decide. You said yourself that people can't know about your existence. Samson will never agree..."

"Samson would never do such a thing without asking me. We are not an army, we are family, he loves us and respects our wishes and opinions."

Kimberly released a heavy sigh. "And then what? They were my best friends, we were just girls. It'll never be the same. The two of them . . . they've known each other for so long, they have such a strong bond."

"I know where this is coming from," said Ruben. "It's because Eleanor and Hanna couldn't be with you today." Ruben put his hands on her shoulders. "Look at me," he said, turning her towards him. "They are still your friends, and I'm not going anywhere without you."

Kimberly's face changed and the sadness in her eyes faded.

"Who's Eleanor?" She squinted. "We don't have an Eleanor in our class." She smiled.

"That's better," said Ruben, pulling her closer.

"That's why I tried not to look at you," said Kimberly, resting her head on his chest. "You're worse than a witch. You can wipe my memory with one glance."

Chapter Ten

THREE HUNTERS WERE MORE than enough to check out the crypt. So when Riley, Ned, and Eleanor left, Ruben and Hanna waited until dark and headed to Alec's place to recover Nicole's body.

Hanna hit the brakes before they reached the house, and both of them stared at the police car parked out front.

"Crap," said Hanna through gritted teeth. "What do we do?"

But before Ruben could say anything, they heard a muted pop. A gunshot. They looked at each other, then around at the empty street. They leaped out of the car and dashed toward the front door.

The moment they walked in, a pungent, caustic smell hit their noses.

"It's gotten much worse." Hanna pressed her palm to her nose. "It's revolting."

They passed the threshold and stopped under the arch. The living room was illuminated by two lamps. The sheaves of yellow light they cast on the walls looked like huge dandelions. Next to one of them stood a tall, robust vampire who wrestled a policeman in his grip.

At the spot where Mrs. Stafford's body lay before, now lay a long, black bag with two handles, while Mr. Stafford's legs still stuck out from behind the couch.

The vampire spotted Ruben and Hanna and wrapped his arm around the policeman's neck. "Ha!" he smirked. "Look who's here."

"I'm glad you recognized us. Now let him go before I rip your head off," said Ruben, glaring at the vampire.

"No," said the vampire, baring his fangs. "If you take another step, I'll rip *his* off."

The choking policeman clung to the arm of the vampire.

"I don't see how it's going to help you stay alive," said Hanna.

They heard heavy footsteps, followed by the sound of something rubbing against the floor. A second vampire came out from the basement, dragging another body bag by the handle.

"Put her down," hissed Hanna.

The vampire gazed at her, then turned to his partner. "Roy?"

Hanna dashed toward him and clutched his throat. "I said put her down." As he dropped the bag, Hanna threw him across the room. The vampire slammed against the big TV hanging on the wall and crashed to the floor.

Ruben looked at the wheezing policeman. The moment he got Ruben's attention, the officer rolled his eyes toward the window. Ruben followed the gaze and saw the policeman's gun on the floor, under the sill.

"According to you two, we're gonna die anyway," said the vampire called Roy. "So I have a last wish." He sank his fangs into the policeman's neck.

"Stop," said Ruben. "I have an offer."

Roy pulled his head up, licking the blood from his lips. "I'm all ears," he said, sneering.

"We take the policeman and the girl's body, and after you clean up your mess, you can get the hell out of here."

"He saw us," said Roy, pointing at the policeman. "He saw

you. We can't let him go."

"It's not your concern. We'll take care of it."

"I don't trust you," growled Roy.

Ruben glanced at Roy, who was almost a head taller than the policeman. He walked to the window and picked up the gun. "Like you have a choice," said Ruben, and he shot the vampire in the forehead. Roy swayed and dropped to the floor. The policeman, who had crashed on top of him, jumped to his feet.

Ruben turned to the second vampire, still standing next to the lopsided TV. "When he comes around, you two better do as I said, or I might change my mind." As the vampire nodded, Ruben looked at the policeman. "Don't try anything stupid. We can't let you go right away, but we're not going to hurt you. And we need your help."

The policeman stared at the gun in Ruben's hand. Ruben stepped back to the sill and put the gun down.

"Ruben," whispered Hanna, pulling him aside. "How are we going to . . . we don't have a witch to erase his memory."

"He'll stay with us until we find one."

"You better hurry, then," said the vampire, nodding toward the policeman.

Holding the gun with both hands and pointing it at the vampire, the policeman was slowly moving to the front door. The moment Ruben moved, the policeman aimed at him.

"Stop, or I'll shoot," he shouted.

Ruben stopped. The man was around forty, had a strong body. With a gun in his hand, he seemed confident that he was back in control. But to his disappointment, Ruben took another step and then, in a flash, he stood right next to him, the gun in Ruben's hand.

The shocked man stared at him. "How did you do that?"

"What's your name?" asked Ruben. He looked at the holes on the man's neck and the collar of his shirt, soaked in blood.

"Mike."

"Listen to me carefully, Mike. This," said Ruben calmly, putting the gun into the holster on the policeman's belt, "can't help you. The bullets can't stop any of us."

The man closed his open mouth and swallowed. "It stopped him," he said, turning to Roy.

"He's not dead."

"You shot him in the head," said the policeman indignantly, pointing his hand at the vampire.

"In a few minutes, he'll be as good as new. Sorry." Ruben gave a fake smile. "But you won't be here to witness the miracle. We have to do this very quickly. First-- what were you doing here?"

"We got an anonymous call that there might be a robbery."

"Did you come alone?"

"Yes."

"Good." Ruben thought for a few seconds, then said, "You'll tell everybody who asks that it was a false alarm. That Mr. and Mrs. Stafford are spending time in their cabin and needed a few things from the house. Their friends came to pick up the stuff and you even helped them." He turned to Hanna. "Go get his car."

"No," said Hanna. "His car will attract attention."

"Right." Ruben frowned. "Go get yours. Park it with the trunk to the porch."

He walked to the black bag holding Nicole's body. "Come here," he said to the policeman, taking one handle. "Grab the other one."

"We can't do this," protested the policeman. "This is a crime scene. These are dead people," he said, pointing at the bags. "What if someone heard the gunshots?"

"There was no one outside. Besides, I have perfect hearing, and even I barely heard it."

"But what if..."

"You'll come up with something. Listen, Mike," said Ruben firmly, "I need to get out of here. The moment I'm gone, you'll become stuffing for one of those bags." Still holding the handle on one side of the bag, he beckoned his head. "I said grab the other one."

When Hanna said that it was safe to come out, Ruben and Mike carried the bag to the car and put it in the trunk.

"You'll come with us," Ruben said to Mike. "But first we need to find some place where we can park that--" he nodded toward the police car "--for a couple of hours."

∼

WHEN BOTH CARS stopped in a dark alley, Ruben turned to Mike. "Do you have an emergency kit?"

"It's in the trunk," said Mike grimly.

Hanna got out of her car and walked to Ruben as he waited for Mike to rummage through his trunk.

"Where are we going to take her?" she asked quietly.

"Somewhere outside of town." Ruben looked at Hanna's tear-filled eyes. "I'm sorry, Hanna."

"It's my fault. It's all my fault," she said bitterly. "I saw him at the party. I should have known that bastard was one of them."

"No, it's not your fault. I was there, too, and I didn't sense it either."

"Here," said Mike, handing the emergency kit to Ruben.

Ruben opened it, found a bandage.

"Let me," said Hanna, taking the bandage out of Ruben's hand. She approached Mike. "Can I see your neck? You'll have to come up with some story about how you got injured." She put the bandage on his wound. "And you'll have to change your shirt before getting back to the station."

"Why can't I go now?" asked Mike, looking angry. "Where are you taking me?"

"Because," said Ruben, putting the emergency kit back in the trunk, "as I said, we need your help. Let's go. I'll explain on the way."

Pressing his lips together, Mike followed them to Hanna's car.

"This girl in the trunk is Nicole Price," said Ruben as they drove.

"Nicole Price?" Mike frowned. "That's the girl we have been looking for."

"Yes. She was the innocent victim of a fight she knew nothing about. We went to the house to get her body before those monsters took her somewhere she would never be found. We did it because she didn't deserve to go that way. We need you to see where we put her so you can call the police and tell them you found her. You can do it today, or you can do it tomorrow––it's up to you to decide when and how. Can you do that, Mike?"

Mike swallowed. "Yes, I can do that," he said, running his fingers through the short, gray hair at his temples. "Did you know her?"

Ruben looked into the rearview mirror. Sitting in the back seat, Hanna turned her head and looked at the trunk.

"Yes. She was my friend," she said. "We're just trying to do the right thing. Her parents deserve to say goodbye to their daughter, to bury her properly." She sighed. "Otherwise they'll never find peace."

Mike took a deep breath. "Listen, I understand that you mean well, but . . . what about the other two bodies? I can still call backup, maybe we could—"

"You can't," said Ruben. "Believe me. I know what I'm talking about."

"I've been a policeman for sixteen years. I've seen things. I've seen a lot of things. But what I saw today . . ." Mike gazed at Ruben. "Who are they?"

"I can't tell you. And even if I did, you'd never believe me."

"Maybe I would." Mike shrugged. "That man bit me. I felt him sucking my blood."

Ruben threw a glance in the mirror. Hanna closed her eyes and shook her head.

"What's even more interesting, and also very disturbing," continued Mike, "is that those men were afraid of you." He looked at Ruben, waiting for a reaction.

"Because we know who they are and how to fight them," said Ruben.

"You said that the man you shot will come back to life, that a bullet can't stop any of you."

"I only said that to stop you from—"

"Don't." Mike waved his hand. "Don't do that. It's too late to backpedal." He took another deep breath. "Why do you think I didn't try to escape, or fight you? I'm a policeman. I'm twice as old as you, I have a gun, and I'm not a coward."

"No, you're not a coward," said Ruben, stopping the car at a red light. "You just witnessed some very weird things, and it surprises me it didn't scare you." He looked at the intersection. "Which way is shorter to the highway? I think if I turn left. . . ."

"Just drive forward," said Mike. "You're in the wrong lane."

"Nothing we can't fix," said Ruben, stepping on the gas pedal and turning the wheel. The car swung to the left, filling the gap between two cars as they drove across. Several horns beeped loudly around them. Mike shook his head.

After a few more minutes, they turned into a quiet alley, leaving behind the busy streets.

Mike began tapping the door handle with two fingers. "My father was a believer," he said, looking absently through the window glass.

"Was he a policeman, too?" asked Ruben.

"No, he was a carpenter." Mike paused for a moment, then spoke again in a lower voice. "He was also a hunter. Twice a year they gathered with friends for a big hunt. But the rest of the year he hunted alone. Once, when he came back from the woods, I heard him telling my mother that he saw something in there. I was thirteen years old. I was already in bed when I heard his truck. When I came downstairs, I heard him saying, 'I saw it. I'm sure it was one of them.' My mom laughed and said, 'Henry, it's just a legend.' 'Aren't you listening?' said my father. 'I'm telling you, I saw it. A young man on a horse disappeared right in front of my eyes. It was like he went through something and vanished, and the air rippled behind him.'" Mike cleared his throat, then continued. "I was hiding behind the kitchen door. I was afraid that if my father saw me, he'd stop talking. He was so excited. 'That was it,' he said. 'The invisible wall. I found it.'"

Ruben could feel Hanna's stare on him, but he didn't glance back. "Did you believe him?" he asked Mike.

"Yeah, I did then," said Mike. "He told the story to his hunter friends. At first they made jokes, asking how many beers he had that day, but then they asked him to show them the spot. But my father never found it again. So it became one of those stories that hunters tell each other in the dark woods around the fire."

The Hunters had been powerless for such a long time, but they weren't forgotten. Somewhere inside Ruben, sudden joy, like a little ball of sunshine, spread warmth throughout his whole body.

"That's how the legend stays alive," he said quietly, his eyes fixed on the road. He knew Mike was looking at him from the corner of his eye, but he couldn't suppress his smile.

They drove a couple of miles down the highway before Ruben noticed a narrow exit. He pulled over and parked the car in between the trees. After they put the body on the ground and covered it with branches, they drove Mike back to his car.

"You understand you can't tell anyone what you saw today," said Ruben.

Mike nodded and pushed the door open.

"It's for your own safety," said Hanna.

"I know," said Mike. He was about to get out of the car, but he stopped and turned to Ruben again. "I just don't get it. Why did you let them go?"

"There were already four bodies in that house. We couldn't let the police find them, and if I'd killed those two, it would be me who had to get rid of them all. I needed them to clean up their mess. But don't worry, we won't let them get away with this."

Mike nodded again. Ruben and Hanna sat in silence until he got in his car. Only when he drove away did they look at each other, exchanging a smile.

"That was a nice story," said Hanna.

"Yeah," said Ruben, starting the engine.

∼

FRAY PACED HIS STUDY, hands clenched into fists. It was such a pleasure to feel his blood burn in his veins again, to feel this enormous power fill up his body. It was back, all of it, and he couldn't wait to get into the last fight to crush Samson's kingdom, to kill off his precious family and watch him suffer alone forever.

All those years he had to move from place to place to keep the Hunters away from everything he was hiding—the Book, the daggers, the transitioning vampires. If he destroyed Samson's empire, he wouldn't have to do it anymore. He would finally be able to return to the castle, to his home where he belonged and which he missed so much. His secret mansion in Williamsburg where he lived with Joanne, and which he had kept safe all these years, was very dear to him, but it couldn't replace the castle. When the mansion was detached from the other estates, he could avoid meeting people. Now the place was surrounded by houses, which made it harder for him to stay there unnoticed.

He couldn't wait for the day when he'd be able to show Joanne the castle. She'd fall in love with it. It wouldn't be easy for her to wake up to this different, new world. The castle would be a perfect place for her to live while adjusting.

All he needed to make his dreams come true was a couple of weeks. That's how long it would take for the transitioning vampires to wake up. Without them, he was in danger of losing everything. When the Hunters were powerless, it was easy to get away from them. But now he had to be extremely careful. His plan to distract, to mislead the Hunters, was working. He didn't care how many of his vampires he had to sacrifice to get what he wanted. There were only a few who were truly valuable; the oldest ones, who had been with him from the beginning, the ones chosen by him and turned by Joanne the first year after they met.

Right now he was very vulnerable, so he chose to stay hidden. He was sure that finding him would be the number one item on the Hunters to-do list. But based on the information he had, they were looking for the bodies and not him. Why? What was the point of finding the bodies, if they had nothing to kill them with? Shouldn't they be trying to get the daggers first?

Samson was planning something. He wouldn't have closed the Book or sacrificed Eleanor's life just to lose them all over again right after bringing them back to life. Samson was the true First Hunter and the Keeper of the Book. He was the only one who had ever met the Higher Powers and could read the golden pages. There was something in that Book, something that gave him the strength to do what he did, and Fray supposed Craig knew what that something was. Otherwise he would never forgive Samson for taking Eleanor away from him for one and a half centuries.

What was Samson up to?

Fray's cellphone rang. He picked it up. "How did it go, Roy?" asked Fray.

"The place is clean. We took care of the Staffords' and Bob's bodies."

Fray distinctly remembered there being four bodies to be removed from the house. "What about the fourth body?"

"Yeah . . . about that . . ."

"What is it?"

"We had some complications," mumbled Roy.

"What complications?" Fray demanded, losing his patience.

"There was a policeman. Before I could take care of him, the Hunters showed up. Ruben and Hanna."

"Why? What did they want? And how are you still alive?"

"They came for that girl, the fourth body. They left us alive to clean up the rest of the mess."

"What about the policeman? He's a witness."

"They took him, too."

Fray hung up, confused. That girl was one of Hanna's friends, he remembered now. They used her to get information about Amanda. Why would the Hunters waste their time, drop everything and come there just to get her body, instead of . . .

Ralph entered the study.

"Any news?" asked Fray.

"No. There's no trace of Samson, and Craig is gone, too."

"Find them," shouted Fray.

"And then what?" roared Ralph. "Even if I find them, I can't follow them. Who am I against Samson? It's nothing like before. They have their powers back, they'll sense me if I get close to them. At least give me the dagger so I have something to protect myself with."

"I can't give you the dagger. I can't risk it."

"So what do you expect me to do? After all we've been through together, you're sending me out to die for nothing."

"I need to know where he's heading, what he's up to. You are my strongest."

"Yeah, and I'm also the one who put the dagger to Hanna's throat. Or do you think they forgot that? You promised you'd turn me the day the Book opened. Instead you're sending me on a suicide mission."

"I can't put to sleep all the oldest and strongest and leave myself with only newborns at such a crucial moment," said Fray, lowering his voice. "Alec's transformation won't take long. Only a couple more days. I promise—as soon as he's awake, I'll turn you."

"Meanwhile, I'm staying alive so I can be there when it happens," snapped Ralph.

"Fine." Fray glared at him. "I'll find another way."

Chapter Eleven

ELEANOR LAY in the bath in Craig's bedroom, covered in fluffy bubbles. She tried to relax, to convince herself that everything would be fine. But her boiling blood and every thought in her head fought against that concept, blocking her attempt to find and manifest something positive. She was in a fury, and it wasn't easy to hide it. Gabriella, Melinda, and Nicole were dead, and who knew how many would die before they'd found a way to stop these monsters. She couldn't ignore the fact that at this point they had nothing. No Book, no daggers, and they didn't know where Fray, Alec, or the transitioning vampires were. When she asked Riley about Samson's plan and Craig's part in it, Riley only offered that it was a secret mission and *our job is to find the transitioning bodies.*

But it seemed like Riley himself knew what the mission was. Eleanor trusted Samson. She had been a part of his secret mission once, and she knew there must be a reason why Riley couldn't tell her the truth. But her brain resisted cooperating with her feelings. She had died to prove her devotion to the Hunters' mission, and it seemed unfair to her to be kept in the dark. She had to ask again. She needed to know that the plan would work, that Fray and Alec would get what they deserved. She owed them pain, and she had to be sure that, when the time came, she'd get to pay her debt.

She walked downstairs, the smell of frying meat and onion guiding her. She headed to the kitchen, where she found Riley with a big knife in his hand, cutting mushrooms at the counter loaded with vegetables. On the stove behind him, the steaming pan crackled.

"What are you doing?" asked Eleanor, surprised.

"Making dinner," said Riley, shifting the mushrooms into the pan.

"Since when do you cook?"

Riley grinned.

"This is nothing." Eleanor heard Ruben's voice behind her. "You should see him sewing on buttons."

"I'm hungry," Hanna said, following him. She stepped to the counter and grabbed a bell pepper ring from the plate of sliced vegetables.

"You're back," said Ned as he came through the door, holding a bottle of red wine in each hand.

"Are we celebrating something?" asked Hanna. She kissed him. "Did you find something in the crypt?"

"No. At least not what we were looking for," said Riley. "But it doesn't mean we're not allowed a glass of wine with food."

"It was a waste of time," said Eleanor.

"I wouldn't say so," disagreed Ned. "We killed the vampires, didn't we? You yourself literally unscrewed two heads, and we staked the rest. Now all eight of them can sleep in their coffins forever."

Eleanor caught the concerned look that Hanna exchanged with Riley. "What?" She shrugged. "They got what they deserve."

"How about you?" asked Riley, sliding chopped tomatoes into a bowl. "Did you get the girl's body?"

"Yes." Hanna nodded gloomily, and she and Ruben told the others everything that had happened at Alec's house.

"You let the vampires go?" Eleanor frowned.

"I didn't have a choice," said Ruben, uncorking one of the wine bottles.

"So you just let them go," repeated Eleanor angrily.

"Yeah. You see, first I thought we'd have to kill them, then we'd clean the place and it would be nobody's business if we carried out six dead bodies from someone's house. But then I thought, what if all six bodies wouldn't fit in the trunk?"

Riley burst out laughing.

"This isn't funny," said Eleanor, shooting an angry glance at Riley. "What about the policeman? He saw you. What do we do if he shows up with ten others on our doorstep?"

"I wouldn't worry about the policeman," said Hanna. "He's not going to tell on us."

"What makes you so sure?" asked Ned.

"What is he going to tell?" said Ruben, filling the wine glasses. "That a vampire bit him and he helped us cover the killer's tracks? Wherever he ends up after saying that, I'll feel obligated to visit him at least once."

"Okay," said Riley. "Set the table, the food's almost ready."

After the dinner, Hanna and Eleanor volunteered to clean up the table and do the dishes. The boys grabbed a bottle of whiskey and went to the backyard.

Hanna turned to Eleanor. "How are you?" she asked gently. "Eleanor, I'm worried about you."

"Why? I'm okay," said Eleanor, putting the dirty plates in the dishwasher.

"No, you're not. You're angry. Tell me what's wrong."

"I don't know." Eleanor sighed.

"Is it because of Craig? Because Samson took him away?"

"I miss him, yes. But it's not that. I think it's much worse for him. After waiting all these years . . ."

"Don't worry about him," said Hanna, handing her a wine

glass. "He was prepared for this. He knew as soon as the Book was opened, he'd have to leave."

"Hanna." Eleanor put the glass back on the table. "Do you know what they're up to?"

"No, I don't."

"Are you lying to me?"

"Of course not. I think Riley and Ruben know, but they won't tell."

"Why not? Since when can we not be trusted? I died for this, and I just want to know that after everything, we have a chance to make it right again."

"It's not about trust. This mission . . ." Hanna sat down. "It has something to do with the golden pages. Gabriella died because Samson shared one of those secrets with her. I think he is trying to protect us."

That night Eleanor didn't go home. She spent the rest of the evening with the others, planning their next move. It was around midnight that she went upstairs to Craig's bedroom. She turned on the lamp on the nightstand, sat on the bed, and looked around. She remembered the night when she snuck up here, and how embarrassed she was when Craig and Melinda found her in Craig's bed. That was only a week ago. So much had changed since then. She was Eleanor now, and everybody in this house was her real family. Now, nothing could make more sense, and nothing would make her happier than to see Craig walk through that door.

But Craig was far away. And it was Fray's fault. Every bad thing that happened to her and her family was Fray's fault.

Her phone rang.

"Hi," Craig's voice said.

"Hi," she replied. She pulled her legs up and sat on the bed, leaning on the headboard. "Where are you?"

"We're in the Vaernes airport. We need to get to this little place called Hommelvik. Samson's renting a car."

"What is in the Hom... Homvik?"

"Hommelvik." Eleanor could feel Craig smile. "It's surrounded by woods. That's where we're headed."

"Woods? What's in the woods?"

"Eleanor, I know you're curious, but . . . I wish I could tell you more."

"I know." Eleanor breathed heavily. "Just tell me you're not in danger. Are you?"

"I'm not. It's you I'm worried about. I talked to Riley. He thinks you're a little on edge. Promise me you won't do anything reckless."

"Riley said?" Eleanor rolled her eyes. "I'm killing vampires. Isn't that what we're supposed to do?"

"Promise me," insisted Craig.

"Okay, I promise, and don't worry, I'm fine." She took the pillow sitting next to her and pressed it to her chest.

"What time is it there?" asked Craig.

"It's midnight. What time is it in Norway?"

"Nine a.m. Are you at home?"

"No. I'm in your bed. Planning to fall asleep hugging your pillow."

"I miss you so much," said Craig with longing.

"I miss you, too." Eleanor sighed.

"Samson's coming."

"Go. See you in my dreams," said Eleanor.

But Eleanor's dreams weren't as pleasant as she wished them to be. In her dream, she was back in the old times. The whole night was spent with a stake in her hand; she was chasing a vampire. A woman in a black gown. They were running through the woods first, but following the woman, Eleanor came out to a small, moonlit field. The woman ran toward the house standing on the other side of it. Before she could cross the field, Eleanor caught up with her. When Eleanor grabbed the woman's shoulder to turn her around, the woman vanished. The next moment, Eleanor was back in the woods, chasing the same woman all over again.

Chapter Twelve

CRAIG PUSHED the phone into the back pocket of his jeans and strode across the terminal toward Samson.

"Ready to go?" asked Samson.

Craig nodded, and as Samson headed to the exit, he followed, still thinking about Eleanor, recalling the sound of her voice. After waiting all those years for his Eleanor to come back to him, he had to leave her the day it happened, and there was nothing he could do about it because the mission always came first.

After her death, it took him a long time to understand it, to forgive her for secretly signing up for that suicide mission. But she was back now, and so were those forgotten feelings, the lust and passion. She was in his room, lying in his bed, and he wished to be the pillow she was hugging right now. That thought brought a smile to his face, but it faded the second he remembered their conversation. The questions he couldn't answer, just like when she was Amanda. Craig could only imagine how angry it must make her. He didn't want to have secrets from Eleanor, and he would gladly tell her everything he knew about this trip, especially the fact that she was a big part of Samson's plan. But Samson said he had to give her time to become the Eleanor she used to be before dropping her into a new assignment. Besides, it wasn't safe for any of them to know where he and Samson were heading and the meaning of their trip.

The rental, a gray Jeep Cherokee, waited for them in the parking lot. They got into the car, and a short moment later they were driving down highway E6, stretching along the fjord. It was a warm, sunny morning, but the howling wind blowing from the fjord was strong enough to rock the car. Craig reached into the bag in the back seat and pulled out his sunglasses. He put them on and looked at the clear blue sky. An airliner neared the low bridge crossing the highway, only a hundred meters ahead of them. It was decreasing, landing. Roaring, the plane sank lower, and its massive wheels touched the concrete of the bridge. At that moment the Jeep slid under the bridge, and when they came out on the other side, the plane was far away.

"The bridge is a part of the landing strip," said Samson.

"Impressive. I've driven here before but hadn't caught the blockbuster scene. It felt like it was landing on my head." Craig grinned. He glanced at the big, yellow road sign with destinations. The name Hommelvik wasn't there. "How far is it?" he asked.

"Ten to fifteen minutes."

"The witch, does she know we're coming?"

"No. Last time I met her was long ago." Samson looked at Craig, then at the road again. "But she knew that the moment Eleanor was back, I'd come to her."

"What if she isn't home?"

Samson's hand ran over his forehead and down his shoulder length hair. "We're not going to her home. We're going to an old, abandoned house. We're meeting there so she can hand over the box."

"Why didn't you call her? She could be anywhere."

"She probably knew Eleanor was back the moment it happened. I'm sure she's nearby."

"How? You mean witches can sense that?"

"No. But she can. She isn't an ordinary witch." Samson glanced at Craig. "She's like me. She's the First Witch."

Craig stared at him. "The First Witch? How come we never heard about her? Why didn't you tell us?"

"Because I read about her on the golden pages and, as you know, that's secret information. I'm glad I followed the rules and never told Fray about her. During all those years, she was my safest harbor."

"Is she as old as you are?" Craig asked, still processing the news.

"Oh no. She's much older."

Craig looked at the dagger, imprinted on Samson's forearm. "Does she have a sign, too? What is it?" He chuckled. "A cauldron?"

Samson smiled. "It's a pentagram. It's colorful and shaped a little differently than ours."

Craig glanced at the fjord. Not far from its shore was a small island covered with pointed coniferous trees and resembling a giant hedgehog.

"Samson, you chose me for this," said Craig. "It means you trust me. Don't you think that it's time to fill me in?"

"I'll tell you everything you need to know to fulfill your mission. The rest you'll find out yourself."

"How do you do that?" Craig shook his head.

"Do what?" Samson gazed at him.

"You're eight hundred years old and still full of secrets. How do you keep all those secrets without exploding?"

"Oh, that." Samson sighed heavily. "I take my duty seriously. So should you. After a while, I started feeling good about it. It gave me power."

"Like you need more of that. You are the most powerful man on the planet."

"No. Not that kind of power, not physically. I mean knowing

something no one else does. Knowledge can be a very powerful weapon."

Craig looked at him, at the man who seemed only a few years older than Craig himself. At the man who was always confident, determined, poised, and in control. "That's why the Higher Powers chose you. They knew you could do it. All of it."

"I don't know. I always thought that it was dumb luck." Samson beamed. "Never got a chance to ask, never seen them since."

It was nice to see him smile. Time wasn't dead anymore. The clock was ticking again, counting minutes, and each minute brought him closer to his goal.

The blue road sign informed them that the tunnel ahead was three hundred meters long. Before entering it, Samson pulled his sunglasses to the top of his head. The glasses weren't that black and he could see even if the tunnel didn't have any lights at all, but after a hundred and sixty-two powerless years, he had acquired the habit.

They drove for a few more minutes along the shore. As they passed a gas station, a bus stop appeared, and Samson slowed down. He parked the car next to a one-story red building—Cafe Rampa. Across the street was a grocery store. And that was pretty much it—the center of Hommelvik. From the foot of a mountain, tidy houses decorated with potted flowers stretched up to the woods. From between them the pointed top of a church stuck out.

They had breakfast in the cafe. While Craig was finishing his coffee, Samson went to the grocery store.

"What is that for?" asked Craig when he came back with food and bottles of water in a plastic bag. "You said it's only a few miles from here."

"Just in case," said Samson. "As I said, she isn't there yet." He locked the car. "We'll go on foot from here."

The area was sheltered by mountains, and the wind was much

weaker. They crossed the road, rounded the store, and went up the street. As they passed the last house at the end of the lane, the asphalt pavement changed to a dirt road, wet from passed rains.

They kept to the path at first, but after a while Samson veered off it, taking a shortcut. It didn't take long until the old, gray, two-story house showed up in the small clearing.

"It looks like it might collapse the moment we pull open the door," said Craig, looking at Samson sideways.

"It's been like that for a very long time. That, and the hearsay that the house is haunted keep people away from it. Mostly."

As they came closer, Craig saw a small wooden sign with a few native words scrawled on it. The words were written in red, looking like blood. Not far from it, in a small hole in the ground, a thermos sat with a sticker reading COFFEE and a few plastic cups for the passersby.

"Did she do all this?" Craig asked.

"Of course not." Samson went toward the porch. "People like mystery, and they're trying to keep it alive." He stepped to the door and pulled it open. "Many searched this place out of curiosity, and after they did, they all said the same thing: that they didn't find anybody in the house, but the candle was lit and a cup of steaming coffee sat on the table, like someone just put it there."

Craig passed the threshold and stopped in the corridor. There were two doors, one to the left and one to the right. In front of him, running along the wall, was a staircase. The door to the right was open, and Craig looked through it into the kitchen. It seemed like nobody had changed anything here since WWII. There was no dust, and everything was old but clean, like in a museum.

Craig followed Samson, climbing up the squeaking stairs. As he reached the second floor, he saw the room with old furniture, where in the middle of the simple wooden table stood a candlestick with one lit candle, and next to an open book sat a steaming cup of coffee.

"There was nobody around, and if no one lives here. . . ?" Craig started his question.

"Magic," Samson answered before he could finish. "It's not just a cup of coffee. Pick it up."

Craig approached the table and looked at the small cup on a saucer. When he lifted the cup, it weighed at least five times heavier than it was supposed to. "Okay," he said, putting it down. "Then, what's it doing here? I'm sure it has some meaning."

Samson stepped to the table and picked it up. "You have to take a sip from it," he said, and sipped the coffee. "That's how you summon the Witch. Now she knows that someone is here."

Craig pondered for a moment, then said with a grin, "Couldn't you just text her?"

Samson chuckled. "Last time I met her, cellphones didn't exist yet. We were followed by vampires most of the time. I couldn't take a chance." He picked up a pencil lying next to the book and wrote his name on its page. The next moment, the writing was gone.

"Message received," said Samson.

Craig ran his hand over the printed page. He tried to look at the cover, but the book didn't budge. Samson's gaze was still fixed upon the page, and a few seconds later it shone with golden words: *See you at midnight.*

Craig pointed at the words. "Is this . . . this reminds me of our bracelets."

"Who do you think enchanted them? And the spell to summon the Hunters, which we—and she, of course—passed to witches. Where do you think I know it from?"

"I thought you learned it from the Book."

"It's a Book of Power, not a Book of Spells." Samson chuckled again. He glanced at his watch. "We have more than twelve hours. Let's go."

"Where are we going?" asked Craig, following him outside. "Is there a hotel nearby?"

Samson shook his head. He pulled a bottle of water out of the bag and took a few gulps from it. "There's a cabin in the woods, not too far. We can wait there."

"I don't get it. Isn't it too easy?" said Craig, still thinking about what he'd just learned. "The people who search the house may think that it's just a coffee and try it as well. That means that anyone can summon her."

"That's what the weight of the cup is for. It's not normal, and at a mysterious place like this, people wouldn't risk it. Besides, it wouldn't work without a message. She has to know who summons her, otherwise she wouldn't show up. That's how witches communicated with her before. And not just any witches. Only the heads of covens knew about this place. I'm sure they use phones now."

They took a trail, stretching up into the woods. Between the thick trunks of big pines, Craig saw a waterfall running down the craggy mountain wall. He thought about the house they had just left, about its secret. All those centuries, he had thought there was nothing supernatural in this world he didn't know about. To find out there was somebody like them walking upon this Earth, and the fact that she was even older than Samson, was overwhelming. This exciting discovery brought up a lot of questions.

"If she is the First Witch," Craig asked, "does it mean that there are other immortal witches out there?"

"No, there's just her."

"So she can't turn people, like you do?"

"No, but she can slow down the aging of chosen ones."

"For how long?"

"Hundred and fifty, two hundred years."

"That's horrible." Craig felt sorry for the Witch. "Live forever and not have anyone with you for that never-ending journey."

"Yeah," sighed Samson. "That's why it made her very happy when I showed up. I was thinking of introducing her to Fray. But in the end, we decided to stick to the handbook. And predicting your next question," said Samson, his eyes on a squirrel as it prepared to jump from the branch of one tree to another. "No, we never had an intimate relationship. When we first met, she had someone, and by the time he was gone, we were good friends and kept it that way."

"You would make a sweet couple," smirked Craig. "The Hunter and the Witch."

"I was with a witch, long before I met Gabriella. She was the head of a coven. Believe me, it wasn't fun. Especially when she tapped into the black magic. It wasn't fun for her either, because, thanks to the Higher Powers, her magic never worked on me. For example, things like mind control—to discover my secrets, use my power for her dark purposes, to convince me to turn her. When word got to Runa, she stripped her of her powers."

"You mean the Witch? She can do that?" asked Craig, feeling like a freshman on his first day of school.

"Oh, yes. She has stronger punishments for the ones who breaks the rules. She and I—we have to support each other. We have a code. Otherwise, I would never trust her enough to give her the only key to my goal for safe-keeping. Plus, Fray and his vampires have killed dozens of witches. She wants to punish him as much as we do."

"I still don't understand. The witches, they always knew about us, that we exist. Why couldn't we know about Runa?"

"The witches are mortal humans. We needed each other. Many of them didn't believe we were real until we showed up. They don't believe Runa is real, either. To them, she is a legend. She is their god. Among them, Runa pretended to be just another witch. As I said, only the heads of covens know about her existence, and they take that secret to their graves."

Samson took a deep breath. "In the beginning, it was just me and Fray. Even then he wasn't always honest with me, and I wasn't sure I could trust him. I didn't keep this secret from you, I kept it from him. Who knows how it would have ended up if he had met her?"

They were off the trail now and soon reached a big glade. On its edge stood the cabin. In front of it was a long wooden table with benches on both sides. There was also a fire pit, furred with rough stones.

Samson opened the cabin door, and the both of them stepped in. It was one big room with two lower and two upper bunks. Since the whole place had only one window, it was dark and damp, smelling of smoky wood. In the corner, next to the door, was a stove with an old kettle on the top and a stack of logs on its side. By the window stood a small square table with a few shelves on the wall next to it.

Craig eyed the shelves, stocked with a jar with plastic cutlery, disposable plates, a jar with granulated coffee, about a dozen candles, paper and glass cups, as well as a bag of rice, some sugar and matches, and a bundle of other useful items. "Does anyone live here?"

"No," said Samson, dropping the bag on the bunk. "This place belongs to the community. People come here to spend weekends with family and friends. They leave those things here, in case someone needs them. Hikers, for example, or passers-by, like us."

Craig glanced at the table. A couple of glasses with half burned candles in them, a mug stuffed with pens and pencils, and an open journal sat there. It was a guest book. The last record informed that, "Stian and Mona stayed here last weekend."

He took a pen from the mug. "Let's do this. For the history." He threw a glance at Samson. "I mean, for our family history," he said in a low voice. He wrote down the date and put his name next to it. Then he handed the pen to Samson. They turned to each other, and their eyes met in a sad, lingering look.

"Craig . . ." started Samson.

But Craig raised his hand, stopping him. "You don't need to say anything. You made your decision, and I respect it. What I am trying to tell you is . . ." He swallowed. "It's such an honor to be here with you today. Thank you for believing in me."

Samson nodded and took the pen. Next to Craig's name, he wrote, *and Samson*.

Chapter Thirteen

"DO you think they can do it?" asked Craig quietly. "Find the bodies?"

"It's not an easy task, and they don't have much time." Samson brushed back his hair with both hands. His hands stopped on his forehead, and it took a moment before he dropped them down. "They know that their lives and our mission depend on it, and I'm sure they'll do their best."

Craig dropped down on the bunk.

"Listen," said Samson, sitting on the bunk across from him. "I know you're worried about her, but she'll be all right."

"Yeah. It's just . . ." Craig hesitated. "It's only been a few days since we got our powers back, and I feel this rush of energy. You know it, because you feel it, too. So do they, and so does Fray. Our blood is boiling. What if he's in Green Hill? What if she's not able to control her rage when she meets him? She blew up that gas station. Riley tried to make it sound casual, but I could tell he was worried, too."

"We knew this would happen. She's grieving. She lost people she cared about, and it causes her pain to think what you went through all those years. Grief and power are a dangerous combination. But I'm sure the daggers are well hidden. Fray wouldn't risk bringing them out now, when he is all alone. Riley and Ruben will look after her, they will all look after each other. And don't forget —she has a protector on the enemy's side." Samson stood up. "By the way. That rush of energy you were talking about? Let's go make use of it."

They walked outside and Samson pointed at another small stack of logs under the wall. "There's not much wood left. Let's find some dry lumber."

Next to the logs, an ax was stuck in a tree stump. Craig pulled it out. Samson went behind the house and came back with a chainsaw.

It felt good to do something physical. A few hours later, when the work was done, Craig was more relaxed and really hungry. They ate outside, sitting next to the fire Craig made in the pit. It was nearly eight, but the sky above the glade was still bright.

"It'll get darker after ten," said Samson, looking up. "End of May is the beginning of white nights in Norway." From the bag on the ground, Samson pulled out a bottle of whiskey and two glasses.

"Why Norway?" asked Craig, thinking about the Witch. "Runa. Is it...?"

"It's Norse." Samson poured the whiskey into the glasses and handed one of them to Craig. "That's why she chose this place. She was born somewhere around here."

"Where does she live? I mean, she was alone, and she couldn't turn people. Does she have a castle, too, or just a secret house somewhere?"

"She has a castle. It's in Scotland, hidden in the woods. It's not as big as ours, but very quaint. I've been there only a couple of times. You know how it was, the communication, the distance, each busy with own mission."

"How did she summon you?"

"Same as the other witches. With the Map. But she used a

different spell. It showed a golden spot on the location where she expected me."

Craig was amazed by this revelation. It was like opening an arcane door. There, somewhere, was another castle hidden behind a veil. The Map showed golden spots, and none of them had ever seen or known about it. Samson had dated a witch. From the day Craig became a Hunter, Gabriella was there, and it never occurred to him to ask Samson about his love life before her. Gabriella. Did she know all of this, or did he have to keep it from her, as well?

His eyes narrowed as he glanced at Samson. "I'm not the first person you're telling this to, am I?"

"No," he said quietly, looking at the burning logs. "Gabriella knew. I told her not long before she died." He leaned forward and with a stick in his hand pushed the burning logs toward each other. "That day it was only the two of us in the castle. When I went to check the Map, she came with me. I opened the Map, and there it was, the golden mark, calling me to New York. She couldn't believe her eyes, started asking questions. I kept it together until she began making suggestions. Her imagination flew so far and in such horrifying directions that I couldn't hold it anymore. I burst out laughing." Samson smiled. "I said that if she'd give me her word to keep it a secret, I'd tell her what it meant. You know what she said?" He glanced at Craig. "She said 'I swear on your life.'" Still grinning, Samson shook his head.

"Good one." Craig smiled.

They sat in silence for a moment, then Craig asked, "How did she take it? When you told her?"

"She was stunned. She wanted to meet Runa, but her biggest desire was to see the castle. I asked Runa's permission." Samson's face darkened. He sipped from his glass. "I don't know if you remember, but that day, when you all returned from France, we said that we were planning to go to New Orleans. From there I was going to take her to Scotland, to Runa's castle."

Craig remembered the last time all of them saw Gabriella alive.

They'd just returned from Paris. Eleanor and Hanna went to see Margaret. The rest of them were in the small living room, having brandy, gathered around the fireplace. That's when Gabriella told them that she and Samson were going to New Orleans.

Craig took a big gulp from his glass. There was another long moment of silence, after which Samson said, "You don't have to keep it from Eleanor. In fact, after we win this war, it doesn't have to be a secret anymore. I am very proud of my family. Nobody got tempted by Fray's dark ideas, nobody changed sides. Those past two centuries have proven how loyal each member of our family is to our mission. Especially Riley. He has been with me for six hundred years. I owe him so much."

"That's why my being here . . ." Craig spread his hands. "Samson, it feels wrong. It should have been him."

"We've talked about this," said Samson firmly. "Stop feeling guilty. When I told him about my plan, he didn't hesitate for a second. Neither did Ruben. They had plenty of time to change their minds, but they didn't." Samson sighed. "Just like me and you, Riley has suffered all these years. He lost the love of his life, too. His wings are broken, just like mine, and he and I, we both know that this mission needs someone whole, someone who is still able to fly."

It was dark now. They talked and reminisced next to a crackling fire, something they hadn't done for a very long time. This evening was a checkpoint of both of their lives. Craig enjoyed and valued every moment of it, and he was going to treasure it for the rest of his existence.

∽

AT MIDNIGHT, Samson and Craig crossed the dark threshold of the old house and climbed up the stairs. In the dim light of the single candle, Craig saw the silhouette of a woman standing in the furthest corner. Her hands were up and she was slowly moving them around, like she was feeling the air surrounding her.

"Hello, Runa," said Samson.

Runa dropped her hands. "Sorry," she said in a soft voice. "I was scanning the area, making sure there are no strangers around." The next moment, dozens of big candles illuminated the room, and Runa came forward.

Tall and slender, she looked about Samson's age. Her black hair had purple stripes, which were beautifully gathered up in ringlets. On her long neck hung an antique medallion with unreadable text. The black fitted dress she wore had a wide silver belt, which looked like two hands reaching to each other. In between the tips of their fingers was the buckle, a large oval, a dark-blue stone in a silver setting.

"It's good to see you again, Samson," she said, and her wine lips curled up in a smile. She turned to Craig. "Hello. I am Runa." She came closer and held out her hand.

"I'm Craig. It's nice to finally meet you," said Craig, and as he took her hand, she pierced him with her gaze. Staring back, Craig tried to convince himself that the vertical stripes of fire in her black pupils were just a reflection from the candles. But then, why was his chest warming up?

"So do you approve?" asked Samson.

She blinked once and the fire stripes were gone from her eyes, and so was the heat in Craig's chest.

"I approve. You made a good choice." She stared at Craig for another second, then turned to Samson. "He has what it takes."

Craig shifted uncomfortably as he realized they were talking about him.

"I know he has it," said Samson. "And I wanted you to know it, too. I wanted you to know you can trust him."

Runa glanced at Craig. "By the way, we have met before." She tilted her head. "You just didn't know who I was."

Craig glanced at Samson, then at Runa, trying to remember if he had seen this face before.

"Don't torture yourself. It was long ago, and, if I remember it right, my hair was blonde and short then. It has been a long while," she said, now addressing Samson. "Decades. You knew that I couldn't summon you—after your Book closed, your Map stopped working. What's your excuse?"

"I have been followed by vampires most of the time. I couldn't risk coming here," said Samson. "You have enough of your own problems. I didn't want to add mine to your pile. That would be a poor payment for your kindness."

"I knew the Book had been opened the moment it happened. I've been expecting you. How have you been?" she asked with concern. "The transitioning bodies? Did you find them?"

"No." Samson slowly shook his head. "But now, with our powers back, we might succeed."

"I wish I could help you, but I can't locate them." She spread her hands. "I have nothing to work with. They don't have souls or heartbeats, we know nothing about them, and we don't have even a drop of their blood or any of their personal possessions. But," she raised her finger, "you were right when you said that Fray didn't move them too far. They are there, somewhere around Green Hill. I can sense an enormous power awakening in that area."

"I felt that, too." Samson's eyes narrowed. "But I thought it was us."

"No," said Runa, moving toward the table. "It's bigger, it's much bigger, and it keeps growing."

"Thank you. It's good to know that we are looking in the right place."

Samson moved closer to the table, too, and his eyes stopped at the square, mahogany box lying on it. It was two inches high and about eight inches wide. The box had a golden pentacle on its top, and its sides were covered with familiar golden symbols.

"I already had it with me when you called." Runa picked up the box and ran her long fingers over the top before handing it to Samson. "Go on, open it. I know you want to make sure it's there." She smiled.

"I know it's there," said Samson, returning the smile. "I can feel it." He took the box.

As Samson lifted the lid, Craig drew closer and looked inside. On the brown velvet lay a golden disc about five inches in diameter, with a large hole in it. Its surface was covered with symbols.

"This is the Key?" Craig asked, a little surprised.

"You didn't expect it to look like a regular key, did you?" asked Runa, raising her brow.

"This is the Key," said Samson with tangible delight. He placed his hand on the disc and closed his eyes. "And its power is back," he muttered. Samson closed the box and put it at the bottom of the bag hanging on his shoulder.

"Do you have one, too?" Craig asked Runa.

"I did," said Runa with a deep sigh. "But it's gone now."

"What do you mean, gone?"

"The Key can be used only once. I used mine centuries ago, to save my witches from being burned in fires all over the world." Runa rounded the table and picked up an envelope from a chest of drawers. It was dark brown with a big stamp in the middle—a glittering, colorful pentagram. She stroked the stamp. Then she put the envelope into a leather folder, zipped it, and handed it to Samson.

"I'll deliver it safely," said Samson, and he deposited the folder in the bag.

They looked at each other for a long moment. Craig felt like he was intruding in some private, wordless conversation and looked away.

"Samson, are you sure you want to do this?" Runa asked quietly.

"I am sure," said Samson.

Runa nodded with understanding.

He held out his hand and, as she took it, he said, "Thank you for everything. Goodbye, Runa."

"We'll meet again." A mysterious smile crossed Runa's face. "And sooner than you think."

Chapter Fourteen

THE SINGLE, tender ray of sunlight, which snuck in through a narrow gap between the curtains, fell on Eleanor's cheek. Enjoying its warmth, she lay motionless for a few more minutes, but as it reached her eyes, she pulled herself up. She sat in bed and thought about her dream. She was hunting, and there was nothing special or unnatural about it—she had been chasing vampires for decades—but the fact that it kept repeating itself over and over made her wonder.

Someone knocked on the door, and before Eleanor could react to it, it opened.

"You're awake," said Hanna, coming inside. "How was it, sleeping at the new place? Did you dream about Craig?" She grinned. Hanna pulled open the curtains, then pushed aside the duvet and dropped on the bed at Eleanor's feet.

"It was my first night in his bedroom and I hoped to," said Eleanor. "But instead I had this --"

"Don't tell me that you had another nightmare," interrupted Hanna.

"No, it wasn't a nightmare. I was hunting a vampire, a woman in a black dress. But the dream kept repeating, like a worn out record. It was weird."

Hanna's eyes unfocused, her mind seeming to be somewhere else.

"Are you okay?" asked Eleanor.

"Yeah. It's just . . . I missed this so much," she said, looking at Eleanor fondly. "You know . . . I missed us. It wasn't that long for you, but for me. . . ."

"Of course, I know." Eleanor leaned forward and squeezed Hanna's hands with her own. "I missed us, too. We have a lot of catching up to do."

"I was thinking," Hanna said thoughtfully, "how hard it must be for Kimberly now."

"I know." Eleanor nodded. "We need to spend more time with her. But we need to be careful, because I think we're freaking her out."

"I already called her. Since there's no school and we're not going to the warehouse with the boys, I asked her if she wanted to go out with us."

"When are we meeting?"

"In an hour, so you better get up."

After a quick shower, Eleanor went downstairs. Hanna was waiting for her in the kitchen with freshly made coffee.

Ruben, Riley, and Ned were about to leave. They were already in the hallway when Hanna called them back.

"Guys, come here. Look," she said, pointing at the kitchen window.

All five of them stood a good distance from the window and looked out. There, in their driveway, sat a police car.

"It's Mike," said Ruben. "He found us."

"How?" asked Hanna.

"He's a policeman, Hanna," Riley said. "You rode him around in your car and you ask how?"

"I knew it," grumbled Eleanor. "You shouldn't have let

him go."

They watched Mike get out of the car. For a moment he just stood there, looking at the house. Then he approached the mailbox and put something in it. Mike looked at the house again, scanning from porch to roof like he was trying to memorize it, then got in his car and drove away.

"I'll get it," said Ruben, and dashed out. He came back with a small envelope in his hand. The envelope wasn't sealed. He sat down, pulled out the piece of paper in it, and read it aloud.

"Everything is taken care of. The girl's parents have been notified. I wrote down my phone number, in case you need my help. Mike. PS: Sorry, couldn't keep my mouth shut—"

"Oh, no," gasped Hanna.

"I went to the cemetery today," Ruben continued reading, "to visit my father's grave. I told him everything. Thought he would like to know."

The five of them stood in silence for a moment, then Riley said, "Come on, we have work to do."

∽

"RUBEN TOLD me that you managed to recover Nicole's body," said Kimberly as she, Hanna and Eleanor sat at an outside table at a small cafe.

"Yes, we did," said Hanna.

"That's good," said Kimberly quietly. "Any news about Alec?"

"No." Hanna shook her head. "We didn't have much time to . . ." Hanna looked at Eleanor, then turned to Kimberly again. "We were a little busy."

"Kimberly, we're sorry we couldn't come to school yesterday," said Eleanor. She put her forearms on the table and leaned forward. "We didn't mean—"

The waitress wedged between them, holding a plastic tray with three cappuccinos. Eleanor removed her arms from the table and leaned back again.

"That's okay. I understand." Kimberly shrugged. "It's not important for you anymore."

"Who said it's not?" protested Eleanor.

"Of course it's important," said Hanna. "It's not like I've finished high school a hundred times."

"Kimberly, this is my first time in high school," said Eleanor. "The three of us went there together for three years. Like you, I want to finish it properly."

"Really?" Kimberly's face brightened. "So you're coming to graduation tomorrow?"

"Graduation is tomorrow?" Eleanor looked taken aback.

"Oh. I see." Kimberly pulled her cup closer. "You already have plans."

"No. That's not what I meant." Eleanor smiled apologetically. They didn't yet have plans for tomorrow, but to spend the whole day at school seemed like a waste of time at the moment. "I meant that today I'll have to go back to my house and find my cap and gown. We ordered it a while ago. I don't remember where I put it."

"You'll have to go back to your house? Where've you been?"

Eleanor was trying to make things better, but it seemed she was only making them worse. Her attempt to show Kimberly that nothing had changed between them was backfiring, proving the fact that she and Hanna had been together the whole time, leaving Kimberly alone and out of the loop.

"She stayed at our place last night," Hanna said, coming to the rescue.

"My dad is still in LA," said Eleanor. "I didn't feel like staying alone in the empty house after Melinda's . . . you know."

"Yeah," said Kimberly. "I understand."

To make Kimberly feel more involved, Hanna and Eleanor told her everything that had happened in the past two days, up until the moment when Mike showed up in their driveway. When they got back to the graduation theme, Kimberly pulled out her phone and read a message.

"I gotta go," she said.

"Now?" asked Hanna.

"Yeah," said Kimberly. "He's waiting."

"He? He who?"

"James. I'm meeting James." Kimberly grabbed her bag off the back of her chair and stood up.

"You're meeting James?" Eleanor raised one brow. "You mean your ex?"

"I need him to help me with something. See you later." Kimberly waved and walked away.

"What's going on?" asked Eleanor, staring at Hanna.

"I don't know." Hanna shook her head.

They remained pinned to their seats for a few more minutes, then, with a heavy sigh, Eleanor stood up. "If we're going to graduation, then I really need to go home."

The moment Eleanor walked into the house and closed the front door behind her, she was plunged into dreary silence. She threw a quick glance at the empty kitchen and went upstairs to her room. Next to her bed, on the floor, she saw her notebook. She picked it up, opened a random page, and read the first sentence.

She looked at his face and then touched the wound on his cheek. The blood seeped into her silky glove, but the next moment it was dry, and the wound healed right in front of her eyes.

A shiver ran down Eleanor's spine. She turned a few pages:

Those short meetings in the lodge were the source of her happiness, but with the baby growing inside her . . ."

Eleanor closed the notebook. There was no need to read more. She knew that everything she had written in the past two years was the history of her previous life, of her life with Craig from the moment she first met him. She had shown Hanna and Kimberly a couple of her short stories, but never this. This was her first attempt to write a novel, and she wanted to finish it first. Otherwise, Hanna and Craig would have known who Amanda was long ago.

Eleanor looked at her laptop on the edge of the bed. It was dead. She plugged in the charger, then walked to the closet and pulled out a pair of jeans and a fresh T-shirt.

As she put the jeans on, a noise came from downstairs. With the T-shirt in her hands, she went to her bedroom door, but before she reached it, the front door slammed.

"Melinda," came her father's voice from the hallway.

"Oh my God," whispered Eleanor. She stopped, paralyzed. She had planned to call him, but the last few days passed so quickly, and after everything that had happened, it had absolutely slipped her mind.

"Melinda?" her father called again. "Amanda, are you home?"

"Yes," she said, putting on the T-shirt. "I'm here." Wearing a big smile, she ran down the stairs.

"Hi, Dad." She hugged him.

"Hi, honey."

"You startled me." She pulled back. "I didn't know you were coming today. Why didn't you call?"

"I did," said Lindsey, taking off his jacket. "I thought you were at school, so I called Melinda. I called several times, but she didn't answer. Where is she?" He headed to the kitchen.

Eleanor was paralyzed again. She didn't know what to say, she hadn't prepared the answer to this question. In a few seconds, dozens of thoughts crossed her mind. She wasn't ready to tell him the truth yet. Maybe she should say that Melinda was visiting her relatives? No. Melinda didn't have family, her father knew that.

"Did she go to the store?" he asked.

"No," she said, shaking her head. "Melinda left. This morning."

"What do you mean, 'left?'" Lindsey frowned. "She wouldn't do that without warning me."

"When I say left . . . her old friend is sick . . . dying. She has no one to look after her, so Melinda had to . . ." Eleanor's cheeks warmed.

"That's very nice of her. But why didn't she answer my calls?"

"She lost her phone," Eleanor said with more confidence.

"Really?"

"Yes, at the grocery store. She asked me to warn you, but. . . . She said she'll call as soon as she buys a new one. So, how are you, Dad? Did they accept your project?" Eleanor tried to change the subject.

"Yes, they did, but on some conditions," said Lindsey. With a suspicious look on his face, he glanced around the cold, unwelcoming kitchen. "It's just so not like her," he said, his eyes stopping on the empty pot of the coffee maker. He pulled it out. "Would you like some coffee?" He filled the pot with water. "I promise, I'll cook something tomorrow, but today we'll order pizza. Deal?"

"Yay. Good to have you back, Dad." She beamed, thinking the absolute opposite. Eleanor knew his presence would complicate things. Not only because she'd have to keep lying to him, but because being her father automatically put him in danger, and she had no idea how she'd explain to him that he couldn't invite people into his house and that he had to stay inside after dark.

After a little catch up talk over a cup of coffee, they both went to their rooms—Lindsey to unpack his suitcase and Eleanor to prepare her graduation gown.

Except Eleanor didn't need to do anything. Melinda had prepared it for her a week ago, and now it hung in the closet, ready to wear. Eleanor ran her hand over the gown. "Thank you," she whispered with a heavy sigh.

She picked up her phone and sent a message to Hanna, telling her that her father was back, and then she asked about the warehouse. The reply was disappointing, but not unexpected: the warehouse was just another trap.

Eleanor looked at the laptop. She sat in the middle of the bed and pulled it closer. She hadn't used it since she and Alec took off three days ago. His website was still open on the screen, showing the picture of her old house. She saved the image and was about to close the window when the About Me tab on the top of the page caught her eye. She clicked on it.

The short text didn't tell her anything she didn't already know. It was just a blurb. Next to it was Alec's photograph. He was standing with his hands crossed over his chest, leaning on an antique dresser. On the wall above it hung three different sized pictures—two paintings and one drawing. Though most of the paintings were hidden behind Alec, Eleanor could tell that they were landscapes. But the drawing, which she could see clearly, was a woman—just her face, a beautiful face. Judging by the hairstyle and the collar of her dress, the woman lived in the nineteenth century. The drawing seemed old. It was yellowish and looked like it was scratched or cracked in several places. As she looked at it closer, she heard a deep "hmm," then realized she was the source of the sound. The woman, whose cold blue eyes pierced her from the screen, looked familiar. Eleanor closed her eyes, trying to remember where she could've seen this drawing before. This photograph of Alec wasn't taken in his house, Eleanor was sure of it. It was nothing like his room, and his house was modern. Besides, even if the drawing was hanging in one of the rooms of his house, how could she have seen it, if she'd never been in that room? She opened her eyes and looked at the drawing again. Hoping to find the artist's name, Eleanor zoomed in on the picture.

There was no signature, but in the bottom corner she saw some numbers, a date—1834. Eleanor *hmmed* again. "This is the year I became a Hunter," she murmured. It was probably just a coincidence. But something told her this memory wasn't new, and it wasn't Amanda's, but Eleanor's. She picked up her phone and took a picture of the drawing.

Later in the afternoon, Eleanor and Lindsey, each with large slices of pizza in their hands, sat on the couch in front of the TV, watching *The Vampire Diaries*. Eleanor chose the show on purpose, except she didn't exactly know why, what exactly she was trying to achieve by making her skeptic father watch a show about vampires and werewolves.

"Who comes up with this stuff?" Lindsey said with a sneer. "Gosh, look at her. She could at least clean the blood from her face before kissing him. It's disgusting."

"I know. But they don't mind. They love blood, remember? It's their food."

"So?" Lindsey scoffed. "We love salsa, but we don't walk around with it dripping down our chin. Imagine somebody kissing you with bacon fat all over his face."

"Ew, Dad." Eleanor wrinkled her nose.

Chewing his pizza, Lindsey watched the show without comment for about five more minutes, then he sneered again. "They can walk under the sun because they have a daylight ring?"

"Yeah, right," said Eleanor with sarcasm, taking a bite of her pizza. "Only in movies. In reality nothing can protect them from the sun except—"

"In reality?" Lindsey turned to her, looking perplexed.

Eleanor choked. She tried to swallow the pieces of pizza in her mouth but coughed, spitting out chunks of food.

"Honey, are you okay?" Lindsey asked, clapping her on the back.

"I'm fine, Dad," she said, clearing her throat. But when she looked at Lindsey, she saw a smile on his face, which was slowly growing into a laughter.

"What?" asked Eleanor, wiping her mouth with the back of her hand. "Oh, very nice, Dad. Did you imagine someone kissing me right now?" As she childishly poked him in the shoulder, she realized that for a moment, she was Amanda again. Her anger, her grief, her urge for revenge were gone. But only for that one short moment. Keeping the grin on her face, she stood up. "I'll go wash up."

While she washed, the restless thoughts began buzzing in her head again. Three days had passed without any results. They had no idea where to look for the transitioning bodies or where Fray was. Every wasted day got him closer to his goal. They needed a new plan.

"I need to make some calls," said Lindsey after they cleaned up the living room. "Are you going somewhere?" he asked, as Eleanor grabbed the car keys.

"I'm meeting Hanna. You know, to prepare some stuff for the post-graduation party."

"It *is* tomorrow, right?" asked Lindsey.

"Right," said Eleanor.

Chapter Fifteen

WHEN SHE ARRIVED at Hanna's house and opened the front door, she heard arguing voices. Kimberly sat curled up on the couch, looking from one to another.

"What's going on?" asked Eleanor. "Did something happen?"

"That's the thing, you see," said Hanna with an edge in her voice. "Nothing is happening."

"I'm glad that you're aware of that," said Eleanor.

"I appreciate the irony, Eleanor," Riley grumbled. "Maybe you have some thoughts? The floor is yours."

"Maybe," said Eleanor, sitting next to Kimberly.

"Well?" asked Ruben, who stood behind the couch with his hands on Kimberly's shoulders.

"I was thinking that maybe, instead of looking for bodies, we should look for Fray."

"That's what I was thinking, too," said Hanna.

"We can't," said Riley. "Samson said to find the bodies. So that's what we need to do right now."

"Listen, guys," said Eleanor. "Now is the best time to go after him. It's five of us, and all he's got is a bunch of vampires."

"No," said Riley firmly. "We tried it once, remember? We were seven then, and you still had to die. Who knows how many vampires he has now. We can't risk it."

"Let's say we got him, locked him up somewhere," said Ruben. "Then what? It's not going to make him hand over The Book and the daggers."

"No. But I'm sure if we find him, we find the rest."

"Not now, not when Fray expects us to go after him. Samson thinks he would definitely use the Book the moment he got it back. But not the daggers. He thinks that the daggers are hidden separately. Fray is not going to go near them until the last moment. When the transitioning vampires wake up, the risk of losing the daggers will be minimal. Samson knows what he's doing and we'll do as he says. We'll look for the bodies."

Eleanor couldn't argue with Riley, because he knew what Samson was up to, and she didn't.

"Where do we look? You should know something," said Eleanor. "I haven't been here, but you have been watching him all those years. Are there any specific places he spent the most of time, for example?"

"We did keep an eye on him," said Ruben. "But he's moved around a lot. We couldn't follow him everywhere."

"Sometimes we lost him for years," said Riley. "But he always showed up when some of your descendants were about to turn eighteen."

"And sometimes, Samson asked witches to do a locator spell," added Hanna.

"Yes," said Ned. "That's how he found that Chinese warlock's house. The witch did a spell and located Fray in that house. I tailed him from that day until he came here."

"Does he have a residence?" asked Eleanor.

"We never came across one," said Ruben. "But I wouldn't be surprised if he has a home somewhere."

"Today, in the warehouse, we tried to beat some information out of the vampires," said Riley. "But they didn't know anything."

Ruben rounded the couch and sat on the other side of Kimberly. Eleanor pulled out her phone and showed Ruben the drawing she'd found on Alec's website.

"Does this look familiar to you?"

Ruben looked at the half of Alec's face on the left side of the screen. His forehead crinkled. "Do I look like I have amnesia?"

"Not Alec." Eleanor rolled her eyes. "The drawing."

Ruben looked at the screen again, then shook his head. "Should it?"

"I don't know. I think I've seen it before. This face . . .And look at the date." She enlarged the picture.

"Isn't this the year Samson turned you?"

"Yeah. It might be a coincidence, but I can't shake this feeling . . . look." She passed the phone to Riley beside her in the armchair. "Do you recognize this?"

"No," said Riley, studying the photo.

"Let me see," said Hanna, taking the phone from Riley. She and Ned looked at the picture for a long moment. "No," said Hanna, returning the phone to Eleanor. "Doesn't ring a bell. Where did you find this?"

"On Alec's website. This picture was taken in some house. Not his, I'm sure of it."

"Are you saying it might be Fray's house?" said Riley.

"Why not," said Eleanor excitedly. "If Fray trusted Alec with the Book and the dagger, it means they're close."

"If they're close, why would Fray kill his parents?" asked Ruben.

Eleanor stood up and began pacing. Riley went to the small table with drinks and poured himself a glass of whiskey.

"Alec's parents didn't spend much time with him," said Eleanor, stopping abruptly. "When he showed me his website, I was surprised to see photographs from all over the world. He traveled a lot, not with his parents, but with his uncle. He said his uncle started taking him places when he was twelve."

Ruben leaned forward and looked up at Eleanor. "Uncle?"

"So they're *that* close," said Ned.

"I think they are," said Eleanor. "The only picture he took while hiking with his father was the picture of my old house."

"And that was a lie," said Hanna. "Because it was definitely Fray who showed him that place."

Eleanor took another few steps back and forth, then stopped again. "I am sure he's transitioning right now," she said grimly. "But he'll show up eventually."

"And when he does—" Kimberly spoke for the first time. "You might want to ask him why his family changed their last name before they moved to LA."

All five pairs of eyes turned to her at once.

"How do you know that?" asked Ruben.

"I did some research. After Alec . . . after he killed Melinda." She paused for a second, then continued with a sigh. "I wouldn't believe it if I hadn't seen everything with my own eyes. I liked him a lot. I was trying to find out if something like that had happened before, if he had a criminal background. I knew he moved to Green Hill from LA. I had to break into the school database to see if they had any records on him. I couldn't do it by myself, so I asked James to help me."

"Who's James?" asked Ruben.

"He's . . ." Kimberly hesitated. "He's my ex."

Ruben cleared his throat and leaned back on the cushions of the sofa.

"What?" Kimberly gazed at a chortling Riley. "He's good with the computer stuff."

"So." Ruben leaned forward again, looking softly at Kimberly. "Did he help you?"

"Yes," said Kimberly with a deep breath. "We found out that Alec lived in LA only a year. His school records said he moved there from Williamsburg, Virginia. James researched further. There are only three high schools in Williamsburg, but there was no Alec Stafford in any of them. There was only one Alec there—Alec Mayson, who graduated two years ago."

"Maybe it's not him?" Hanna said.

"It's him. There was no picture, but everything matches. He was the captain of the school football team, took photographs for school events, and the parent names are the same—Matilda and Clark."

"Actually, it makes sense," said Hanna. "I took Craig's last name and changed my age so I could go to high school with you." She glanced at Eleanor. "Fray did the same with Alec."

"We have to dig deeper," said Eleanor, agitated. "It might help us find something new about Fray."

"I'll contact Mike tomorrow, see if he can help," said Ruben.

"Okay," Eleanor said with a sigh. Realizing that there was nothing more to add to the subject, she headed to the basement door, muttering, "Where is that punching bag?"

Chapter Sixteen

AS ELEANOR, Hanna, and Kimberly walked to the school's backyard, all three of them beamed. The atmosphere was saturated with excitement. Most of the graduates had already taken their seats, and the rows of red caps and gowns looked like a poppy field. Behind them was a colorful garden bed of festively dressed up parents. Eleanor's eyes searched for Lindsey. She found him sitting in the last chair of the first row, next to Kimberly's mother.

"Your father's the only one she knows here," said Kimberly, looking in the same direction. "Let's go sit."

"There," said Hanna, pointing at the three empty seats in the fifth row.

The podium was decorated with white and yellow flowers. Ms. Finch fixed the crooked pile of diplomas. Above her, an arch of balloons stretched from one end of the podium to another.

"Isn't this exciting?" said Hanna.

"Don't tell me that you haven't done this before," said Kimberly, looking at her sideways.

"Twice. But I never enjoyed it; I never had friends like you. Now, when the mission is accomplished," she glanced at Eleanor, "nothing in the world would make me go through high school again. So, yes, I'm excited."

The ceremony started, and the principal invited the first speaker to the microphone. After two more speeches, the principal began calling the names to hand out diplomas. Kimberly was the first of three of them to receive her scroll, tied with a thin golden ribbon. Then next was Hanna. Eleanor's turn came shortly after. On her way back to her seat, she looked toward her father. A tall man in a fine suit stood right in front of Lindsey with his back to the podium, and somebody was placing an extra chair for him. Lindsey looked out from behind the man. Eleanor raised the scroll of paper in her hand and waved to her beaming father.

There were only a few diplomas left on the table when the principal called, "Alec Stafford."

"Yeah, right," Hanna chuckled.

But the principal waited with a smile, looking at the further rows. Following the principal's gaze, Hanna, Kimberly, and Eleanor turned their heads.

"You son of a bitch," Hanna muttered as she saw Alec, with a huge grin across his face, pop out from between the students.

"He looks too happy for someone whose parents just died," said Kimberly.

"Maybe he doesn't know yet," said Hanna. "Maybe he was transitioning, and after he woke up, nobody told him."

Eleanor's heart pounded. "It can't be . . . Hanna, he couldn't." With narrowed eyes, she carefully watched his moves. His gait seemed a little different, like he was measuring his every step. "After what he'd done, he had to transition for at least four days. Today is the fourth day and he's already awake? No."

"Yes," said Hanna. "Otherwise, he wouldn't dare show up."

As Alec received the diploma, he glanced at the graduates. It took him two seconds to find Eleanor. The moment their eyes met, Eleanor's hands clenched into fists. Turning his eyes away, Alec looked above the red caps, at the rows of parents sitting behind them, and waved his hand.

"If his parents aren't here, who is he waving to?" asked Hanna.

"Let me guess," said Kimberly. "To his *uncle*?"

Eleanor and Hanna stared at her.

"No," said Eleanor, rage rising in her voice. Craning her neck, she looked back. On the extra chair, next to Lindsey, sat Fray. Her hand shaking with anger, she pulled out her phone and called Ruben. "Where are you?"

"I'm on my way to meet Mike. Tell Kimberly I'll be there soon," she heard Ruben's voice on the other end.

"You need to come now. Call Riley and Ned. Tell them to come, too."

"Is something wrong? Eleanor, what's going on?"

"Fray is here. They both are." Eleanor hung up and turned to Hanna. "Ruben will take care of Kimberly. You, Riley, and Ned need to keep an eye on Fray. Let him see you, but don't engage. He didn't sit next to my father by accident. But the sun is up, and that means there are no vampires to help him. With you around, he can't do anything. He knows that. This is just a show."

"And you?" asked Hanna. "What are *you* going to do?"

"I'm going to have a little chat with his nephew."

"Eleanor, be careful," said Hanna. "You know that this isn't just a show. This is a warning."

"So what? I have to sit here and do nothing?" said Eleanor, trying to keep her voice down.

The next ten minutes felt like forever. When the ceremony was finally over, she stood up and looked back. Alec was heading toward Fray, who was talking to her father. Not far behind them, she saw Riley standing in front of a big banner. Ned was on the other end of the rows, leaning on a tree trunk.

"Nothing is going to happen to him," Ruben said.

Eleanor turned around to see him standing next to Kimberly.

"Your father will be fine."

"I know," said Eleanor.

Suppressing her urge to run, she walked toward her dad.

"Here she is," said Lindsey as she approached the three men. He pulled her in and kissed her on the forehead. "Congratulations, honey."

Eleanor barely hugged her father. As Lindsey let go of her, she locked her hands behind her back, fingers piercing her palms. Eleanor looked at Fray, who gazed at her smugly.

"This is my daughter, Amanda," said Lindsey. "I don't know if you've met before. Amanda, this is Alec's uncle."

The hatred was choking Eleanor, but she unclenched her tightly shut lips and forced a smile. "Yes, we've met before."

"I'm so happy to see you, Amanda," said Fray sardonically.

"Oh, I'm sure we'll meet again, Mr. Wald," said Eleanor, looking straight into his eyes. "But Alec and I, we have to go." She turned to her father. "There's a cake waiting for us. See you later, Dad." She kissed Lindsey on the cheek and walked away. Eleanor didn't look at Alec once, but she heard him follow her.

She led him to the classroom at the end of the corridor, where they had cake before the ceremony.

"Sorry, no cake for you," she said, looking at the three end-to-end tables with empty cake trays and dirty paper plates lying on them.

"Amanda," said Alec quietly.

But before he could say another word, she turned around and grabbed him by his clothes. "You don't get to speak," she hissed, shoving him toward the blackboard. She swung her hand to hit him, but Alec caught it and pushed back.

Eleanor sneered. "You hatched quickly." She fisted her other hand and punched him in the face. Alec's head tilted back and hit the blackboard.

"Amanda, stop it," said Alec. She let go of him. "Let me explain," he said, taking off his crooked gown.

"Filth like you doesn't deserve those powers."

"I killed someone you cared about. I'm sorry—"

"You're sorry?" Eleanor glared at him. "You think I'll forgive you because you said you're sorry?"

"Of course not. I just want you to know I'm really sorry."

"Let's see how sorry you are. Fray has the daggers. That means someone else I care about might die. Or me."

"I'll never let anything happen to you. Amanda, I know what you're going to ask. Fray is the only one who knows where the daggers are. He wouldn't tell anybody. Not even me. But I'm not going to lie to you. Even if I knew, I wouldn't tell you. I wouldn't do that to him."

"You wouldn't do that to him?" Eleanor looked at him, astonished. "He killed your parents," she shouted.

"They weren't my parents," said Alec. "He hired them."

"What?" She stared at him in disbelief, then said. "So it's okay then?"

"I didn't say that—"

"That's how sorry you are. You know," she said, panting with rage, "we have this rule not to harm humans. I'm glad you're not a mortal human anymore." She took off her gown, too, and threw it aside. "Now, at least, I can kick your ass." She sent a blow into his chest. Alec flew back and hit the wall.

He restored his balance and stepped to her again. "You can do whatever you want. I'm not going to fight you."

"Because you know your powers are not enough. You'll have to learn a lot to match me."

"No. Because I know what I did was wrong, and I deserve to be punished." Alec frowned, his voice became sharper. "But I did what I had to do so Fray would turn me. I had to be like you so I could be with you. I did it because I love you."

"Stop lying," shouted Eleanor. "You knew that you'd turn before you came to Green Hill, before you even met me."

"I always knew who you are. I knew everything about you," said Alec, stepping closer. "I fell in love with you from the moment

Fray first told me about you and showed me your picture." He stopped, his blue eyes piercing hers. "And I couldn't wait to meet you."

"If you knew everything, then you also had to know that I love Craig." Eleanor pushed him away with both hands. "That he's the love of my life, and next to him you're nothing. You killed Melinda not because you wanted to be with me, but because Fray told you so."

"No. Fray told me to kill *you*. But I didn't."

"So instead of killing me, you killed Melinda. Do you hear yourself? Do you expect me to feel better?"

"No. I'm just saying I didn't have a choice."

"Everybody has a choice. You made yours when you chose Fray."

"You don't understand. Amanda, when I—"

"Stop calling me that." She punched him. "Forget Amanda." She punched him again. "My name is Eleanor. I can't kill you. Yet," she said, glaring at him. "But I can make you feel what she felt." She grabbed the knife from the cake tray and, gazing into his eyes, she stabbed him into his stomach. Moaning, Alec doubled over. She pulled the knife out and took a step back. "Do you know what they did to Craig? I can make you feel that, too." She raised the knife to stab him in the heart, but someone stronger than her clutched her wrist.

"Stop," said Ruben.

"Why?" Eleanor's lips trembled. "Why are you protecting him?"

"I'm not protecting him," said Ruben calmly. He pushed her hand down. "I'm protecting you."

Eleanor looked back. Standing in the classroom doorway, Kimberly stared at her with wide eyes. Eleanor gasped. "Kimberly." She looked at Alec, pressing both of his hands to his stomach as he slid down the wall and sat on the floor. "Kimberly, you shouldn't have . . ." Wiping a tear from her face, Eleanor rushed toward her.

"I'm sorry," she whispered. She threw her arm around Kimberly's shaking shoulders and hurried her away.

∽

"STAY AWAY FROM HER," said Ruben, looking down at Alec. "Stop trying to get in her good book. That will never happen. Not just because you're on the wrong side. She sacrificed herself for the greater good, and everything you did, you did for yourself. You killed someone to get what you want. She'll never forgive you, if that's what you're after. And I think that's what you're hoping for. You're not so stupid to let your imagination go further than that." Ruben left the room.

"Eternity is a long time," muttered Alec under his breath. He remained sitting for a minute, then got to his feet and pulled up his shirt. The wound was almost healed.

"I see you got your first injury."

Alec turned around to see Fray standing in the doorway.

"It's nothing," said Alec. "It's almost gone."

"It must be a very deep cut, to take so long to heal," said Fray in a casual tone. "But I wasn't speaking about your physical wound. I meant your emotional trauma."

Alec glared at him. "I'm fine."

"Are you? I'm sure she showed you who she really is, that she is not the Amanda you knew."

"No, she isn't. She's much better now. Beautiful, strong, smart. Daring. Everything I desired."

"But she is Eleanor, who loves Craig. She stabbed you because she hates you. Aren't you disappointed? Your heart isn't broken?"

"I'm not an idiot." Alec looked at the blood on his shirt. He picked up his graduation gown. "After what I've done, I didn't expect anything better."

"After what you've done?" Fray chuckled. "The fight hasn't even begun."

"I understand that," Alec said, pulling on the gown. "And you can count on me."

Fray gazed at him. "I need to know I can trust you. What we're planning will make everything much worse for you. It'll make her hate you even more. Are you ready for that?"

"I said I'm in. I'll do whatever you need me to do, but on one condition—Eleanor stays alive."

"Alec, think what you're asking for." Fray's voice hardened. "If she had the dagger right now, she would have killed you."

"You're right." Alec nodded. "But in the end, she was glad it wasn't the dagger she stabbed me with. You know why? Because she would have become a killer, like me. She knows I did what I did because you told me to. It's not me she really hates, it's you. I'm not saying she wouldn't try to hurt me again. But she knows that hurting me will not make her pain go away. You're the one she wants to kill. You ruined her life, and if she could, she would kill you without a second of hesitation." Alec paused for a few seconds. Looking at Fray's frowning face, he stepped closer. "I know you care about me," he said softly. "And you don't want anything bad to happen to me. I'm the only human you've ever been close to. I care about you, too. You're the only real parent I've ever had. And I want you to know I'll never betray you. I'm ready and I'm with you. I'll do whatever it takes. But she stays alive—that's all I'm asking." He looked into Fray's eyes, waiting. And when Fray finally nodded, he spoke again. "You've been waiting for Joanne to wake up for all these decades. I can wait, too. I'll wait as long as it takes for Eleanor to forgive me."

Alec left the room, and only when he was about to exit the school did he hear the echo of Fray's footsteps at the other end of the long, empty hallway.

Chapter Seventeen

STANDING NEXT to the podium and still keeping her hold on Kimberly, Eleanor looked at the crowd. Happy, celebrating their first step into adult life, graduates threw their red caps, smiled to the cameras, and hugged their classmates goodbye. There were fewer parents now. Eleanor didn't find Lindsey among them. Riley and Ned were gone, too, but Hanna was still there, waiting for her.

"Where's my father?" Eleanor asked. "Is he okay?"

"Don't worry, he's fine," said Hanna. "Riley and Ned are escorting him home. What about Alec?"

"Not now," said Eleanor grimly.

Hanna turned to Kimberly. "What are you doing here? I thought Ruben took you home." She looked around. "Where is he?"

"He's inside," said Kimberly.

"With Alec?" Hanna gazed at Eleanor. "What's going on? And why are you holding her?"

Eleanor took her hand off Kimberly's shoulder.

"It's nothing," said Kimberly. "Look," she said, pointing at Ruben as he came out of the school entrance. "There he is. We can go now."

The four of them arrived at Hanna's place. Eleanor dashed upstairs the moment they walked inside. When she opened the door to Craig's bedroom, she heard Hanna's voice from down the hall.

"I suppose the conversation with Alec was intense?" she said. "The whole way home she didn't say a word. Ruben, what happened? She didn't kill him, did she?"

"No. He got lucky. The kitchen knife didn't do the trick, and the dagger was nowhere around," said Ruben with sarcasm.

"I knew it." Hanna sighed. "So, there's two of them now. Wait. Are you saying she stabbed him?" There was a pause. Eleanor assumed that Ruben nodded. "But after she knew he'd turned, right?"

"Yes."

Eleanor stepped into the bedroom and shut the door. Yes, she knew the knife wouldn't kill Alec when she stabbed him. But what if she had the dagger? Of course, in that case, Alec wouldn't just stand there, waiting for her to kill him. But the question was, would she do it? Would she kill him?

Eleanor sat on the bed and ran her hand over the pillow, thinking of Craig. If only he could be here. She missed him so much. He was the one who could give her some desperately needed comfort.

The sound of footsteps approached and ceased behind her door, followed by a knock.

"What?" said Eleanor loudly.

The door opened and Ruben walked in.

"Don't start lecturing me." She looked away from him.

"I'm not." With his hands in his pockets, Ruben moved forward and stopped in front of her. "I saw that you were sorry. I just thought you might want to talk about it."

"The only thing I'm sorry about is that Kimberly saw it."

"That's because I got there in time. If you had stabbed him in the heart, you would be sorry for more than that."

"How can you say that, after what they did to you and Craig?"

"Yeah. They tortured us. And it wasn't the first time."

Eleanor stared at him.

"This surprises you?" Ruben shook his head. "Eleanor, why do you think after all these years we don't know where the daggers or the transitioning bodies are? Every time we got close to them, the vampires sniffed us out and locked us up. Do you know what they did to Samson? They tortured him for weeks until we found a way to get him out. That's how helpless we were. But they're the monsters. We don't do that, we don't torture people. If you had stabbed Alec in the heart, it would have changed you."

"You mean to say that I would become like them," said Eleanor.

"We may be powerful and immortal," said Ruben, sitting down next to her, "but we're still humans."

"Human or not, Alec is with them. He killed Melinda."

"Yes. She didn't see it coming, she didn't protect herself, and he stabbed her in cold blood. He's a killer. You don't want to be like him. That's why we're different. None of us would do such a thing."

Eleanor fixed her eyes on her lap and said quietly, "Samson did." She looked at Ruben from the corner of her eyes. "He's done it many times. He stopped their transition because they were killers."

Ruben stared at her. He stood up. "Eleanor, how can you compare that? Almost all those people were dying in the first place. By turning them, he was trying to save their lives, like he saved me, you, and Craig. Being responsible for our mission, and as a leader, he had to make tough decisions. You think it was easy for him?"

"I didn't say that. What I mean is Alec is a killer, too. You said yourself that they are waiting for the transitioning vampires to wake up so they can kill us all."

"Alec got powers he doesn't deserve, and if it comes to that, we'll kill him. But we're not going to sneak up on him, like he did, or torture him, Eleanor. We'll do it in a fair fight." Ruben sat next to her again. "Eleanor, you're angry with him, I understand. We all are. But he is who he is because of Fray. He's just a bug. While Fray is alive, everyone we love, we and our mission are in danger. I want you to concentrate your energy on destroying Fray. He's using every possible way to distract us, and it's working."

The bedroom door opened.

"They're back," said Hanna. "Riley wants you two downstairs."

~

RILEY STOOD in the doorway of the backyard with his hands behind his back. He turned to face the room at the sound of footsteps.

"Things are becoming more complicated," he said, running his hand over his shaved head. The serious tone made his voice lower than usual. "We didn't expect Fray to just sit there and wait for us to find his coffins, but we didn't think he'd show up here himself. Now, when Alec has turned," he continued, coming forward, "it's two of them out there, and it's dangerous. They're not vampires, they can walk under the sunlight, and they don't need an invitation to get into any house they want." He looked at Eleanor. "We followed your father's car and then waited for him to get inside, but it doesn't mean he's safe there. Same goes for you, Kimberly." He glanced at her, and at Ruben sitting next to her. "Fray is trying to keep us occupied. He knows we'll do anything to keep our people safe. But we can't afford to guard them twenty-four hours a day. We need to find some other way to protect them."

"We need a witch," said Ruben.

"We should ask Samson," said Hanna. "He knows them better. Maybe he could recommend one."

"I've tried to call him," said Riley, "but he's out of reach. They're probably still in the woods." After a short pause, he glanced at Eleanor. "I think you should talk to your father. It's easier with Kimberly because she knows what's going on. One day he'll find out who you are anyway. Maybe you should come clean now?"

"And tell him what, Riley?" Eleanor stared at him. "Hi, Dad. I'm your God-knows-how-many-times great, great-grandmother?"

"We'll think about it. We'll find the right way to do it. And I'll try to contact Samson later, ask him to find a witch." Riley waved his hand, signaling that the subject was closed. "Now about the coffins. Those places we've been . . . none of us believed those coffins were the ones we're looking for, but we still had to check, to make sure. Samson thinks those bodies are too important to Fray to hurl around like that."

"Then where does he think they might be?" asked Eleanor.

"He thinks the transitioning bodies are where he hid them after he turned them, that he hasn't moved them since. That night, when you—" Riley cleared his throat. "After what happened in the church, we left. To be sure that we were nowhere around, Fray's vampires followed us all the way to the castle. The next day, when Samson returned to that place, they were gone and the barn was empty. He still had a little of Fray's blood, but after the Book was closed, the Map lost its power. When he finally found Fray with the help of witches, he was already in New York. Even without powers, his well-prepared plan worked, because he had strong and fast vampires on his side, ready to do his bidding.

"During those years, Samson checked dozens of places where he supposed Fray could've hidden the bodies; the places he thought were significant to him. But Fray had secrets. You all remember that, when he lived with us, he could disappear for months, and nobody knew where he was." Riley walked to the armchair and sat down. "We have to dig deeper, try to remember some details, find some clues. So, Eleanor, instead of trying to cut Alec into pieces, maybe you could use his feelings for you and fish out some information."

Eleanor gazed at him, bubbling with anger.

Riley leaned forward, arms on his knees. "Eleanor, this isn't the right moment for a vendetta. When the time comes, you can do the honors." He sighed. "Listen, Fray doesn't care how many of his vampires we kill. But you said yourself that he and Alec are close. If you harm his, he'll harm yours, and we have enough problems already. You've let your steam out. Now you have to calm down and look at the big picture. When you see Alec next time, use him wisely."

"I already tried," said Eleanor. Everybody looked at her, waiting. "When he said he was sorry," she rolled her eyes, "for what he did, I said he can prove it by telling me where Fray hides the daggers before he kills somebody else. But Alec said Fray wouldn't tell anyone, not even him."

"He's lying," said Hanna.

"No." Eleanor shook her head. "He also said he wouldn't tell even if he knew, that he would never do that to Fray."

"Unbelievable," said Hanna. "After what Fray did to his parents."

"They weren't his parents."

"Wait. What?" Hanna stared at her.

"Really?" said Ned. "You mean he was adopted?"

"Nope. Fray hired them."

"I can't believe this." Hanna shook her head.

"So Alec is an orphan," said Ned.

"Apparently, 'Uncle' isn't some conspiracy name," said Kimberly. "That means Fray took care of him. The house Alec lived in in Williamsburg wasn't Matilda's and Clark's. It probably belonged to Fray."

"As I said before." Eleanor tilted her head and raised her eyebrows as she looked at Riley.

"The coffins can't be there," said Riley. "Virginia is too far. Samson said the one thing he's sure about is they're somewhere around here. But the house is a start. It can help us untangle the knot."

"We should find out what happened to the house after Alec moved out," said Ruben. "I'll go see Mike. He said he'll be at the station." Ruben kissed Kimberly on the temple and got up. "Wait here. I'll be back soon."

Kimberly's eyes followed Ruben as he walked away.

"I need to drink something cold and refreshing," said Hanna. "Who's with me?" She headed to the kitchen.

"Me. I'll always be with you," said Ned in a jocular way. "Even if you'd jump from a plane, fall from a cliff, run into fire..."

"What would that be?" chuckled Hanna. "Some kind of immortality test?"

"What?" said Ned, spreading his hands. "It'll still hurt."

"I'm with you, too, little sis," Riley said with a smile. "But no tests. I just want a beer."

When the three of them disappeared to the kitchen, Eleanor looked at Kimberly. The moment their eyes met, Kimberly smiled unnaturally, then got up and followed the others.

Eleanor's heart sank. Kimberly had already looked at her like she was some kind of alien. Now it was much worse. Kimberly was afraid of her.

Less than two weeks ago, they were just three girls having fun at the lake, thinking about what they'd wear to an upcoming party, talking about boys. Sure, Hanna knew that everything might change at any moment, but she enjoyed their time together as much as Amanda and Kimberly did. If what happened to Amanda meant awakening, finding her true self, to Kimberly it was the opposite. Everything she liked about her life—her friends, their plans for the future, her new love—everything was slipping away. Seeing Riley snap vampires' necks, seeing Alec kill Melinda, dead bodies lying all around Eleanor's old house—it wasn't how she expected to spend her last days of high school, and watching her best friend stab her classmate wasn't how she planned to celebrate her graduation. Kimberly deserved better than that.

Eleanor bit her lip. She felt guilty, angry, and embarrassed at the same time. She wouldn't be able to fix it today, and who knew what would happen tomorrow—the real fight hadn't even begun. But staying away from Kimberly would only expand the distance between them.

She got up and went to the kitchen. "I want something, too," she said opening the fridge. "Something cold, yellowish with bubbles." She pulled out a bottle of champagne. Eleanor glanced at Kimberly. Expecting to have an exciting day, she wore a new, gorgeous blue dress. And now she stood there, her hands crossed over her chest, her eyes sad. Eleanor put three glasses on the table and uncorked the bottle. "You guys may have your beer," she said to Riley and Ned, filling up the glasses. "But we," she handed the glasses to Kimberly and Hanna, "we'll celebrate our big day, no matter what. Happy graduation!"

"Happy graduation!" said Hanna, putting down the glass of soda she held in her other hand.

Kimberly pressed her lips together, then with a weak but this time real smile, said, "Happy graduation."

"Happy graduation!" Riley and Ned chimed together, raising their beers.

Riley and Ned each grabbed another beer and went to the backyard.

"I'm going to frame my diploma and put it next to the other two," smirked Hanna.

"When I received mine, Mr. Hancock actually blinked at me with his small round eyes," grinned Eleanor.

"I can't believe it's over," said Kimberly. Eleanor heard the sad note in her voice. "A week ago I couldn't wait for it to happen, but now . . ." She took a sip from her champagne.

"You think you'll miss it?" asked Hanna.

"I'll miss us," said Kimberly, looking into her glass.

"Hey, you know where we live now." Hanna beamed. "The address is Eternity Road, Invisible Wall number 1."

"Besides," said Eleanor, "weren't we planning to go to the same college?"

Kimberly stared at her. "You mean you still want to go to college?"

"Why not? I've never been to one. Hunters need education, too. Look how the world has changed after my first li—after I die-- You know. We have to keep up, to fit in."

Kimberly's eyes glittered. She looked at Hanna for approval.

"I would like that. I finished one, but it was decades ago. I went to Columbia. We didn't have much time for colleges. Me, Ned, and Ruben went to high school a couple of times each. We had to. Riley and Craig went to wars to keep Eleanor's posterity safe." She looked at Eleanor, grinning. "Sorry, your ancestors." She turned to Kimberly again. "Now, one mission is accomplished. Eleanor is back. And after we put down Fray, we can do whatever we want."

They talked more about colleges, what they would like to study, and Kimberly's mood seemed to be much better, but every time her and Eleanor's eyes were about to meet, she turned away.

When the front door slammed, Kimberly rushed to the hallway. Eleanor and Hanna waited a minute. When Kimberly didn't come back, they went after her.

Still standing in front of the door, Kimberly and Ruben were kissing. Hanna beamed, and took a step forward, but Eleanor turned her around and pushed her back to the kitchen.

The news Ruben brought from the police station didn't untangle anything; instead it brought them to a deadlock.

"Mike contacted the Williamsburg police," said Ruben. "It took them a few minutes to find out that after the Maysons moved out, the house was empty for about two months. Then it was sold to a middle-aged couple with two kids."

"So, maybe it wasn't Fray's, maybe it belonged to the Maysons?" asked Ned.

"I don't know. It isn't just some house. They said it's a big mansion from the nineteenth century."

"Even if it's his," Riley said, "he wouldn't sell the house with the bodies in it."

Hanna sighed. "Now we are back where we started."

"It's getting dark. I gotta go," said Eleanor. "I don't want to leave my father alone."

"Kimberly, Hanna will stay with you tonight," said Riley.

"No," said Ruben. "I'll do it myself. I'll stay with her."

"How're you going to do that?" asked Eleanor. "David will never allow it."

"Did your husband Richard allow Craig to spend nights in your bedroom?" asked Ruben, raising an eyebrow.

Riley and Hanna chuckled.

"Times may have changed, but here's the good news, Eleanor," said Ruben, index finger in the air. "Bedrooms still have windows."

"Then if Ruben's staying with Kimberly," said Riley, "Hanna can stay with Eleanor. If Fray decides to show up, you'll need some backup." He looked at Eleanor's bracelet. He was wearing his, too. He raised his hand and pointed at it. "Their powers are back, and I think we should all start wearing them. For emergencies. It's quicker and more reliable than phones."

∽

STANDING IN ELEANOR'S BEDROOM, Hanna looked at the back side of a painting leaning against a dresser. She picked it up and flipped it. It was Amanda's birthday present from Alec. "You took it down," she said. "I'm surprised it's still in one piece." "I was going to tear it apart, but I couldn't," said Eleanor. "It's Amanda. I'll never be *her* again. I know I have plenty of photographs to remember her by, but this is different. The way I look here—"

"You mean the way he saw you?"

"I'll never be like that again. When he showed it to me, part of me felt so sad, and the other part was glowing, like I already knew." Eleanor sat on the bed, but then stood up again, took off her dress and slid under the duvet.

"He used a secret ingredient," said Hanna, putting the painting back on the floor. "It's called love."

"About that. I'm worried about our love birds. What do you think is going to happen to them?"

"I don't know," said Hanna. She pulled off her pants and lay down on the other side of the bed. "Kimberly loves Ruben, but she's not ready for any of this. At least not yet. She's still in shock."

They turned to each other.

"She's changed," said Eleanor. "She's been so quiet lately, and it's so not like her."

"Yeah, I miss her snappy comebacks." Hanna took a deep breath. "She'll come around."

"After what happened today. . . . It'll never be the same. She hates me, Hanna."

"No, she doesn't. She's just a bit scared. It'll be fine, give her time."

"Today I was angry, and maybe I went a little overboard, but the thing is—we're Hunters. We do kill. So does Ruben. How is she going to be with him if she's scared of everything? She hasn't even seen him in action. What'll happen when she sees him ripping vampires heads off, or hearts out?"

"Hey, I warned him, and I was the one who was trying to keep them away from each other, remember? But it's too late now. I've never seen Ruben like this," said Hanna quietly. "He's in love. All we can do is wait and see what happens."

∽

RUBEN STOPPED the car in front of Kimberly's house. When she got out, he drove a little farther and parked next to the neighbor's trash cans. He waited for Kimberly to walk inside, then got out and, keeping close to the bushes, snuck into the backyard. A few minutes later, without turning on the lights, Kimberly opened her bedroom window.

"Step back," whispered Ruben before he jumped.

As he got in, Kimberly went back to the door and locked it. "My brother is asleep, and mom and David are watching a movie downstairs," she said quietly, walking toward him.

"'Die Hard' right?" asked Ruben, listening.

"You can hear it? All I hear is noise."

"I have perfect hearing, remember?"

Before he could say another word, she leaned into him and pressed her lips against his cheekbone. Ruben's hands slid up her back. He looked at her lips, and as he kissed them, her body trembled and her hands slipped under his shirt. When he pulled her closer, breathing heavily, Kimberly released a short "Ah" and her eyes flew open.

"Oh God, Kimberly," said Ruben, letting go of her. "Did I hurt you? I'm sorry,"

Kimberly smiled. "Got you."

"Don't scare me like that," he said softly, taking her face in his hands. "What is this, revenge?"

"Revenge is still coming."

Ruben looked into her mischievously glittering eyes. He had planned to talk to her about Eleanor, about what happened today, but when he returned from the police station her mood was much better. He didn't want to ruin it and decided to save the tough talk for some other time. Tonight he'd make her forget everything, banish her thoughts about what had happened, and take away her worries about what might happen tomorrow.

As he bowed his head to kiss her, her lips parted. Her soft hands slid under his shirt and pulled it off.

Chapter Eighteen

RUBEN WAS AWAKE. His eyes were fixed on Kimberly's ginger curls covering her naked back. It was Sunday morning, and it was pretty quiet outside, except this single chirping coming from the open window. He lifted his head and looked toward it.

The bird was a magpie. It sat on a long branch a few feet away. Ruben remembered how once, long ago, Craig told him that in Scotland people believed a single magpie seen near the house was a bad sign. It was a sign of—

Kimberly's hand moved, searching for something. Ruben leaned over her, took her hand, and kissed her shoulder. The chirping became louder. The magpie was much closer now. Craig said that to prevent the bad luck you had to salute the bird by doing something like taking off your hat.

Why would he suddenly remember this? He had never been superstitious. People believed in weird things when they cared and worried about someone. He smiled. It was true then—love made people stupid.

A light breeze filled the room with chilly air. Ruben carefully pulled his hand out of Kimberly's, but the moment he tried to cover her back, she began searching again. His hand slid under the duvet and lay around her belly. At his touch, she rolled over and buried her face in his chest. The next second her warm lips were gliding up his neck, sending a pleasant shiver down his body.

Kimberly turned on her back and lay on Ruben's arm.

"Good morning," he said, kissing her temple.

"Good morning," she whispered. "I don't remember the last time I slept so relaxed. Without nightmares, without any dreams at all."

"Are you sure? You jolted a couple of times."

"Maybe I just don't remember them. Why should I? My dream was next to me the whole night," she said, still whispering. "I don't need other dreams."

"You don't have to whisper." Ruben turned her to him. "They're gone."

"Oh, right, the picnic. Gone?" she asked a little louder. "What time is it?"

"It's almost ten."

"Really? How long have you been awake?"

"For a while."

"Oh, that's so selfish of me." She leaned over him. "I left my dream alone and bored."

The swinging tips of her hair tickled his chest. "I wasn't bored. I was watching my dream, making sure it was comfy," said Ruben. He reached for her neck and pulled her face closer. "I also learned a lot," he said, kissing her lips. "Now I know that your mom's name is Sharon," he kissed the corner of her mouth, "your brother's name is Luke," his lips moved down to her neck, "and he couldn't wait to meet his friends."

"Yeah." Kimberly's eyelids slid down, and her breathing became deeper. "That picnic is for him. It's kind of a breakfast with friends. It won't take long."

"We need to go, anyway," murmured Ruben into her ear. "We'll continue this pulse-raising conversation tonight."

"God," moaned Kimberly. "What the hell is wrong with that

bird?"

"It's alone," said Ruben quietly. "It's probably looking for a mate."

"You think so?"

Ruben nodded.

She leaned back and glanced at the magpie. "Poor bird," she said with compassion. "I hope it finds someone." Kimberly looked at Ruben. "Someone good, and they'll always be together." Stroking his cheekbones, her fingers slid up and sank into his hair. Her soft lips covered his face with gentle kisses. Then she pulled back a few inches, and her hazel eyes looked deep into his with such tenderness, as if searching in them for a way to his soul.

Ruben's heart hammered. He knew what was coming, what she was going to say, and he couldn't let her do that, no matter how badly he wanted to hear it. He had lived long enough to know how vital those three little words could be. She wasn't ready for them, there was so much she didn't know about him yet.

"Ruben," she whispered.

Ruben swallowed and, before she could say another word, he said, "I'm here." He turned her on her back and buried her in kisses.

∽

HER EYES barely opened as Eleanor reached for her phone to check the time. She unlocked it, her eyes lingering on its background picture. It was a photo of her and Craig, which she took at the castle's front yard right before he left. When she looked at the small numbers on the top of the screen, she muttered to herself and jumped out of the bed.

"Hanna," called Eleanor, putting her clothes on. "Hanna, wake up."

Hanna didn't move. Her face buried in the pillow, she was still asleep.

Eleanor picked up Hanna's pants and threw them at her. Hanna slowly lifted her head.

"What? Is it coffee time?"

"Get up," said Eleanor.

Hanna turned around. "What's the rush?" she asked, sitting up.

"My Dad is going to a meeting," said Eleanor, brushing her hair. "We need to make sure he gets to his office safely, that nobody follows him there."

"Meeting? Isn't it Sunday?"

"His team wants to see him today. They want to know the details about the deal he made in L.A."

They followed Lindsey's car, keeping a good distance. Hanna drove while Eleanor looked around, searching for anything suspicious. When Lindsey parked the car and walked into the building, they waited for a few more minutes to make sure that the coast was clear, then drove away.

Last night Eleanor had the same dream from two nights ago. She was chasing the same vampire woman in the woods, over and over again, and every time she reached her, the woman vanished. It wasn't just a dream, and she knew if she could catch the woman and see her face, she'd understand what it meant.

"Don't worry," Hanna said. "He'll be fine."

"What?" asked Eleanor, awakening from her thoughts.

"I'm saying nobody knows he's at the office. He'll be fine," said Hanna.

"I hope so," said Eleanor.

"Are you okay? You seem a little off."

"It's just that dream." Eleanor sighed. "Last night I had the same dream, and I can't figure out what it means."

"About the vampire woman?"

"Yes."

"Eleanor, it doesn't necessarily have to mean anything. You just got back. It might be some memory flash from your past." Hanna pondered for a moment, then added, "Maybe back then a vampire woman got away from you, and now you're feeling some kind of unfinished business effect."

"Maybe," said Eleanor. "I like your theory. It makes sense. Of course, it also makes me feel dead. I mean, the 'unfinished business' part. Like I'm some kind of ghost."

"Relax." Hanna grinned. "It's just an analogy."

Hanna looked into the rearview mirror when they neared the house. "Ruben and Kimberly are here. Everyone is home."

Eleanor looked back. Ruben and Kimberly were right behind their car in Craig's black Jeep. "Not everybody," she said with longing.

"Oops." Hanna bit her lip. "Sorry."

The cars drove into the front yard and parked next to each other in front of the house.

"She looks happy," said Eleanor, glancing at Kimberly.

"Who wouldn't be? Look at the guy next to her." Hanna chuckled. "He doesn't need to work all night to make her glow like that. He just has to be there."

Ruben was already out of the car. He cracked a smile. "Thanks, sis."

"You shouldn't eavesdrop," said Hanna, pushing her door open. She and Eleanor waved to Kimberly and headed to the front door.

"Did you say something?" asked Kimberly, getting out from the Jeep.

"Nope." Ruben shook his head.

Hanna inhaled the scent of coffee coming from the kitchen. She darted to Ned at the table and dropped into his lap. Kissing him, she pulled the cup out of his hand. "Did you miss me?" she asked as she sipped the coffee. "How did you sleep?"

"Diagonally," said Ned. "Like I have for the last three years."

Hanna arched her lips, then kissed his wavy blond hair.

Riley was standing next to the counter and waiting for the toasts to pop out of the toaster. He wore a gray, sleeveless T-shirt that made his shoulders and arms seem even bigger.

"Toast, anyone?" asked Riley as they popped out.

"Me." Hanna raised her hand.

Riley put the toasts on two plates and handed one of them to Hanna. Then he pulled butter and jam from the fridge. "Anyone else?" he asked, adding another two pieces of bread to the toaster.

"Hi," said Ruben, as he and Kimberly walked into the kitchen.

"Riley, did you speak to Samson?" asked Eleanor.

"I just called him," said Riley. "They were checking into a hotel. He said he'd call back."

"Hotel where?" asked Eleanor. "Craig sent me a message. He said they're done in Norway."

"They're done in Trondheim. Now they're in Oslo, and their flight to Egypt is tomorrow." The phone rang. Riley put it on speaker.

"Hey, there," said Samson. "How are you doing? Is there any progress?"

"No," said Riley. "All those places were just traps. The only news is that Fray is here. He showed up yesterday with that boy, Alec."

"The one who killed Melinda?"

"Yeah, that one. And he's invincible now."

"Samson, after what he did, his transition took only three days," said Eleanor. "How's that possible?"

As Samson always said, if the person had evil inside him, was cruel, violent, or have killed someone, the transition would take more than four days. Alec killed Melinda, and Eleanor couldn't understand what made his transitioning process different.

"There is one thing that can affect the process. It's remorse. It happened once before, and that is what the golden text told me then. But I stopped the transition anyway. I couldn't take the risk. And I'll advise you the same—be careful with him. Even if he feels sorry, it doesn't mean he'll never kill again. His remorse might be a result of personal feelings for that particular victim. It might not stop him from doing the same thing to some stranger, or a person he dislikes."

"Fray isn't here because he missed us," said Ruben. "He showed up next to Eleanor's father. We need at least some protection spells around Eleanor's and Kimberly's houses."

"I've already thought about it, and I spoke to a coven in Chicago. They're sending a witch. She'll arrive tomorrow. But I don't think that protection spell will help much with Fray and Alec around."

"I know," said Ruben. "But it's still an alarm, a head start."

"There's one more thing I wanted to ask you," said Eleanor. She pulled out her phone. "Craig, I'm sending a picture to your phone. Can you both look at it?"

"That's a photo of Alec," said Craig, disappointed. "You keep his photo in your phone?"

"Oh, God." Hanna grinned. "You're still jealous. That's so sweet. Don't worry, she hates him as much as I do. She stabbed him the moment she got the chance."

Eleanor glared at Hanna.

"What?" Now Craig sounded almost angry. "Eleanor, if Fray was there . . . you promised to be careful."

"Yeah," Riley cleared his throat. "That's how we found out he's immortal."

Eleanor turned her glare to Riley.

"Eleanor," came Samson's voice. "What did you want us to look at?"

"Zoom in on the picture," said Eleanor. "Look at the drawing on the wall. Have any of you seen this drawing or that woman before?"

There were a few seconds of silence.

"No, I don't think so," said Craig.

"The date is suspicious," said Samson. "But I don't think I've seen that face before."

"She looks familiar to me," said Eleanor. "And I think it has something to do with Fray. Kimberly dug into Alec's past. It helped us to find out that the house Alec lived in, before he moved here, belonged to Fray. I think this picture of Alec was taken in that house."

"Fray?" asked Samson. There was another pause. "Gabriella told me once—Yes, it was the day he left. When she went to talk to him. She said she saw the drawing of a woman in his hand. She said he was looking for it so he could take it with him. She supposed he was in love with her."

"I don't understand," murmured Eleanor. "Where do I know her from? If none of you have seen her before . . ."

"Maybe some of us did, but we don't remember," said Samson. "Too much has happened since then. Your memories about the time when Fray lived with us are more fresh than ours."

"Samson, we're stuck," said Riley. "We're not getting anywhere. Any advice?"

"You said Alec lived in Fray's house. Did you check it? Where is it?"

"It's a mansion in Virginia," said Ruben. "But it was sold a couple of months after Alec moved out."

"As I've told you before, there is always a loophole. You found an entire mansion that we never knew existed because of Alec. He was the loophole. That mansion itself might be another one. And there's still the drawing. Fray's plans always worked, but that doesn't mean they were flawless. Is Kimberly there?" asked Samson.

Everybody looked at Kimberly. Kimberly's eyebrows jumped up in surprise.

"Yes," said Ruben.

"Good job, Kimberly. Thank you," said Samson.

Kimberly turned pink. "I'm glad to help," she said quietly.

"We've been stewing in this for too long," said Samson. "It can make us blind to details. We think there's nothing we don't already know. A new perspective can reveal something we may not see." He paused for a second, then said, "Tell Eleanor about the places we've checked, show her my records. It's not much, but maybe it'll trigger something."

"We will," said Riley.

"Keep us updated."

"Eleanor, I'll call you later," said Craig.

"Craig." Ruben bent closer to the phone. "You're almost there. Good luck, brother."

"Thanks," said Craig with perceptible excitement in his voice.

Eleanor pierced Ruben with her gaze. "Good luck with what?" she asked with frustration as soon as Riley hung up.

"Eleanor, they didn't go for a walk," said Ruben. "I wished them good luck with everything they're doing."

"All right, keep your secrets. You tortured me with them while I was Amanda, and now, when I'm Eleanor, you torture me again." She rolled her eyes and stormed out of the kitchen.

Ruben followed her. As she stopped in the living room, facing the fireplace, he turned her around.

"Eleanor, I know it seems unfair that, after everything you've been through, we're keeping secrets from you. But I gave Samson my word that I wouldn't tell anyone, not even you."

"I know," Eleanor said with a sigh.

He locked his hands behind her back and kissed her on the forehead. "I know how much you miss him, and I know you're worried about him. But it won't be long now. He'll be home soon."

Eleanor dropped her head to his shoulder. "It's just . . . when I kept a secret from Craig, I. . . . Promise me he isn't in danger." She looked into his eyes.

"I promise. If it were something like that, why would I be glad he's almost there?"

"Right. I'm being stupid."

"Yeah." Ruben smiled. "Love does that to people. It makes them stupid."

Chapter Nineteen

THE NEXT FEW hours they spent in the study, sitting around a big table, unfolding old maps, one after another. Riley, Ruben, Hanna, and Ned showed Eleanor the marked areas and told her the stories behind them.

Ruben wasn't the only one who noticed Kimberley's excitement as she listened.

"Kimberly's in heaven," smirked Hanna as Riley finished the story about the ruins, marked on one of the maps. "I bet you would love to go and dig up all those places, wouldn't you?"

"Definitely," said Kimberly. "But you know what? I just realized that no matter where I go and how deep I dig, I'll never be able to find a bigger archaeological treasure than the one talking to me right now."

They all laughed.

Ned turned to Hanna. "I never thought about that," he said, narrowing his eyes and looking at her closer.

"Hey, don't you dare." Chortling, Hanna pushed him away. "Her Ruben is much older than me."

Kimberly leaned to Ruben and kissed him.

"Riley is much older than me," said Ruben.

Riley beamed. "Next to Samson, I feel like a boy. That's who is really antique."

"And he knows my name," said Kimberly. "You're all too old and have seen too much to understand how creepy that is."

It was already dark outside. Eleanor called her father to check if the meeting was over. The moment she put away her phone, Kimberly pulled out hers.

"It's my mom," she said, reading a message.

"What is it?" asked Ruben. "Is everything all right?"

"She says she needs me. She wants me to come home."

"Sounds serious," said Hanna. "Ruben, you didn't forget your socks under the bed, did you?"

"It's probably the usual—they're going out and want me to stay with Luke," said Kimberly with a sigh. "I gotta go."

Ruben drove Kimberly home. It was too early for him to go inside. Kimberly said she'd call later to let him know when the best time for him to come back would be. When she walked into the house, he waited for a few minutes, listening, and after making sure that everything was calm and quiet, he drove away.

Ruben was halfway back when his phone vibrated. He jerked it out of his pocket, expecting to see Kimberly's name on it. But to his surprise, it was Mike.

"Mike," said Ruben. "What's up?"

"I need your help," said Mike, breathing heavily.

Ruben heard screams. "Mike, what's going on?"

"There are too many of them. I don't know what to do."

"Where are you?"

"It's . . . Wilson Alley . . . two houses at Wilson Alley."

"I'm on my way." Ruben hung up and called Riley. "Take the others and get to Wilson Alley. There's a vampire attack there, Mike says it's bad."

A few minutes later, Ruben stopped the Jeep next to Mike's police car. Young people ran screaming up and down the street.

Some of them had bloodstains on their clothes or around their necks. Ruben opened the trunk and pulled out two stakes.

"Did you call for backup?" he asked, hurrying toward Mike.

"No. The police can't do much here. But my partner is here somewhere, he might have called," said Mike.

"Are you hurt?" asked Ruben, noticing the blood on his shirt.

"It's not mine, I was helping a guy. Those kids . . . they were having a party . . . Ruben, nothing works. I shot all the rounds I had. It didn't even slow them down."

"You have to shoot in the head. Take this," Ruben handed him a stake. "Just in case. To protect yourself."

Hanna's car stopped next to them. In a flash, Riley was standing beside Mike.

"It's not just this house," said Ruben. Pointing his hand down the street, he showed Riley the second one.

"You, Eleanor, and Hanna take this one," said Riley. "Ned and I will take the other. Ned, let's go." In the next second, the two of them were gone.

"This is Debra's house," Ruben heard Eleanor's voice behind him.

"Let me guess—she invited Mark to her graduation party. This time I'll get that son of a bitch," grumbled Hanna, and she and Eleanor stormed in.

Astonished, Mike looked after them.

Ruben ran toward the house and jumped in through the second floor window. He landed in the bedroom. Right before his feet was a body. It was a young man. He heard a cry but didn't react to it. He glared at the vampire sucking blood from the neck of a girl pressed to the wall. Ruben grabbed him and turned him around.

The vampire's eyes widened as he looked at Ruben.

"It's you," he muttered.

"Oh yes, it's me," said Ruben, thrusting the stake into his heart. He looked at the girl. Her eyes half-closed, wobbling, she took a step and almost fell. Ruben caught her and put her down on the bed.

The bedroom door swung open. Another vampire flew in and crashed to the floor.

"Finish him," Eleanor spat from the hallway and ran after another one.

The vampire tried to get up, but Ruben stepped on his chest, nailing him to the floor. As he staked the vampire, he heard the cry again. It came from the closet.

Ruben pulled aside the mirrored door and saw a girl sitting in the corner, on top of the shoe boxes.

"It's okay," said Ruben, looking at the trembling girl. "You'll be fine."

From outside came the wail of several sirens. Ruben saw police cars driving down the street. Two ambulances stopped in front of the house. "Come with me," he said to the girl in the closet, then he took the one lying on the bed into his arms and rushed out.

On the staircase he saw Hanna, who had found Debra and was now shouting at her.

"I told you to stay away from Mark. Look what he did." Hanna pinned her to the wall with her gaze. "Where is he?"

"I don't . . . I don't know," said Debra, stammering.

Three vampires—two women and a man—darted out the front door. "Come on, Hanna," Ruben said. "They're running away."

The girl in his arms was getting paler. When he got outside, he saw the paramedics pulling out a stretcher from one of the vans. "She's lost a lot of blood," he told them, putting the girl down. When he looked around for the second girl, he saw a red-haired girl covered in blood sitting on the step bar of another ambulance. Ruben's heart stopped, thinking of Kimberly. He turned to the house and saw Hanna and Eleanor running out of it.

Ruben darted toward them and clutched Eleanor's arm, stopping her. "Get to your father. Now. This was a distraction."

The next second he was beside his car. "She's all right," he kept repeating to himself. "She's all right." He drove as fast as possible, but when he finally arrived at Kimberly's house, he remained in the car for a few seconds, listening. The lights on the first floor were on, but Ruben couldn't hear any voices or sounds coming from there. The street was quiet, too, except the hum of an engine coming from one of the cars parked down the lane.

With the stake in his hand, he got out of the car and ran past the garbage cans to the backyard. Kimberly's bedroom window was open and the light was on. He heard a weak cry. It was Kimberly.

"I don't know," she said, sobbing, "I don't know."

Ruben froze for a moment, thinking maybe she was having an unpleasant conversation with her mother. But then a husky voice said, "You're lying," and Kimberly screamed.

Ruben jumped. Once in the room, he saw blond hair and a fancy gray suit bend down to Kimberly where she lay on the bed. He grabbed the vampire and hurled him across the room. Another one in a black jacket stood on the other side of the bed.

Ruben threw one quick glance at Kimberly, at her pale, terrified face as she sobbed, her shirt stained with blood, and his chest heaved with fury. He felt an irresistible desire not just to kill the vampires, but to hurt them, make them suffer. Ruben threw away the stake.

He turned to the vampire in the jacket. By the look on his face, Ruben knew he was trying to overcome his fear. The vampire bared his fangs and jumped. Before the vampire could reach him, Ruben struck him in the chest with his open hand. The vampire flew back and hit the dresser, shattering its mirror into pieces. The first vampire was on his feet again, and his fist was next to Ruben's face when he caught it. Pushing it back with one hand, Ruben punched him in the nose with the other, then twisted his arm. With the edge of his free hand, he hit the vampire's elbow. It bent backwards. Screaming in pain, the vampire fell on his knees.

The second vampire jumped forward and was about to kick Ruben in the chest, but Ruben bounced back, grabbed his foot, and rolled it.

There was the sound of cracking bone. Ruben threw him back. Howling, the vampire crashed to the other side of the bed. Ruben turned to the blond vampire, pulled him up, and pressed him to the wall. Blow after blow, he beat the vampire up until his face was a red mess. Blood rained from it onto his gray suit.

"How dare you touch *my* girl?" hissed Ruben. He thrust his hand into the vampire's chest and ripped out his heart. He threw it away, stepped to the other one, and clutched his throat. His teeth clenched, and his glare fixed on the vampire's horrified face, Ruben ripped open his jacket. His fingers pierced the vampire's chest, and the next moment another heart fell on the floor. He dropped the body and looked at the blood dripping from his fist as he squeezed it tight. Suddenly, he remembered the suppressed scream he heard a second ago.

He turned to Kimberly. She sat on the bed, her hand over her mouth and staring at him with eyes full of tears. Her whole body shaking, she got up. When Ruben stepped to her, she pushed him aside, yelling "Mom? Mom!" as she rushed downstairs.

Realization hit Ruben as he followed her down the steps.

Kimberly's mother lay on the kitchen floor. Her eyes were closed, face pale, and there was a small puddle of blood next to her neck. She was dead.

Thinking of Kimberly's brother and stepfather, Ruben looked around. He didn't see any traces of blood. He went to the living room, then ran upstairs and checked the other two bedrooms and the bathroom. There was no one else in the house.

For a second, he stopped in the threshold of Kimberly's room and looked inside. He wouldn't be able to clean this up. There was too much blood.

Kimberly knelt next to her mother and held her hand, sobbing. Ruben put his hands on her shuddering shoulders.

"Kimberly, we have to go," he said quietly. She didn't move or say anything. "Kimberly, we can't stay here," he said again. "We need to go before someone sees us. The last thing you need right now is police asking you questions you can't answer."

He heard a car outside. Kimberly sobbed harder. He pulled her up, took her in his arms, and ran to her bedroom. When the front door opened, he pressed her to his chest and jumped out of the window.

He put Kimberly down, supporting her as he led her through the neighbor's backyard, then through the next one, before going out into the street. Making sure that there was nobody around, he left Kimberly standing under a tree while he got his car.

They drove in silence. Kimberly wasn't crying anymore; her red eyes stared into nowhere. When they arrived, Ruben carried her to his room and put her on the bed. He grabbed a clean towel from the bathroom and pressed it to her neck, then quickly washed the blood from his hands and sat next to her.

She lay on her side, eyes open. Ruben didn't know what to say. How could he let this happen? It was his fault, all his fault. If Fray hadn't seen her with him, this would never have happened. Hanna was right; he had to stay away from Kimberly. He wanted to hug her, to comfort her, but he couldn't even do that. After how Kimberly saw him act today, he doubted he'd ever be able to hold her again, that she'd ever let him.

"I'll go make some tea," he said quietly, and went to the kitchen.

While waiting for the water to boil, Ruben thought about what happened in Kimberly's room. It wasn't his first time to rip out a vampire's heart; the Hunters did it often if there was no stake at hand. But the fact that Kimberly saw him do it made him hate himself.

He heard a car in the driveway.

"Ruben." Hanna's voice came from the hallway. The next

moment, she was standing in the kitchen. "What happened? Where is Kimberly?"

"She's in my bedroom." He barely heard his own voice.

"Is she okay?" Hanna moved closer, looking alarmed. Riley and Ned were now behind her, and the three of them stared at him in anticipation.

"No, she isn't. She was bitten." He swallowed. "And her mother is dead."

"Oh, God," Hanna gasped, pressing both hands to her mouth.

"Dammit," said Riley through gritted teeth.

"Do we have any bandages?" Ruben asked.

"Yes," said Hanna, opening one of the drawers. "I kept them just in case, for Eleanor. I mean, for Amanda."

"Hanna, David might call her any minute, and he can't know she was there when it happened."

"I'm on it," said Hanna, and dashed upstairs.

"Did the vampires get there before you?" asked Riley.

Ruben nodded. "They were there, and they still are, with their hearts next to them. There was no time to clean up the mess."

"It doesn't matter," said Riley. "Not after what happened today."

"It matters to her." Ruben took a cup from the shelf. "What about Eleanor's father? Is he okay?"

"He's fine. He was still at the meeting."

"What about the others? The kids at the parties?"

"We killed most of the vampires," said Ned. "But when we got there, there were already two bodies in the house."

"Yeah, I saw one dead guy, too," said Ruben with a sigh. He added honey into the tea, then took the cup and went upstairs.

Hanna's bedroom door was open. Ruben looked inside and saw her rummaging in her closet.

"I need to find something to cover her neck," she said, pulling shirts and sweaters out of the drawer.

"Did they call?" asked Ruben.

"Yes. I did the talking. It wasn't David. It was the police. They thought that they were speaking to Kimberly."

Ruben went to his room. Kimberly sat with her eyes closed, leaning against the headboard. Hanna had already cleaned her wound and put the bandage on it.

Ruben sat on the bed. Choking from guilt, he whispered, "Kimberly."

She opened her eyes and looked at him. Then she looked at the cup in his hand.

"You need to drink this," he said. She closed her eyes again, and tears ran down her pale face. The pain shot through Ruben's heart, tightening his throat. Suspecting that his presence was increasing her suffering, he stood up.

"This will do," said Hanna, walking in. She held a dark-blue cashmere sweater with a turtleneck.

Ruben put the cup on the nightstand. "Make her drink this," he said, and left the room.

Riley and Ned were now in the living room. Ruben poured himself a glass of whiskey and gulped it. "How did Fray know we'd go there?" he asked, looking from Riley to Ned. "If Mike hadn't called—"

"We would have gone anyway," said Riley. "Right after you called me, Eleanor got a message from Alec. It was an invitation to a graduation party at that same address. There was a postscript—'You don't want to be late.'"

"I wonder what the police will tell people," said Ned, "How are they going to explain what happened?"

"This isn't the first time they've encountered the supernatural," said Riley. "These sorts of things happen from time to time. Never this big and obvious, of course, but I'm sure they'll come up with something."

Ruben heard Hanna and Kimberly coming down the stairs. Without looking at either of them, Kimberly went to the front door. Ruben followed her, but Hanna grabbed his arm and pulled him into the kitchen.

"You're not going."

"I won't talk to her. I'll keep my distance."

"That isn't the point. Whatever happened in that house, you're a part of it. Someone could have seen you sneaking in today, or yesterday. The house is full of police. You can't show up there right now."

"I need to know she's safe."

"I'll take care of her," said Hanna softly. "Don't worry."

"Hanna, the house is all messed up." *I'm the one who made that mess,* Ruben added in his head. "They won't be able to stay there. I don't know where her stepfather is planning to go, but I need you to bring her back."

"I will. Call Eleanor. Tell her what happened."

Through the kitchen window, Ruben watched Hanna and Kimberly drive away. Then he called Eleanor and told her everything.

"Oh my God. That's horrible," said Eleanor. "Poor Kimberly. And I can't even go to her."

"No. You need to take care of your father. You can see her tomorrow and maybe you'll be able to talk to her then. She hasn't said a word since . . ."

"I think I'm the last person she would want to talk to, after she saw me—you know."

"After what happened today," said Ruben bitterly, "I think she has a right to hate us all, starting with me."

"You're right. We did this to her."

"*I* did this," said Ruben, pacing up and down the kitchen. "It's all my fault. I shouldn't . . . it doesn't matter now. It's already done, and I can't change it." He stopped. "What I can do is keep her safe."

"Why didn't you go with her and Hanna?" Eleanor asked.

There was a moment of silence, then Ruben asked, "Eleanor,

when you met Craig . . ." He paused, thinking how to phrase the question. "When you saw him killing . . . did it scare you?"

"I fell in love with Craig the moment I saw him. As you know, the day we met, he killed a werewolf right in front of me. Did it scare me? Yes. I was terrified. But I wasn't scared of him. He saved my life. He became my hero."

"Did he rip out the werewolf's heart?" asked Ruben in a much lower voice.

"So that's what this is about." Eleanor sighed.

"When I saw her like that—Eleanor, he was hurting her." Ruben ran his hand through his hair. "I lost it."

"Ruben, you killed monsters. You saved her life. I'm sure she'll understand. She loves you."

"I know. I mean she did, and she was about to say it to me this morning. But I didn't let her, because I knew that she doesn't know me yet, that she doesn't know what being a Hunter really means."

"Knowing it never stopped me, or Gabriella. Give her some time. She has a lot to deal with. She lost her mother tonight."

"That's what bothers me. She was already in so much pain, and I made it even worse."

"All you can do right now is be there for her and be patient," said Eleanor softly.

"Thanks, Eleanor. See you tomorrow."

Ruben returned to the living room just in time to hear Riley say, ". . . and his plan works every time."

"Yeah, he's the winner. Again," said Ned with frustration.

"He didn't win a damn thing," said Ruben, swallowing his anger. "People died because of him, that's true, but it doesn't make him a winner. When he stole the Book, we found him. Eleanor closed the Book and he never enjoyed his victory. He stole the Book a second time and he's still nothing. What he did today only proves that he's a killer, that he's ready to do anything to get what he wants. The vampire didn't just want to kill Kimberly; they were trying to get information."

"They went after Kimberly for information?" asked Riley, looking perplexed.

"I don't know what Fray wanted, but I know whatever it was, he didn't get it. So, no, he didn't win a damn thing. And he's not going to. We need to find the transitioning bodies."

"We still don't know where to look," said Riley.

"To start, someone needs to go to Virginia and look at that house, ask around about the new owners. Maybe they're fake, like the Maysons. I can't leave Kimberly right now, Eleanor needs to look after her father."

"I'll go," said Ned. "I'll see what I can find out."

Chapter Twenty

RUBEN SPENT the rest of the evening pacing in the living room. It seemed to him like he had been waiting forever when around midnight, he heard Hanna's car. He walked into the dark kitchen and looked through the window. As Kimberly opened the passenger door, Ruben breathed a sigh of relief.

Ruben watched through the kitchen doorway as Kimberly passed by and climbed to the second floor.

When he saw Hanna, he came forward. "How is she?" he asked.

"Why don't you ask her yourself?" Hanna gazed at him. "Ruben, what's going on?"

"I don't think she wants to talk to me right now."

"Why? What happened?" Hanna asked, looking confused.

"She saw me kill those vampires and . . . Can we talk about it later? What took you so long?" Ruben switched the subject. "Did the police question her this whole time?"

"No. The police seemed really lost. They didn't even know what to ask. It was David who bombarded them with questions. They told him there was an attack on two other houses and it was probably some new gang in town. When the policeman said that they can't stay in the house, David wanted to know why. He wanted to go upstairs, but they wouldn't let him." Hanna sighed heavily. "I didn't think he'd . . . he was so shocked."

"Hanna, she was his wife, the mother of his son," said Ruben.

"Yeah, but . . ." Hanna's expression froze, and it seemed her thoughts drifted away.

"Then?" asked Ruben, pulling her out from her stupor.

Hanna blinked. "Then we went to a hotel. David was about to book two rooms, but I said it'd be better if Kimberly stayed with me. She went with him to the room, staying until Luke fell asleep. I didn't want to intrude, so I stayed in the lobby."

"Did you talk to her? Did she say anything at all?"

"Just a few things. When she got home, her mom said she didn't send her any messages, that she lost her phone the previous evening. Kimberly knew then that something was wrong. She was about to call you when she heard unfamiliar voices. She went to the hallway and saw two well-dressed men standing in the threshold. They must have been asking for David, because her mother said that he'd be back soon and they could wait for him inside. Kimberly screamed, 'Don't invite them in,' but it was two seconds too late. One of them grabbed her mother, the other one grabbed her."

Ruben looked away as Hanna's sad eyes met his. "When I drove her home, I waited, I looked around, I listened. There was no one there," he said through his clenched teeth. "Where the hell did they come from so quickly?"

"Ruben, they sent the message. They knew you'd come, and they were careful. You need to stop torturing yourself. We can't prevent every dangerous situation."

"Right." Ruben nodded, then went to the living room and poured himself a whiskey.

"I'll check on her and then go to bed," said Hanna, heading upstairs.

About half an hour later, the house fell into total silence.

Ruben sat on the couch, fighting the temptation to go to his room. The thought that Kimberly was there alone after everything she'd been through this long, agonizing day tormented him. But would his appearance make it better? What if being alone was exactly what she needed right now? To think everything through, to cry out her pain without witnesses. Even if she needed someone, it wouldn't be him, not the one who brought this adversity upon her.

Ruben realized he was standing at the bottom of the stairs. He went back to the couch and lay down. In his long life, he had never experienced anything like this. He, Ruben—who always knew what to say to women, how to act around them, what to do when they were in trouble—was absolutely lost. And he knew why. Because he never cared about any of them the way he cared about Kimberly, he wasn't afraid to lose them. He had been in love once, very long ago, but it wasn't the same. They were never that close, and when after many doubts, he finally told her the truth about who he really was, it turned out to be a big mistake.

With Kimberly, everything was different. After seeing her only a couple of times, he wanted to tell her everything. He felt connected to her. Every time she looked into his eyes, it was like she was turning on the light in the darkest places of his heart. Even now, when she knew who he was, she was interested in his life, trying to adjust, even help. And today he had ruined that.

He didn't know how long he lay there, staring at the ceiling when he heard weak footsteps. He looked at the stairs and saw Kimberly coming down them, barefoot, still in her jeans and the dark-blue cashmere sweater.

Ruben sat up. *She's probably thirsty*, he thought. *Or maybe she's hungry? Has she eaten anything tonight?* His palms pressed into the edge of the couch, he watched her until she stopped in the middle of the room, facing him.

He stood up.

"So," she said in a dry voice, "you're just going to sit there?"

The question confused him. He shrugged, pushing his hands into his pockets.

"What the hell is wrong with you? How can you do this to me?"

"Kimberly, I can't tell you how sorry I am. I know I scared you. But when I saw you . . . I couldn't bear . . ." This didn't seem right. He straightened his back. He was sorry, but that didn't mean it would never happen again. He was a Hunter. He pulled his hands out from his pockets, folded them behind his back, and said in a steady voice, "I wanted to hurt them. They got what they deserved."

"Then what are you sorry about?" Kimberly frowned. "I think they got what they deserved, too," she said, her voice full of anger. "And I would have done it myself if I could."

Ruben stared at her. He stepped closer. "Kimberly, you don't mean that," he said softly. "You're saying this because you're hurt."

"Oh, I mean it. After what they did..." Her voice broke, but she swallowed and spoke again. "After all I've witnessed in the last few days. . . . And now they've killed my mother. She was all I had, only one who cared about me." Her eyes flooded with tears. "Now I have no one. So, yes, I mean it," she said with trembling lips.

Ruben hugged her. "You have us, and you have me. You'll always have me."

"Then why have you avoided me all day?" Kimberly broke into a cry.

Ruben's heart sank. He'd done it wrong. He'd done it all wrong. He kissed her on top of her head. "I thought you hated me," he said, pressing her to his chest. "I thought you wanted me to stay away."

"You scared the hell out of me, yes, but I don't hate you. I could never hate you."

She held him tight enough that he could feel her fingers sink into his flesh. He took her in his arms and carried her into the bedroom.

IMMERSED in a leather armchair with his legs up on the low round table, Fray waited for Alec.

"How did it go?" he asked when the front door slammed.

"They're dead. Both of them," said Alec, walking into the dark room. He turned on a lamp. "It was Ruben who killed them."

"And the girl?" asked Fray, taking his legs off from the table.

Alec dropped down on it. "They killed her mother, but she's alive."

"Then we should try again."

"Leave her out of this. She's just a girl."

"She was with them in the castle. She has to know something. There's no one else we can get information from," said Fray. He added sarcastically, "Or maybe you want me to ask Riley?"

"You just lost two of your oldest vampires. Ruben will kill anyone who gets close to her."

"I don't care who he kills." Fray stood up. "I've been waiting for this for too long, and I can't just sit here and wait for Samson to destroy us." He went toward the basement. "I want you to keep a close eye on Eleanor," he said over his shoulder.

Fray opened the basement door and went down the stairs. Mark bent over the pool table, feeding from the young girl laying upon it.

"Enough, you'll kill her," said Fray.

"She's fine," said Mark, raising his head. He bit his wrist and pressed the bleeding wound to the girl's half open mouth. As she swallowed the blood, he broke her neck.

"There's only three of them," said Fray, looking at the other two limp bodies on the couch. "We lost eleven vampires today."

"We couldn't get more. The Hunters showed up. All of them," said Mark, wiping the blood from the corners of his thin lips. "We had to get away."

"All of them? Ruben, too?"

"Yeah, he was the first to arrive."

He ran back to his girl. Clever boy, thought Fray.

"I fled the moment I saw him. I was the one to torture him, remember? And I was the one who grabbed Hanna after that party. If they catch me, they wouldn't just stake me, they'd tear me to pieces."

Fray's vampires were devoted to him, but the oldest and strongest, knowing they were one step away from getting their enormous gift, were becoming too cautious. He couldn't blame them. What chance did they have against the Hunters?

Alec was the only one who couldn't be killed. But even though he had been raised by Fray and trained with him, he wasn't ready for this fight. He lacked the anger, the rage. Alec cared too much. He wasn't a bloodthirsty vampire who would tear apart anyone to get what he wanted. His love for Eleanor weakened him, held him back.

But then, he'd killed the witch, and Fray hoped if Alec's feelings were strong enough, his desire to get rid of Craig would make him fight, eventually.

Fray returned to the living room, turned off the lamp, and sank into the armchair. He looked into the open window in front of him. His eyes fixed on the crescent moon shimmering in between the branches of a young maple, he thought about Joanne. He'd never had a woman like her and he never had such a companion. What they planned together always worked. She was strong, smart, and confident, and the fire in her attracted Fray to her in the first place. He needed her in this fight. But he knew that, of all the vampires he had turned, she would be the last one to wake up, because of her past and her age.

Chapter Twenty-One

AFTER MAKING sure her father had safely arrived at work, Eleanor hurried to Hanna's house to meet Kimberly before she and Ruben went to the hotel. David had to go to the police station and Kimberly wanted to stay with Luke so her five-year-old brother wouldn't have to go with David and listen people discuss his mother's death.

"She's upstairs," said Ruben.

The tension between her and Kimberly the last few days made Eleanor feel a little nervous. She was full of doubts about what Kimberly's reaction might be. She raised her hand to knock, when the bedroom door opened. Eleanor's heart fell as she looked at Kimberly—at her pale face, at the dark circles under her eyes.

The moment they looked at each other, Kimberly's eyes shone with unshed tears. Eleanor pulled her into a hug. "Kimberly, I am so sorry," she whispered. Kimberly's hands tightened around her. "How are you?"

"I don't know. I keep repeating in my head, 'Is it over yet? Can I wake up now?'" Kimberly pulled back. "But it's not me I'm worried about." She brushed away the single tear rolling down her cheek. "It's Luke. He's just a kid."

"I know," Eleanor said with a sigh. "The first few months will be the hardest. But after a while, he'll come around. I know I did. My father helped me. So will David. He'll take care of him."

"Eleanor," said Kimberly. "I want to . . ."

Eleanor supposed it was her surprised look that made Kimberly pause. "You called me Eleanor."

"Yes, you are Eleanor now, and I was wrong expecting you to behave like Amanda." She took Eleanor's hand and pulled her toward the bed. They both sat down. "You lost Gabriella and Melinda, you had to die yourself, and I'm sorry for underestimating your pain. I was scared. Everything changed so fast."

"You don't have to explain," said Eleanor, stroking her hand. "In the last week you have witnessed so much violence. Of course you were scared. But I want you to understand that Ruben is not an ordinary man. We're not ordinary people. Our emotions are much higher, and sometimes it's difficult to control them, especially when we see those monsters hurting someone we care about."

"I know. When those vampires were hurting my mom, I wished I could . . ." Kimberly looked down. "I wished I could kill them myself. What I'm saying is, who knows what I would've done if I had those powers?"

"Since you don't have them, you'll have to stay here, with us, so we can protect you," said Eleanor.

"First I have to talk to David. They won't be able to go home for a while, and I have to make sure Luke is okay where he is. What if he needs me?" She stood up. "We better go downstairs. Riley wanted to have a word with me before I left."

Riley was sitting on the couch with a newspaper in his hands.

"Where's Hanna?" asked Eleanor.

"We sent Ned to Williamsburg to check the mansion. Hanna drove him to the station. Then she went to meet Debra," said Riley, folding the newspaper, "to—in her exact words—'interrogate that bitch.'"

Eleanor pulled the newspaper out of Riley's hand and sat next to him. "How bad is it?"

"Three are dead, and three are missing. Police say that eleven criminals were involved in the attacks and all of them are neutralized. Not a word about who or how. They're looking for the three missing people."

"Oh, I'm sure they'll show up soon," grouched Ruben. "With fangs and red eyes."

"Riley, you wanted to talk to me," said Kimberly.

Riley leaned forward. "Yes. I need to ask you something. Ruben said that yesterday, when he came to—"

"Kimberly," Ruben said, taking over, "before I jumped into your room, I heard the vampires questioning you. What was it about, what did they ask you?"

"We're sorry to bother you with this," said Riley. "But if it was something about us, then we need to know what they wanted."

"I didn't tell them anything," said Kimberly, looking a little startled.

"I know you didn't." Ruben put his hand on her shoulder. "We just want to know what they wanted from you."

Kimberly turned to Riley. "They were asking about Samson, where he is and what he's up to. I told them I don't know anything, I said they're wasting their time, that even Eleanor doesn't know. But they didn't believe me. They thought if I was with you in the castle, I must know things." She looked from one to another, then said again, "I didn't tell them anything. Not about Norway, not about Egypt."

"Kimberly, we know you didn't," said Eleanor softly.

"And we appreciate that," said Riley.

After Kimberly and Ruben left, Eleanor turned to Riley. "You can trust her. I know her, and I know she would never—"

"I believe her," said Riley calmly. "If she had said anything, she would be dead now. Fray created this whole distraction because he needed information. She didn't know much, but anything would be good for those vampires, as long as they didn't have to go back empty handed. That's why they kept her alive. They hoped she'd crack eventually."

Eleanor shook her head. "Riley, we can't let him do this. People are dying."

Riley frowned at her, his mood changing in a second. "What do you want me to do?" He jumped to his feet. "Do you have any idea how stupid I feel, sitting here doing nothing?"

"I do, because I feel the same way," said Eleanor.

"Do you know what it costs me to keep calm?" He sounded angrier with each word. "I want to go find him and beat the crap out of him," he shouted. "But I can't, because if I do that, innocent people will pay the price. I'm tired of being careful. I want to rip him apart. I can't bear the thought that he killed Gabriella and is still alive."

"I know," whispered Eleanor. Riley never spoke about his feelings, but it had to be unbearable for him to keep his pain quiet. And she didn't want him to. She provoked him, wanting him to let it out. "I know how you feel. I know what she meant to you."

"I don't think you do," he said bitterly, turning away from her.

"Actually, I do. She told me."

Riley froze for a moment. When he turned around, his eyes were full of tears. "She told you?" he asked, his lips barely moving.

"Yes," Eleanor said softly. "Riley, you can talk to me about it."

Riley walked to the sofa across from her and sat down. "What did she say? How did she. . . ?" His face sank in anguish. "I opened up to her only a few months before she died, and I was afraid that she. . . . Was she angry with me? Did I disappoint her?"

"Riley, no." Eleanor hurried to reassure him. "She was worried about you. She knew how hard it must be to have feelings for someone who couldn't reciprocate. Gabriella wanted you to be happy and hoped you wouldn't dwell on it. She wanted you to move on with your life."

Riley's face brightened a little. "All these years I've been tortured by the thought that my confession offended her," he said quietly, his eyes fixed on the floor. "That she could consider it as disrespect towards Samson."

"Stop it. You knew her better than that. She was impressed by your decency. So was I. To live under the same roof with the woman you love and keep it in secret for centuries?"

"Yeah," said Riley, taking a deep breath. "I respected them both too much to do anything silly."

"Have you ever spoken about this to someone? Craig or Ruben?"

"No. But they knew. I always felt their compassion. It helped me. I mean, knowing they didn't judge me."

"There was nothing to judge. Love doesn't care what's wrong and what's right. We can't control it. Look at Kimberly. After everything she's been through since she met Ruben, she still loves him."

"We can't let anything happen to her," said Riley. "The pain that I, Samson, and Craig have been through—I don't want Ruben to go through that. He deserves to be happy." Riley narrowed his eyes. "Do you think she'll—"

Eleanor didn't let Riley finish his question. "Oh no, don't ask me that." She waved both her hands, stopping him. "First we have to win this war, then we'll see what happens."

"Right," said Riley.

He looked a little spaced out, and Eleanor gave him a minute before she said, "Samson wanted me to look at his records. Where are they?"

"Not here. They're in the castle."

"Then," said Eleanor, getting up, "while my father is at work, I'll go get them."

"It's not safe for you to go alone. I'll come with you."

"You can't. The witch is arriving today. She can show up any moment. Besides, you don't have to worry about me. I'm not Amanda anymore; I can take care of myself."

Riley stood up. "Eleanor, we can't risk it."

"Riley, I'll be fine."

~

ELEANOR WAS glad to get away from Green Hill for a couple of hours. Too much had happened in the last few days and, sometimes, when Amanda popped up and Eleanor looked at everything from her point of view, it made her uneasy. In those moments she always thought of Kimberly.

Before leaving town, she stopped at a flower shop and bought violets for Gabriella and daisies for Melinda. Then she called Hanna.

"I'm on my way to the castle," she said. "Do you need anything?"

"Why? What's in the castle?" asked Hanna.

"I need to pick up Samson's journals."

"Yeah, I want you to bring me my ring and the bracelet. They're in my bedroom. In that small jewelry casket you bought me in New Orleans."

"Okay. Anything else?"

"No, that's it. Say hi to Amelia."

"I will."

Eleanor thought about the conversation with Riley while she drove. She was glad she made him open up, speak out his doubts. Looking at his brightening face, she could see a huge weight falling from his shoulders. Eleanor didn't want him to be alone for the rest of eternity. She hoped that maybe, after they put down Fray, he'd be able to move on.

Eleanor turned onto the dirt road and drove into the familiar woods. When she had woken up in the castle a week ago, she'd been too shocked to fully appreciate what had happened. Now, when the castle emerged in front of her, Eleanor's heart throbbed from the realization of what a miracle it was to come back to life, to come back to Craig, to come back home.

She ran her hand over one of the big pentacles on the large wooden front doors, then stepped inside and headed for the kitchen. "Amelia," she called.

Amelia, a thin woman with gray shoulder-length hair, showed up in the doorway. She wore a dark purple dress with a black belt around her thin waist.

"Eleanor." Amelia rushed toward her with a warm smile. "It's so nice to see you. How are you? Is everything all right? How's everybody? How's my Hanna?"

Eleanor suppressed a laugh. The way Amelia fired off her questions reminded her of Melinda. "She's fine. She says hi."

"Oh, I miss you all so much. I can't wait until you finally come home. Let's have some tea. I have a nice pie."

Eleanor followed Amelia into the kitchen. It looked different. The old ovens were gone and it was now filled with modern equipment. The furniture was new, but it still had the old-fashioned style—milky-colored wood with light brown scuffs, no plastic or marble, which made it look warm and cozy.

"It must be difficult for you?" asked Eleanor. "To be here alone?"

"It was in the beginning," said Amelia, putting cups on the table. "But not anymore."

Eleanor looked at the white cups with violets and golden stripes around the wavy rims and shrieked with joy. "I remember these! Gabriella bought them in Paris. I can't believe they're still in one piece."

"I use them only on special occasions." Amelia beamed.

"How long have you lived here?" asked Eleanor.

"It's eighteen years now. Before me, it was Melinda. Right after you were born, Melinda moved to Green Hill. Samson sent her there to keep an eye on you. That's when he invited me to manage the household."

"You knew Melinda?"

Amelia poured the tea and put a slice of blueberry pie in front of Eleanor.

"We were close," she said. "We were in the same coven. She was only twenty-six when she came to live here. Melinda was too young for this job, and I know she agreed to it mostly because she had a huge crush on Samson."

"Really?" asked Eleanor, putting down the cup she had just lifted.

"Oh yes," sighed Amelia. "She knew his story and never expected anything to happen. She just wanted to be close, do anything she could to help." She sat across from Eleanor and pulled her cup closer. "It's not easy to cut yourself from the outside world at that age. You Hunters can come and go whenever you want, but we can't. We can go out anytime, but to come back, we need Samson to let us in. She couldn't leave the castle when he wasn't home and didn't want to when he was here. So she never went too far." Amelia sipped her tea. "But she didn't live here for long. Only six years. When you were born, Samson rented her an apartment in Green Hill. And after, when she moved to your house, you were all she talked about. She loved you with her whole heart."

Eleanor's throat tightened. She looked down. "I know. I loved her, too." She took a sip from her cup and changed the subject. "There's so much to do here. It's impossible to keep this place in order alone. How did you do that?"

"Oh, my dear, I didn't do it alone. They all helped me when they were around. And when they weren't, Samson hired one or two men to do the lawn and bushes, cut the trees, fix things. He also hired a couple of women every time I asked him to. They helped me to clean the rooms, the tapestries, to polish the silverware and all of the furniture. After the workers left, all they knew was that they did some work and got paid well for it, and I helped them forget the rest."

After tea, the two of them went to the garden and Eleanor put the flowers on the graves. The violets in front of the white marble and the daisies on the head of the fresh mound.

"I already ordered the stone," said Amelia. "It'll be ready soon."

"Thank you," said Eleanor quietly.

Back in the castle, she went to Samson's study. As she looked at the glass doors of the weapons cabinet and then at the floor, the image of Gabriella's dead body flashed in front of her eyes, and her heart squeezed. She stepped to the desk and looked at Gabriella's picture in the small wooden frame. Eleanor closed her eyes, remembering her last day in this room. Samson's words, *It would kill you* echoed in her mind. *But I'm back, as he promised*, she thought.

Eleanor opened the second drawer on the left side of the desk, as Riley had told her, and pulled out two journals with worn leather covers. She looked around one more time and went to Hanna's bedroom.

When she entered her and Craig's room, she put the journals and Hanna's bracelet and ring on the bed. She had her bracelet on her arm, and Craig told her where he kept the ring.

When she went to the dresser to get it, she heard footsteps. The footsteps were too heavy and measured to be Amelia's. Eleanor turned around and saw Alec standing in the doorway.

"Hi," he said, grinning.

Eleanor's chest heaved with rage. "What the hell are you doing here?" she hissed at him.

"I came to look at my new home," he said in a calm voice, ignoring her reaction.

"This will never be your home. But, of course, everybody is allowed to dream."

"Oh, I did. I've dreamed of seeing this castle since I was ten. Fray brought me here once, to show me the way. All I saw then were trees. But I kept coming, looking at trees, hoping one day I'd be able to cross that veil. And here I am." He leaned on the door frame. "Would you like to show me around?"

"You want a tour? Perfect. Let's start with the garden. There are two graves there. We have you to thank for one of them, and for the other—your precious Fray." She clenched her teeth. "Get out of here."

"I'm a Hunter now, and this castle is mine as much as it's yours."

"You're not a Hunter, you're a killer. And just in case you didn't notice, you are fighting on the wrong side. There's no place for you in this castle." The fury was choking Eleanor, but she remembered Riley's warning and tried to cool down.

"Eleanor, this is temporary." Alec's voice became soft and serious. "When this is all over . . ." He took a step forward. "Everything . . ."

"Take one more step into this room," said Eleanor in a low, menacing voice.

Alec stopped. Standing with his legs shoulder-width apart, he put his hands in his pockets and straightened his back. "Sorry, I forgot my manners. This is your and Craig's bedroom." He frowned. "You think that means anything to me? Only a week ago you kissed me and you liked it."

"Don't fool yourself." Eleanor sniffed. "I didn't know who I was. You know why I did it."

"It doesn't matter *why*. It happened. You didn't hate me. We were close." He flashed forward, and before Eleanor could react, he locked his hands behind her back, pinning her arms to her sides. "I love you," he whispered, his burning gray eyes looking deep into hers.

In two seconds Eleanor thought of half a dozen ways to free herself, but instead of using them, she stared back at him and whispered, "Alec, let go of me."

Alec raised his eyes to the wall in front of him, where a portrait of Eleanor and Craig hung. His grip loosened. Eleanor pushed him aside and stepped away.

"It means nothing," he said mostly to himself, his eyes still on the portrait. He stepped to Eleanor and said, "I'll see you soon." Then he kissed her on the forehead and was gone.

"What just happened?" muttered Eleanor. They all knew that Fray could show up at the castle at any time. But Alec's appearance stunned her. She never thought about the things he just mentioned. He'd called the castle his home. Now she realized that the moment those transitioning vampires woke up, they'd be free to come here.

She heard Amelia's voice. "Eleanor. Eleanor, where are you?"

"I'm here." She ran downstairs.

"Eleanor, who was that young man? How did he get here?" Amelia asked, astonished.

"He's new. Fray turned him. Amelia, he's the one who killed Melinda. I'm afraid you're not safe here anymore."

"That was him?" Amelia's eyebrows jumped up. "So he has the same powers you have?"

"Yes."

"My dear, you don't have to worry about me. Samson's powers are the only ones I can't fight. Magic doesn't work on him. But I'll be able to protect myself from one Hunter."

"You don't understand. The thing is, after those transitioning vampires wake up, they'll be able to cross the veil."

"I hadn't thought of that," said Amelia, pondering. "But it's good you told me. Even with your powers, vampires are vampires. They would be able to cross the veil, but not the castle's threshold, at least not without Fray. Fray, of course, can invite them in. What I need to do is to put protective enchantments around the castle. It'll warn me if someone shows up, and that's good, because this man startled me. I wasn't expecting to see new faces here. It will also buy me some time to see if I can do anything against Fray, maybe somehow block his invitations."

"I still think it would be better for you to leave the castle," Eleanor said.

"My dear, I'm here to take care of it and that's exactly what I'm going to do. This castle is my home. I'm not leaving it." She smiled kindly, took Eleanor's hand, and patted it with hers. "Don't worry about me. I'll be fine."

∼

ALEC WENT TO HIS CAR, parked just before the veil. He got in but took a long moment before he started the engine. He was overloaded with emotions, and he needed to sort them out.

The castle was much more than he imagined. Only now did he understand the longing in Fray's eyes every time he talked about it. The moment Alec crossed the veil, something went through him, and he felt his powers. When he passed the large wooden doors of the castle, he felt a connection to the place. Despite the fact that the people who lived there hated him, and he was, indeed, fighting on the wrong side, he felt like he belonged there. It was like coming home. Seeing and entering the castle made him a part of something big, something old, something powerful. It made him part of the legend.

The other overwhelming sensation came from entering Eleanor's bedroom. He was proud of himself for the way he handled it. He kept his emotions under control, even though his heart was screaming from satisfaction. The glory of it wasn't the surprised expression on Eleanor's face, but letting her know he could come there whenever he wanted. Alec felt so close to her now. The castle was the place where she had lived her previous life, and being able to go there would help him understand her, to know her better, to learn her history. But it hadn't taken long before his first, painful lesson.

It was probably Craig's absence that made Alec constantly forget about his existence. Seeing the portrait didn't just remind him that Craig was real. Looking at that beautiful piece of art, Craig and Eleanor standing together in old-fashioned clothes, stunned him with its truth. The history of their life and love poured out of it, opening Alec's eyes, showing him what he was battling against.

It doesn't mean I can't win, he told himself. *I'll find a way.*

"Did you bring it?" Fray asked the moment Alec opened the front door.

"What?" asked Alec, walking into the living room.

Fray turned from where he stood in front of the window. "What did I send you there for? Craig's blood. Did you bring it?"

"Oh, that," said Alec, whose head was still busy with thoughts of Eleanor. "No. I looked everywhere you told me to, but the vials weren't there: not his, not anybody's."

"Of course they weren't," grumbled Fray under his breath. "He isn't an idiot; he knew I could use their blood for a locator spell." He looked at Alec from under his brows. "But we had to check." He turned to the window again.

Alec knew Fray was angry, mostly with himself. He knew that, no matter what Fray tried, he wouldn't be able to find Samson. After the fight at Eleanor's old house, they all fled: the vampires ran for their lives, and Fray tried to get the Book as far away as possible. But to Fray's surprise, nobody followed them. Only now did Fray realize that Samson wanted them to leave so nobody would track him and Craig.

"Why did she go there?" asked Fray.

"For some old journals," said Alec grimly. "There was also one of those Hunter bracelets. She wears hers; this one was probably for someone else. Where's yours?"

"Why? There's no use for them now. We have phones."

"I want one. As a symbol that I'm one of you now," said Alec, pacing up and down the room with his hands on his hips.

"Have you ever seen me wearing it?" Fray raised one eyebrow. "That would make you one of them, not one of us."

"You're still wearing the ring."

"It's different. I've worn it for almost a thousand years, and I believe it's much older than that. It's different than others, special, like me, and that's what it symbolizes."

"I want one," insisted Alec.

Fray narrowed his eyes. "What happened there? You seem a little off. Besides, you didn't say anything about the castle. Did you like it?"

"It's because you started with the wrong question. It was my first time there, and all you care about is the information."

"So, did you feel it?"

"I felt everything." Alec stopped and threw a glance at Fray. "How could you give it up?"

"I didn't give it up," Fray shouted suddenly. "I left because I hated them all. But it's my home, and I'll get it back."

"Good," said Alec, not paying attention to Fray's change of mood. "So what about the bracelet?"

Fray glared at him. "Samson is the only one who has them."

"Hmm." Alec frowned. "Then you can give me yours."

"This is about her, isn't it? Do you realize what we are up to? We're going to kill all of them, including the man she loves, and you expect her to forgive you for that? She's a Hunter, for God's sake. She'll try to kill you at any cost."

"That's where you're wrong. She liked me. I almost had her. I just needed a few more weeks."

"Alec, she isn't the only woman on this planet," said Fray, taking a step toward him. "You can have any girl you want."

"Those girls, with their boring, mundane lives, never attracted me. She's from the old Hunter's family, she died and came back. She's a mystery, she's unique. There's no one like her, and never will be. You know that," said Alec, gazing at Fray. "I loved her when she was Amanda, and now she's become Eleanor, the woman who was my unattainable dream from the day you told me about her. I'm not giving up. I'm aware of the obstacles, but all I need is time."

Chapter Twenty-Two

WHEN ELEANOR RETURNED, it was almost dark. She walked into the living room and saw a young woman with light-chocolate skin and straight black hair sitting on the couch next to Riley.

Eleanor glanced at him, frankly surprised. *I suppose our conversation was fruitful,* she thought. "Hello," she said, smiling.

Guessing her thoughts, Riley rolled his eyes. "Eleanor, this is Kizzy. The witch," he said, emphasizing the last word.

"Oh, sorry, I'm a little . . . I forgot."

"So you're *her*?" said Kizzy with a crooked smile. "The legendary Eleanor? Such an honor."

"All Hunters are part of the legend," said Eleanor, a little uncomfortable.

"But you're the only one who died and came back to life," said Kizzy, leaning back on the cushions.

"Yeah, whatever," said Eleanor.

"Did you bring my bracelet?" asked Hanna, coming in from the kitchen.

Eleanor opened her handbag, pulled out Hanna's bracelet and the ring, and handed them over.

Hanna put them on. "I missed these," she said nostalgically, pressing the ring to her coin, then to Eleanor's. The green light shone first from coin number seven, then eighth on Eleanor's and Riley's bracelets.

"We have a problem," said Eleanor, dropping on the sofa across from Riley and Kizzy,

"What is it?" asked Riley, looking wary.

"Alec was at the castle."

"You're joking," said Hanna, coming forward.

"You know what that means, right? I couldn't convince Amelia to leave," said Eleanor. She paused. "I don't understand. Alec knew I was there. How?"

"He's probably been following you all this time," said Riley.

"I wasn't followed. So how did he know where I was?"

"Maybe they did a locator spell," suggested Kizzy.

"No. I see it now," said Hanna, musing. "It wasn't a spell; it was Debra."

"Huh?" Eleanor stared at her.

"After you called me, she acted kinda anxious. She fidgeted with her phone. Then she said she had to go. Yeah." Hanna squinted. "Apparently, she was trying to send a message, but she changed her mind because I was still there."

"That's it," said Eleanor. "She's crazy about Alec, she'll do anything for him. She probably organized that graduation party because he told her to."

"After all my warnings," groaned Hanna. "Mark my words—she'll end up like Nicole."

The front door opened, and Ruben and Kimberly walked in.

"Hi," said Ruben, his surprised look stopping on Kizzy.

"Hi," said Kizzy with a broad smile.

"This is Kizzy, the witch. And this is Ruben and Kimberly," said Riley, introducing them to each other.

"It's nice to meet you," said Kizzy, her eyes fixed at Ruben's.

"Well, it's nice to meet you, too," said Ruben drily, looking away.

"I never heard about a Hunter with the name Kimberly," said Kizzy, leaning forward and running her eyes from Kimberly's head to her toes.

"She's not a Hunter," said Ruben. "She's my girlfriend."

"Oh." Kizzy bit her lower lip and leaned back again. She threw one leg over the other, and her short skirt jumped even higher.

"How's Luke?" asked Eleanor.

"He's okay," said Kimberly, sitting next to her. "Ruben and I tried to distract him. We went out for ice cream, took him to a park."

"I think now is a good time to put a protection spell around your house, while David and Luke are staying at the hotel." Eleanor turned to Kizzy. "Are you up for this?"

"Umm, sure." Kizzy shrugged. "If she's in danger."

Something in Kizzy's behavior displeased Eleanor. It was obvious she was really excited to meet the Hunters, but there was also something else. She wouldn't take her eyes off Ruben.

"No," said Ruben. "There's no point."

"What do you mean 'no point'?" asked Hanna.

"David hired people to clean up the house, then he and Luke are leaving," said Kimberly. "They're going to stay with David's mother. David says it'll be better for Luke." Kimberly sighed. "I agree. I don't want Luke to go back to that house right now. A protection spell is not going to stop Fray or Alec."

"What about the funeral?" asked Eleanor.

"They'll come back for that. The police said they want to keep the body for a few days. They're still working on the case and want to examine all three bodies to—" Kimberly swallowed. "So there's nothing we can do right now. David said he'll keep me informed."

"Did he even offer for you to go with them?" asked Hanna indignantly.

Kimberly shook her head. "He said I should go to my mom's cousin's for a while." She shrugged. "I don't even know what she looks like."

"And you don't need to find out," said Ruben. "I'm not letting you out of my sight."

Eleanor read a slight disappointment on Kizzy's face.

"Kimberly." Eleanor took her hand. "I know that in times like these, you might want to be with people who—"

But Kimberly interrupted her. "I don't have such people. There's only Luke, and he's just a kid."

"Right now there is no safer place for you than here, with us," said Eleanor, giving Kimberly a one-armed hug.

After a short moment of silence, Riley stood up. "Eleanor, you and Kizzy should go to your place. It's better to do the spell before your father gets back from work."

"Right, let's do this," said Eleanor, getting up. "Then maybe I'll be able to sleep tonight."

"I just need to pick up some stuff from my suitcase. It's upstairs," said Kizzy. She walked around the sofa, and passing Ruben, run her hand down his back. Ruben didn't look at her, but his jaw tightened in frustration.

Eleanor didn't know if anybody else was paying attention, or if she was the only one who noticed this little game Kizzy had been playing from the moment Ruben entered the room.

"Can I have a word with you?" she said to Ruben and beckoned toward the backyard.

"Ruben, what's going on? Do you know her?" asked Eleanor as he stopped in front of her, looking sour.

"Yeah." Ruben cursed soundlessly.

"Brilliant. That's exactly what we were missing right now."

"Don't look at me like that," said Ruben.

"Like what?"

"Judging. I have a past, and this is a blast from it."

"I'm not judging. I'm just saying that we've already drowned Kimberly in problems and she doesn't need any more stress."

"It's not my fault she's here." Ruben started pacing. "I didn't invite her."

"How do you know her?"

"About a year ago, when we were looking for Fray, Samson sent me to this coven in Chicago. She was the one who helped us."

"How long were you together? Was it serious?"

"No. It was nothing like that. I was only there for a week, then I left, and that's it." Ruben stopped pacing and glanced toward the living room, at Kimberly talking to Hanna. "Do you think I should tell her? Kizzy is unpredictable, and they're going to live under the same roof for a while."

"I don't think that's a good idea. Kimberly is barely keeping it together." Eleanor sighed. "If there's no big drama between you and Kizzy, then I think it'll be fine. She's here temporarily. Just keep your distance."

∽

AFTER HAVING dinner with her father and shrugging and nodding to his bewildered questions and exclamations about Melinda—"How come she hasn't called yet? There's been enough time to buy a phone. How far did she go? I'm worried about her!"--Eleanor went to her room.

She opened the window and looked at the few stars in the dark sky. Her longing for Craig was becoming stronger with each day. When he called earlier that night, she tried to assure him that she was fine, but the yearning in her voice gave her away, and it made it much more difficult for Craig to hang up. She didn't tell him about Alec's visit to the castle, thinking he was too far away to do anything about it, and it would only make him more anxious.

Samson's journals were on the nightstand. Eleanor sat comfortably on her bed and opened one of them, looking at the yellowed pages with the familiar handwriting.

Right from the beginning Samson mentioned that trying to find the Book or the daggers would be like looking for a needle in a haystack. They were small and portable, and wherever Fray kept them, they would be well-guarded. Powerless Hunters wouldn't be able to do much against vampires.

However, it would be much more difficult to hide fifty bodies. All the Hunters needed was to find the place they were hidden. But after a while, Samson realized that wasn't an easy task, either.

So the journals mostly contained short descriptions of their attempts to find locations where Fray could have hidden the transitioning bodies. They followed him all over the world, and most times it ended dramatically.

Ned was captured by vampires while tailing them to South America. After torturing him, they threw him off a cliff.

They lost Fray for a long while, and the next time they found him, he was in India. The fact that he arrived there on a rented ship and stayed about a decade seemed suspicious. This time it was Ruben who followed him. One day he watched Fray and his vampires go down one of the abandoned giant subterranean stepwells. It was about five stories deep and had plenty of rooms—perfect place to hide fifty bodies. Ruben walked away and came back the next day, but after searching the first two stories, he was captured and trapped in one of the rooms. With the help of a witch, Samson and Riley found him a month later.

"It took Ruben a long time to grow back the flesh on his bones," read Eleanor, and a shiver ran through her body.

"The thought that the bodies might be somewhere around never left me, so I decided to use Fray's absence to search familiar areas, starting with the place where the vampires were turned. The barn wasn't there anymore, but even decades later it wasn't hard to find the spot. From there, I planned to check the entire path to the castle.

"One day, when I was coming back from one of my trips, I was grabbed by his vampires. It was late evening and I was about three hours away from the castle. I was crossing a small field, and there was nothing special about that place. But something made me stop and look around. I dismounted from my horse and was walking

towards the woods surrounding the field, when suddenly I saw the vampires coming out from behind the trees..."

When Samson returned to the castle after being tortured for weeks, he wrote,

"All this time I've been asking myself, what made me stop at that field, and why would the vampires be there? It didn't look like they were there by accident.

"I had the same feeling when I returned to the same place a few months later, but I never found anything. It was just a field surrounded by woods."

"Hmm." Eleanor stared at the page for a few seconds, then put away the first journal and opened the second one.

"I was now sure that the bodies were somewhere close and Fray, by going to mysterious places in different countries, was only trying to get us as far away from them as possible.

"But when the witches located him in a ghost town in Connecticut, decades later, Craig—believing that Fray's plan was to scare us off—chased him. Fray had a witch with him who detected Craig the moment he arrived in town. Luckily, Riley was in Virginia at that time. He found Craig three days later, tied to a tree with a stake in his stomach."

"Did you have to be that stubborn?" muttered Eleanor angrily.

The more Eleanor read, the more she realized what a difficult task it was. There were only the six of them, and they didn't have their Hunters' powers or senses. Most of the time the Hunters were busy watching her descendants. Samson also had another important research to do in Egypt. It took him many years to find what he was looking for.

Eleanor closed the journal. Everything she'd just read made her miserable. The pain that each and every one of them had gone through was so much worse than she had imagined.

The day had been long and emotional. Eleanor was tired. She hadn't slept much the night before while guarding her father, but now she had a protective spell around the house. As Kizzy explained, if someone with supernatural powers tried to cross the barrier, something like an electrical wave would go through her body. Eleanor put her head on the pillow and closed her eyes, hoping to sleep until morning without being electrocuted.

Once again clutching the stake in her hand, Eleanor was chasing a vampire in the dark woods. It was the same woman in the black gown. Following her, Eleanor came out to the familiar field with a house at the other end. Halfway across the field, Eleanor caught up with the woman and grabbed her by the shoulder, only this time she didn't vanish. Eleanor turned her around and, as she looked at the vampire's face, she woke up.

The sun was up. Eleanor sat in the bed, took her phone from the nightstand, and checked the time. It was seven twenty-five. She opened Alec's photograph and looked at the drawing of the woman. It was her—the vampire from her dream. That was why her face looked so familiar. Even though Eleanor didn't remember when, she was sure she had seen her before.

The woman whose picture Fray had kept all those years was a vampire. With Fray's lifestyle, it was no surprise. The question was —did Eleanor kill her?

What if it was just a dream? No. Having the same dream over and over again meant something. So what was this dream trying to tell her? Maybe Hanna was right; it was some unfinished business. The woman escaped, she was still alive, and Eleanor had to find and kill her.

Or maybe it had something to do with that field. She thought about the one Samson described in his journal. Could they be the same? No. That field was empty, there was nothing there. Samson went back and never found anything. The field from Eleanor's dream had a whole house on its side.

"Hi, Dad," said Eleanor, walking into the kitchen.

Lindsey didn't reply. He sat at the table with a grim face, reading a newspaper. A few seconds later, he looked up at Eleanor.

"Kimberly's mother is dead?" he asked, putting down the coffee cup clutched in his hand.

Eleanor nodded, then looked away from his piercing gaze.

"And you didn't tell me?" he asked, slowly taking off his glasses. "Why?"

Her eyes now fixed at her feet, Eleanor shrugged. "I thought you knew." She didn't really know why. Probably because it had everything to do with her. Because she, as a Hunter, felt responsible for those deaths, and she was trying to avoid the tough conversation where she had to pretend all the killings were a shocking mystery to her. "It's a big case, all over the news."

"I didn't know it was Kimberly's mother. And those students —did you know them?"

Eleanor nodded again.

"Oh, honey, I'm so sorry." Lindsey got on his feet. "Are you okay?" he asked, putting his hand on her shoulder.

"I'm fine," she muttered. Eleanor wished she could accept his comfort, hug him and tell him everything. Tell him who she was, who the killers were, tell him the truth about Melinda. But the truth would make him think that she was losing her mind, while the comfort would weaken her, and she couldn't afford to be weak right now.

"How's Kimberly?"

"It's hard. We're trying to help. She can't stay at home, so she's staying at Hanna's. I'm going there now."

"Is there anything I can do for her?" said Lindsey, folding the newspaper. "Kimberly's mother was there for us when--"

"When Mom died. I remember, Dad. Don't worry, we're taking care of her." Eleanor looked at the clock on the wall. "You're going to be late," she said, raising one brow, the way Melinda usually said it.

Lindsey smiled weakly, recognizing the gesture. "Yeah, I have to go."

Chapter Twenty-Three

SITTING ALONE at the kitchen table, Hanna was having breakfast. .

"Where is everybody?" asked Eleanor. She noticed the stack of dirty plates sitting next to the sink.

"Riley and Kizzy are having coffee in the backyard," said Hanna, smearing blueberry jam on a piece of waffle. "Ruben and Kimberly are in the basement. I gave her my gun and Ruben is teaching her how to use it."

"Gun? What gun?"

"I have a gun with wooden spikes."

"Really?" Eleanor pointed her thumb in the direction of the basement. "Whose idea was that?"

"Hers. Do you want waffles? I kept some for you," said Hanna, chewing.

"I don't eat breakfast, you know that," said Eleanor.

"I made them, and I kept them warm." Hanna arched her lips, looking at Eleanor with puppy eyes.

"And you're eating alone, cause, let me guess, they all ate while you were making them?"

Hanna nodded. "Yep."

"I see their manners are gone. All right." Eleanor pulled up a chair next to Hanna's and dropped down. "I'll eat with you."

Hanna got up and grabbed a plate from the cupboard.

"Gabriella wouldn't like it," said Eleanor as Hanna returned to the table and put the plate of waffles in front of her.

"What do you mean?" asked Hanna.

"I mean the manners, the traditions. She liked it when . . ." Eleanor pressed her lips together. "I know the times have changed, but when she was around . . ."

"We were a real family?" Hanna sighed.

"Sorry." Eleanor glanced at her. "It's just . . ." Eleanor hesitated.

"I know," said Hanna in a small voice. "I miss her, too."

Eleanor took a deep breath. "It's good that Kimberly wants to learn," she said, changing the subject.

"Yeah. Ruben says she can't sleep at night, that when she falls asleep, it takes only a few minutes before she jumps up, horrified. He thinks training will help her fight her fear, though she doesn't want to admit that she's scared."

"How's Kizzy?" asked Eleanor. Hanna was very sensitive when it came to relationships, and Eleanor wondered if she'd already spotted Kizzy's interest in Ruben. "Is she comfortable here?"

"Too comfortable, I would say. Except I'm not sure she knows what to do with her hands, so she keeps putting them on Ruben. At those moments I just want to rip them off for her, and I would, if I was certain we wouldn't need them in the near future."

"So, you noticed, too?" asked Eleanor, picking up a maple leaf–shaped bottle of Canadian syrup.

"I know Ruben, and I can see what's going on. It happened before, when someone from his past showed up. But it's different now and he needs to stop it, before Kimberly finds out the truth the hard way."

"We all have a past and secrets," said Eleanor quietly. "We lie to the people we love because we don't want to hurt them."

Hanna turned to her. "Are you talking about your father?"

"Hanna, I don't know what to do. How long am I going to lie to him about Melinda? He keeps asking me all these questions, and every time I feel this unbearable guilt for hiding the truth from him."

"Eleanor, I know it's hard, but right now the less he knows, the better it is for him." Hanna poured orange juice into two glasses and put one of them in front of Eleanor. "Drink."

"I had that dream again." Eleanor glanced at her. "This time I got to see the vampire's face."

"And?" asked Hanna, sipping from her glass.

"It's that woman from the drawing."

Hanna's eyes narrowed. "Are you saying Fray had a crush on a vampire?" She shook her head. "Isn't that romantic." Then she chuckled. "People love those stories. You should write a novel about him. Don't lose your opportunity to become a bestselling author."

"Maybe it was just a dream. What if I saw that face because I was thinking about the drawing?"

"Could be," said Hanna.

"Hi," said Kizzy, walking into the kitchen. She wore a black T-shirt and jean shorts. "How was your night?" she asked Eleanor, opening the fridge and pulling out a bottle of water.

"I slept better," said Eleanor. To Eleanor the question sounded like Kizzy wanted credit for her work, and she added, "Thank you."

Kizzy nodded before putting the bottle to her lips.

They heard voices coming from the living room, and in the next moment, one after another, Kimberly, Ruben, and Riley showed up in the kitchen doorway.

"Hi," said Kimberly, coming in first.

"Hi. How did the training go?" asked Eleanor.

"She made two holes in my shirt," said Ruben.

"It's because you let me." Kimberly glanced back at him. "Next time, no cheating." There was a new energy in her voice.

"Next time Riley will be the vampire," said Ruben, punching Riley in the shoulder.

"No way." Riley stroked his chest. "I love all my shirts."

"Then, maybe, guys," said Kizzy playfully, "you should take them off?"

Ruben rolled his eyes. Eleanor was glad Kimberly didn't see it.

"My skin is just as precious to me," Riley said.

Kizzy grinned at him. She opened her mouth, but before she could say another word, Riley turned away from her and looked at Hanna and Eleanor. "So, everyone's here," he said, and his face grew serious. "Let's see what we have for today. Hanna, any news from Ned?"

"He called. But there isn't much to tell. He says the mansion is big and handsome and there's nothing special about the people who live there. They're definitely not vampires. He went to the historical society to check for records. Then, he wants to go back and see if he can sneak into the house."

"We're going to the hotel," said Ruben when Riley glanced at him. "Kimberly wants to see Luke before they leave."

"Make sure they leave safely," said Riley. "If there's anything, call me immediately."

"I will," said Ruben.

"That woman from the picture," said Eleanor as Riley turned to her. "If we could do a locator spell, if we could find her...."

"Do a loc... Eleanor, that picture is from 1834."

"She was a vampire."

"A vampire? How do you know that?"

"I've been seeing her in my dreams. Hunting her. She could still be alive. Or if she was that important to Fray, she might be transitioning right now, and if we find her, we might find all of them. Kizzy, would you be able to do the spell," Eleanor asked in an unsure voice, "if we printed out the photograph?" She raised the phone in her hand.

"You're joking, right?" Kizzy sneered at her. "You want me to do a locator spell using some printed piece of paper?"

"Eleanor, you know it doesn't work like that," said Ruben.

"I know," moaned Eleanor, dropping her hand back on the table. "I just thought that maybe, while I was dead, witches had come up with . . . I don't know . . ." she shrugged. "New technology."

"Is there any way to get the original picture?" asked Kizzy.

"Get it from where?" said Eleanor. "Even if it was in that mansion, the house is sold now."

Hanna got up and opened the dishwasher. "There is another way," she said, cleaning the dirty plates from the table.

"What way?" asked Eleanor, but then immediately shook her head. "No, it's not going to work."

"You can try," said Hanna.

"Try what?" asked Kizzy.

"Guys, I know that Alec has feelings for Eleanor," said Kimberly, "but he already made it clear he'd never do anything that goes against Fray. Even for her."

Simply hearing Alec's name put Eleanor's teeth on edge, but what choice did she have? Time was running out, and the picture of the woman was the only clue they had. She didn't know if this was the right way to go about it, but there was no other. "Hanna's right. We can't just sit and do nothing. We have to give it a shot."

"I don't think it's a good idea," said Ruben.

"How are you going to do this?" asked Kimberly. "You can't just call him, it would be too obvious."

"No," said Hanna. "But if Debra is spying for them, we can use her. I can pay her a visit and—"

"No," said Riley firmly. "It's a pointless risk."

"Riley, that picture might help us," said Eleanor. "Weren't you the one who said I have to use him?"

"I said *use wisely.*" With both hands, Riley leaned on the table and looked at Eleanor where she sat on the other side of it. "Just because Alec won't kill you doesn't make him our friend. Alec wants Fray to win. Kimberly's right; he's not going to help you defeat Fray. If this woman really is a clue to something important, simply mentioning her would be equal to giving away our only weapon."

Eleanor didn't agree with Riley. She was sure she could find a delicate way to get information from Alec without raising suspicion. But she decided not to argue. "So what now?"

"Yesterday, Ruben contacted Mike and asked him to track down Alec's car for us. Mike said he still lives in his house and he isn't alone there. He described a few men staying in the house. Ruben and I recognized two: Mark and Fray."

"Those bastards," grumbled Hanna, putting back the plate she had just picked up from the pile next to the sink. "They aren't even hiding."

"And that's a good thing," said Riley. "Now that I know where he's staying, I'm going to keep an eye on him."

"How are you going to do that?" asked Eleanor. "Just because they're not hiding doesn't mean they're not careful. They know you. And since you're not invisible and they're not blind..."

"I rented a van. Kizzy is new here. She agreed to be my driver."

"All right, then," said Ruben. "If that's it for now, I'll go change."

Eleanor waited until everyone left the kitchen, then stood up and stepped closer to Hanna. "I'm doing it," she said in a low, conspiratorial voice.

Hanna, who just resumed the cleaning, stopped again. "Doing what?"

"Meeting Alec." Eleanor took the plate from Hanna's hand and put it in the dishwasher. "And I need you to visit Debra."

"Eleanor, you heard Riley," said Hanna, sounding a little alarmed. "While Samson is away, he's in charge."

"He doesn't have to know. We'll tell him only if it works."

"If he finds out, he'll kill me."

"Hanna, what else is there? We have nothing else to go on."

Hanna dropped to the chair, and after a moment of consideration, she breathed out, "Okay. What do I say to her?"

"I don't know. Something to hook her."

Hanna absently stared at the syrup bottle for a moment, then said, "I'll say we were worried about her. I'll ask about Mark, then mention you wanted to come, too, but something came up. You had to meet a friend . . . where?" she looked up at Eleanor. "Where do you want to meet him?"

"Meet a friend," repeated Eleanor, thinking. "At the cemetery."

"All right, but not now. If Riley sees us leaving, he'll ask questions, and I can't lie to him, he sees through me. Let's wait until he leaves."

Chapter Twenty-Four

NICOLE WAS BURIED the day after Kimberly's mother was killed, so none of the three girls attended the funeral. Hanna contacted Nicole's parents to find out the name of the cemetery she was buried at, and now, walking between the rows of tombstones, Eleanor looked for Nicole's grave. It didn't take long to find the fresh mound under the low branches of a young willow tree, with a temporary wooden sign containing her name and the dates of her birth and death.

Putting flowers on another grave made Eleanor feel useless. Her job was to protect people, but all she'd done since returning was mourn them. First Melinda, then Nicole, then Kimberly's mother, and there were also three of her schoolmates killed at the party. Those deaths were the consequences of their inaction, but no matter how badly the Hunters wanted to tear Fray apart, Riley was right; they couldn't go against him empty-handed. Beating him up might make them feel better for a little while, but it wouldn't solve any of their problems. It would only bring more deaths and could scare Fray into hiding. At least this way they had one less thing to look for.

Eleanor glanced around. There were no people, except one

woman heading to the gate. A few graves away, under a maple tree, was a bench. Eleanor walked to it and sat down. She didn't know how long she'd have to wait. She wasn't even sure the plan would work, but she was certain that Debra spying on her was Fray's decision, not Alec's. 'Meeting with a friend at the cemetery' sounded mysterious enough to get their attention.

And if Alec showed up, what would she say to him? Alec wouldn't just hand over the picture. She needed to start a conversation and then wriggle it to the point. But even then, she'd need to push the right buttons to crack him, to make him at least consider her request.

Eleanor snorted. That would require a lot of patience. Could she do all of this without punching him in the face?

She heard someone approaching from behind and turned. It was Hanna, and she didn't look happy.

"It didn't work," she said grimly, sitting next to Eleanor.

"What? Debra didn't take the bait?"

"No." Hanna shook her head. "It was the wrong bait," she said quietly. "If I had brought her a blood bag . . ."

"What?" Eleanor jumped to her feet. "No."

Hanna looked up at her. "Her mother said she was in her room, that she didn't feel well. When I got upstairs, I wondered why Debra would close the curtains in the middle of the day, but then I looked at her, at her eyes. She was in pain, transitioning. The moment I walked in, she looked at me with horror and started crying. Then she asked if I'd come to kill her."

"She knows who we are," murmured Eleanor. "What did you do?" She stared at Hanna. "Hanna, did you—"

"How could I?" Hanna stood up, too. "First of all, her mother was home, and second—Eleanor, it's Debra."

Eleanor walked back and forth. Then she stopped and gazed at Hanna. "They turned her and left her at home. Hanna, she'll need to feed soon. She won't be able to control herself and she'll kill anyone near her. That means she might kill her own mother."

"You think I don't know that? There was nothing I could do. I couldn't get her out of there, it's still daylight. Besides, where would I take her?"

"You're right. It's not our job to take care of her." Eleanor pulled the phone out of her pocket and found Alec's name. She tapped it, and he answered almost immediately. "I need to see you," she said, barely holding her anger. "Now."

"Where?" asked Alec.

Eleanor was too angry to sit still and wait for Alec to get to the cemetery from the other end of town. Instead, she preferred to drive toward him. "In the grove, behind the school."

"I'll come with you," said Hanna the moment Eleanor hung up.

"No, there's no need for that. You better get home before Riley is back."

"I can't let you go there alone. And I don't think you should go either. I don't trust him."

"Don't worry, I'll be fine," said Eleanor, rushing to her car. "Go home."

"Not gonna happen," said Hanna, following her. "I'll come a few minutes later so he won't see me. I'll watch you from a distance."

It was getting dark, and the school's parking lot was almost empty. Alec's car was already there. Eleanor got out of her car and looked around. There was nothing suspicious, except a gray Honda with tinted windows standing by the side of the lot. Eleanor went behind the school building, passed the empty football pitch, and checked to make sure no one had followed her before walking into the grove.

Peering into the semi-darkness of the woods, she saw Alec leaning on the thick trunk of an old tree. He straightened when he saw her and took a few steps toward her.

Eleanor glared at him. "How could you let that happen?"

"And by *that* you mean. . . ?" He squinted. "What do you mean?"

"You know what I mean!" said Eleanor with irritation. "How could you let them do that to her?"

"Oooh, you're talking about Debra." He looked at her, puzzled. "Is that why you're here? I thought. . ." He tilted his head.

"You thought what?" Eleanor spread her hands. "That I called you out on a date?"

"No. Wait . . . Actually, I do now," said Alec, pondering. "You never liked Debra. Why would you suddenly care about her? I think you're using her as a reason to see me."

Alec's words caught Eleanor off guard. She blinked.

Alec smirked and drew closer. The smug look on his face stirred Eleanor's blood and brought up the urge to punch him. "You think this is funny?" she said sharply. "She is home with her mother and is getting hungry." Eleanor pushed him away from her. "She might kill her own mother. Her whole family."

"Then maybe you should stop her," said Alec, looking at her seriously. "Isn't that what you do? Kill vampires?"

"You want me to kill her?" Eleanor stared at him. "She would do anything for you."

"I never loved her, she knew that. I didn't get her into this mess," shouted Alec. "She did it all by herself, by trusting Mark, by letting him use her. I told her to stay away from him, and you know what she said?" He lowered his voice. "She said I never treated her as well as he did."

"She was trying to make you jealous. She loves you."

Alec shrugged. "So what? Is that my fault too?" he said indifferently, then added with a crooked smile, "Now she can love me forever."

"This is funny to you?" Eleanor flashed forward and punched him in the chin. Alec flew back a few feet and hit the tree behind him. Eleanor darted to him and raised her hand again, but Alec caught it and pushed it down.

"Don't." His gray eyes gazed into hers. "You might be more experienced, but I'm stronger than you."

Eleanor wrenched her hand out of his and turned away. In a split second, Alec was standing in front of her. He grabbed her by her arms and pressed her against the tree.

"You just got your powers back and still need time to remember how to use them. Fray has been training me for ten years, and from the moment I got the powers, I've been fighting him. He's been teaching me as he taught most of you, as he taught your Craig."

"And in the meantime, he is teaching you to kill people, to be unfeeling like him, to betray people who care about you," said Eleanor, panting from anger.

"This is war," hissed Alec. "I can't save everyone. You're alive, and that's what matters to me." His dangerous glittering eyes were fixed on hers. He put his hand around her neck. Eleanor's hand moved up his spine. Alec closed his eyes from the pleasure, and when he opened them again, his look was softer, happier. He bowed his head, but before his lips could touch hers, she grabbed him by his jacket and threw him aside.

"You know," said Eleanor, walking to him, "Fray never trained me. But I had a few lessons with Samson. You wanna have a go?"

"No." Alec slowly shook his head. "What I'm saying is, I'm not going to be your punching bag. I can fight, too, but I'll never hurt you, you know that."

"Why not? This is war, you said it yourself."

"You know why."

"Because you love me," Eleanor scoffed. "What about Fray? You think he cares about your feelings? He'll kill me the first chance he gets."

"He does, he cares about me. He'd never do that."

Eleanor released a mirthless laugh. "Fray never cared about anyone but himself. He never loved anyone." She frowned. "If he'd known what love is, he would never dare to kill Gabriella." At these words Eleanor realized that, even though she didn't do it knowingly, she had brought the conversation to the right subject, to the reason she wanted to meet Alec in the first place. "I've known him a bit longer than you have," she said, "and believe me, I know him much better. Did you ever ask yourself why he's alone? The man has lived eight hundred years and has no one but vampires. Samson could turn a woman for him, but he never brought one, because he never loved anyone. He had no friends."

"That's not true," said Alec, his eyes burning with anger. "He told me everything. Everyone Fray asked Samson to turn for him ended up dead. Samson killed them. And he had a woman, but she was different, and Fray knew Samson would kill her, too. That's why—"

"Don't say another word," said a voice from between the trees.

It was already dark, and Eleanor couldn't see any more than the man's silhouette. But she didn't need to. She would recognize that voice from a million others.

"Don't you see what she's doing?" said Fray, coming forward. "She's fishing for information."

Eleanor could see him now. "You brought him with you?" She glared at Alec.

But Alec looked as shocked as Eleanor herself. "What the hell are you doing here?" he said, clenching his teeth. "Were you spying on me?"

"I can see you're still in one piece," said Fray, ignoring Alec's question. "You know why? Because she's playing you."

"Stop it. I'm not an idiot, I know she's here for a reason." He turned to Eleanor. "I didn't know. I came alone."

"Yes, you did. But she didn't," said Fray with a gloat.

Eleanor's narrowed eyes peered into the trees behind him. In the light coming from the football pitch, she saw several figures moving toward them. The figures got darker as they walked into the grove, but Eleanor already recognized the one in the middle. Her heart fell.

"She brought her," said Fray, pointing at Hanna, who now stood behind him. She was surrounded by seven vampires.

"She didn't bring me," snapped Hanna. "I came because I knew you would come up with something. I know what a son of a bitch you are."

A blade shone in the hand of the vampire standing next to her. But before he could jab her with it, Fray raised his hand.

"Yes, you're right, little firecracker," he sneered. "I'm full of surprises. Now." He looked at Eleanor. "I came for information, too. I want to know where Samson is and what he's up to."

"Why? Are you scared?" Eleanor started toward him, but Alec grabbed her by the arm and pulled back. Eleanor jerked her hand away. "Don't touch me."

"You'll tell me what he's planning," said Fray furiously, "or I'll kill your Hanna."

Two vampires clutched Hanna's arms. The one behind her gripped her neck, but Hanna managed to swing her head backwards and hit him in the chin.

"You bitch," hissed the vampire, grabbing Hanna by the hair.

Eleanor rushed forward, but Alec caught her again.

Something moved in between the trees. Eleanor stopped. A shadow flashed behind Hanna and the vampires. The next moment, she felt the air shift behind her. It seemed that Alec noticed too, as they both looked back at the same time.

It was Riley. He stood a few steps away from them. Eleanor froze, part of her relieved, the other part abashed, as if she were a criminal caught in the act.

Riley didn't look at her. His eyes were fixed on Fray. "How are you going to kill her?" he asked calmly. "Did you bring the dagger?"

They heard a moan. The vampires clutching Hanna's neck and holding her left arm dropped simultaneously, and Eleanor saw Ruben. The moment Hanna's arm was free, she punched the vampire on her right, jerked her hand out of his grip, and snapped his neck. Ruben killed two more, but he didn't follow when the rest ran away. He pulled Hanna behind him and stepped to Fray.

"Your vampires tortured us for decades," said Ruben, gazing at him. "But they aren't much help now, are they?"

"You just wait. I'll kill you all," growled Fray. He glared at Riley. "Starting with you." He turned his eyes on Eleanor. "This is all your fault. If you hadn't closed the Book . . . I'll make you suffer." He walked to her. "I'll rip your Craig to pieces and make you wa—"

Riley didn't let him finish the word. He flashed forward, and his fist landed on Fray's face.

Fray shuddered and took several steps back. "Is that it?" he laughed. "Is that all you got?"

Riley sent another blow, this time to his chest. Fray flew back and fell on the ground between the trees ten feet away.

Now it was Alec who moved forward. But Eleanor pulled him back. "Let the grown-ups handle this," she said, then added, "Don't worry, he can fight back, he knows how."

Fray got up and walked back to Riley. But to Eleanor's, and everyone else's surprise, Fray didn't hit back. "I'm stronger than you, and you know that," he said, catching his breath. "But I'm not going to fight you."

"Why not?"

"Because he doesn't have it," said Ruben. "It isn't fun without the dagger, is it, Fray?"

Riley glanced at Eleanor and nodded toward the football pitch.

"Get Debra out of the house," Eleanor said to Alec, gazing at him over her shoulder.

Riley crossed to Fray. "You know how badly I want to rip your guts out. But I can't," he said in a stony voice. "If you get near anyone in my family again, I'll crucify you in the backyard of the castle and watch you dry out under the sun, without food or water. I might put your boy next to you, for company." Riley walked away.

"We'll see about that," Fray threw after him. "Your days are numbered."

Eleanor wanted to have a few words with Hanna before getting home, but as they were driving back in separate cars, she didn't get a chance.

Eleanor and Hanna were the first to arrive, and when they walked into the house, Kimberly, who was pacing in front of Kizzy on the couch, rushed to Hanna. "Oh my God. Ruben called to check on me and he told me what happened. Are you okay?" Kimberly, hugged her.

"I'm all right," said Hanna softly. But the moment Kimberly let go of her, she burst out in anger, "Why is it always me? I hate when those bloodsuckers touch me."

A car door slammed. Ruben was the first to show up in the doorway.

"You're dead. You know that, right?" he said, gazing at Eleanor.

A second later Riley stormed in and stopped in front of her. "What the hell did you think you were doing?" he shouted.

"Riley, I'm sorry. I—"

"Are you trying to get yourself killed?" Riley went on. "I made a promise to Craig. Ruben and I gave him our word that we'd keep you safe. You're lucky Fray didn't have the dagger on him. He could've kidnapped Hanna, could've killed her, and done the same to you."

"Riley, we're stuck, we're not getting anywhere. I was just trying to—"

"I know why you went there. And even though I told you not to, you did it anyway." Riley spun to Hanna. "And you—"

"Don't," said Eleanor. "She came only because she didn't want me to go alone."

"You think I don't know that?" said Riley, gazing back at her. "Hanna can be a huge pain in the ass sometimes, but she would never disobey me."

"How did . . . how did you know we were there?" asked Hanna, stuttering.

"That's the thing. I didn't."

"Then how did you find us?"

Riley drew away from Eleanor. "I told you this morning I was going to keep an eye on Fray," he said, lowering his voice. "Kizzy and I saw him drive into the school parking lot. There were a few cars there. All of them had tinted windows and were parked next to each other. Fray approached one of the cars and talked to the driver, and it was obvious the cars had been waiting for him and were full of vampires."

"It wasn't obvious to me, was it?" said Hanna. "As you said, those cars were parked next to each other. I didn't want Alec to see me. My car, standing alone, would strike the eye, so I parked in between them."

Riley shook his head.

"Hanna." Eleanor looked at her, astonished.

"What?" Hanna shrugged. "There are plenty of cars out there with tinted glass, and not all of them belong to vampires, you know."

"Did you see them grab Hanna?" asked Eleanor, looking at Riley.

"No." Riley shook his head. "I didn't see her at all. We retreated. It was a big open place, and we didn't want to expose ourselves. I also didn't want to lose Fray. I knew he didn't come for a walk. It was almost dark and I could go on foot. Since I didn't know how many of them were out there and what they were planning, I called Ruben and sent Kizzy home to stay with Kimberly."

Eleanor's heart throbbed. She realized just how lucky they were that Riley and Ruben had found them. If something had happened to Hanna, she never would've forgiven herself. Her stubbornness could have cost them their lives. Riley was right to be angry with her.

"Riley, I'm so sorry," she said, taking his hand.

"Eleanor, you can't go and do things without telling me. I'm responsible for you, we're all responsible for each other."

"I should've listened to you. I promise, it'll never happen again." Eleanor stepped to Hanna and pulled her into a hug. "I'm sorry," she whispered into her ear. "I put you in danger."

"Don't sweat it," said Hanna, rubbing her back. But when Eleanor let go of her, she burst out again. "It's just, those bastards, they always go for the hair. I hate that."

"All's well that ends well, as people used to say," Ruben quipped. He crossed the room and picked up a bottle of whiskey from the small table loaded with alcohol. "Now we all need a drink."

The front door opened. All of them turned their heads.

"Ned," shrieked Hanna. She dashed toward him and hung from his neck. "I'm so glad you're back."

"I was only gone for two days," said Ned, looking surprised. "You missed me that much?"

"Yes. Today I was ambushed, and I really need . . ." She looked back at everyone, then said, "Comfort. I need your comfort."

Ruben chuckled. "That means the rest of us will need safety belts and earplugs."

Riley rolled his eyes. "Kids," he murmured. "Centuries-old kids."

"Ambushed?" Ned stared at everyone. "What happened?"

They told Ned what happened, avoiding the part where Eleanor and Hanna's wildcat act was Eleanor's idea.

"You think Alec was in on the plan?" asked Ned.

"No," said Eleanor. "When Fray showed up, Alec almost attacked him."

"Maybe he was acting?"

"No," said Hanna. "Eleanor's right. He was shocked, and he kept throwing furious looks at Fray."

"If they didn't plan it, then Fray will think we did," said Ruben. "Fray will think this whole thing was a setup, that we used Eleanor and Hanna as bait to make him bring out the dagger."

"He probably thought it was suspicious us doing nothing this whole time, not going after him, just sitting and waiting for his next attack," said Hanna. "He had nothing to worry about, except Samson. Now . . ."

"*Now*, we're screwed," grumbled Riley. "And I can give back the van, because *now* he'll go into hiding. And he was the one who was supposed to lead us to the Book and the daggers."

"Maybe we shouldn't have left," said Eleanor. "Maybe we should've followed them."

"How? He was there, watching us from behind the building, waiting for us to leave. From now on he'll be watching his own shadow."

"I can do a locator spell," said Kizzy.

"On what? He's a Hunter, a personal item wouldn't work. We'll need his blood to do it. Same goes for Alec. We had some of Fray's blood left after the Book was closed, but Samson used it during those years."

"So, Ned," sighed Ruben, handing everyone a glass of whiskey. "How was your trip? Did you find anything?"

"Sorry, but there isn't much I can tell," said Ned, dropping down on the couch. Hanna curled up next to him. "I went to the historical society," he continued. "They said they don't know who the original owner was—the old records were lost a long time ago. But for the last fifty-seven years, it belonged to William Thatcher, who didn't live there himself. He renovated the mansion twice, in 1969 and 2002. The Maysons bought the house ten years ago.

"When I came back from the historical society, I saw that both cars parked in the front yard in the morning were gone. There was no one in the mansion. I snuck in through the second floor window. The only thing I can say for sure is that Eleanor was right —the house belonged to Fray, and I think it still does. The furniture, all the antique items, the weapons. His weapons. Remember the axes and the sword with his initials engraved on them? They were there, hanging on the wall."

There was a deep silence. After a moment of absently looking at the floor, Hanna said, "Fray actually has his own house. A mansion. That's something I would really like to see."

There was another pause, until Eleanor broke the silence. "Ned, I sent you a message this morning."

"Yeah, about that. I found the room Alec's picture was taken in. The paintings were still hanging on the wall, but the drawing was gone."

"Dammit." Eleanor crossed her hands over her chest, exasperated.

"So you didn't find anything suspicious?" asked Riley.

"No." Ned shook his head. "He has a big cellar. I checked it out. I tried to pull the wine shelves, thinking there might be some secret door or something. I even went Indiana Jones and pushed some bricks in the wall, you know, just in case, but nothing happened."

Eleanor fell into the armchair. "And we're right back where we started," she huffed.

"I think we need another drink," said Ruben.

Chapter Twenty-Five

FRAY AND ALEC looked at each other, but the moment Alec opened his mouth to speak, Fray raised his hand, stopping him. "We need to make sure that they're all gone," he said, beckoning toward the football pitch.

Standing in the corner of the school building, Fray saw Hanna's and Eleanor's cars take off. After exchanging a few words, Riley and Ruben got into the black Jeep and sped away as well.

"We can't go back to the house," said Fray as he and Alec walked to the parking lot. "We'll stay with the vampires. Get in the car."

Alec didn't move. "Why did you follow me?"

"I said get in the car. We have to go."

"Fine." Alec threw him a dark look and marched to his car.

"Not yours. Mine," said Fray.

"I can't. There's something I need to do first."

"I said we have to leave now. That estate is the only safe house we have here. If they see you—"

"If someone tails me, I'll notice."

"Like you noticed the vampires following you here?"

Alec dashed back to Fray. "Oh, I saw that car," he said furiously. "But I thought you sent them to keep an eye on me in case something went wrong, not spy on me and then call you and your escort."

"I have a feeling you've got something to say," said Fray. "Why wait?" Though he didn't doubt Alec's loyalty, he was afraid Alec's obsession with Eleanor might change him, sow wrong thoughts into his mind, make him question their ambitions.

"All right," said Alec. "Why didn't you hit him back? You're stronger than he is."

"Yes, I'm stronger, and I wanted to fight him. I wasn't in danger," said Fray in a low but firm voice. "The problem is that all those things Riley threatened to do—they could do it to you."

"They wouldn't. When Eleanor was about to stab me in the heart, Ruben stopped her."

"Ruben stopped her because he didn't want Eleanor to get dirty, he didn't want her to break the 'never torture humans' rule. But after what we did to Ruben during all those decades, he would gladly stab you himself. He and Riley are old enough not only to break the rules, but to create their own. Or they might take you away and lock you up for the simple reason of making me weaker."

"And you couldn't let that happen," said Alec, heavy irony in his voice.

"Of course I couldn't," said Fray, opening the car door.

"Why? Because you care about me? Or because you need me?"

"Both." Fray closed the door again and drew closer to Alec. "What is this? Is it because of what she said to you? Alec, she needed information and was trying to get under your skin."

"No, it's not that. It's . . ." Alec hesitated.

"What? Spit it out."

"They're like a real family," said Alec carefully. "They care about each other."

"And we're not?"

"I don't know. Sometimes I think you only took care of me because you needed me."

"How can you say that? You're the only human I ever turned. I gave you everything. I've always shared my thoughts, my desires with you, discussed my plans with you."

"For now, yes. But what's going to happen when your Joanne wakes up? Will I still fit? Will my opinion still matter? Or will I be left alone again?"

Fray knew what Alec wanted to hear. Like any other human, he didn't want to be alone, he wanted to be loved, know that he was an important part of someone's life. "You are like a son to me," he said, and he saw Alec's look soften. "And, as I've shown you in the past ten years," Fray continued, "I'm nothing like your alcoholic parents. It's time for you to let go of your past. I'm immortal and you'll never be alone again. Even when Joanne is back, I'll feel the same way. The thing is," Fray put his hand on Alec's shoulder, "it's you I'm worried about."

"What the hell is that supposed to mean?"

"You and I, we were a family. But now that Eleanor's back, she's all you care about. Don't you see what she's doing? She's turning you against me. She has awakened this aggression in you that I never knew you had. It's a weapon." Fray walked back to his car and opened the door again. "Turn it on the right target. I'm not your enemy."

As Fray took off, he glanced into the mirror. Alec hadn't moved. He was looking after Fray. Leaving him confused, standing alone in the middle of that big, dark, empty parking lot, made Fray's heart ache. It reminded him of the days when Alec was a boy and Fray came to visit him at the mansion. His visits were short and Alec begged him to stay longer. But he couldn't, and every time he left, Alec was standing and looking after the speeding car, like he did now.

Everyone has a weakness. Fray never knew Alec was his until that moment. He and Alec were close; there was a bond between them. But the way he felt now was different, new. He never cared about anybody like this before.

He had Joanne. But Joanne wasn't human. Watching Alec, that mortal boy, grow up, teaching him to be a strong, confident man, making sure he was safe, was a new experience. Alec needed him. Joanne was a two hundred and thirty-three year old vampire when they met. What drew them to each other was passion and their love of freedom and power. The only thing Joanne had to know was how to avoid the Hunters, and Fray showed her their pictures and taught her how to stay away from them.

Of course, there was always a chance of losing her. And once, he nearly did.

Even before meeting Fray and learning about the Hunters, Joanne had always been careful, always covered her tracks. However, one day she almost got killed. By Eleanor.

It was a couple of years after Fray had found her. Joanne was always on the move, and so was Fray. Communication was a problem, and they needed some permanent place where they could meet or leave messages for each other. Their first house was hours from the castle. For security reasons, Joanne always went there alone, and nobody knew about its existence. The house had a field in front of it and a forest behind it. Joanne liked the place. It had an extra exit through the basement leading to the woods, where she could walk even at daytime, if it wasn't too sunny.

Fray had never had his own place, and it felt good to have one. Joanne was the first member of his own family, and the time they spent there together was exciting for both of them.

That evening he was going to meet Joanne. He was in his room, preparing to leave. He heard a neighing, and as he looked out of the window, he saw Craig and Eleanor mount their horses and gallop into the woods. He assumed they were going for a ride, but when he came out of his room, he heard Gabriella's voice coming from Samson's study.

"Are you sure that the two of them will be enough?" she asked. "Maybe I should go with them?"

"I'm sure," said Samson. "There is nothing big there."

"What's going on?" asked Fray, walking in.

"There was an attack," said Samson. "It's a full moon, it's probably just a couple of werewolves."

"Where?"

"Not far, only two or three hours away."

That's how far his house was from the Castle. Trying to hide his anxiety, Fray asked again, "Where?"

"Why? As I said, there's nothing big." Samson got up from his desk. "Besides, didn't you say you were leaving?"

"I was about to, and that's why I ask. It might be somewhere on my way."

"Here," said Samson, pointing at the small red stain on the still open Map. "Next to the Clear Pond."

As Fray looked at the location, the blood rushed to his head.

"Fray." He heard Gabriella's voice.

His thoughts buzzing, he slowly turned his head to look at her.

"Is that where you're going?" she asked.

"Yes." He nodded. "If I catch the wolves, or whoever they are, I'll let you know." He threw a glance at Samson's bracelet and dashed out of the room.

When Fray arrived at the house, Joanne wasn't there. He looked up at the moon. The Hunters being summoned wasn't her fault, he was sure of that. He knew how careful Joanne was, he knew if she was hungry and she killed someone, she wouldn't just leave the body lying around. She loved it here and she would never do anything to compromise this place.

Standing in the middle of the field and listening to the silence, Fray looked around. Craig and Eleanor would've had to move fast, but if they were somewhere close, they wouldn't be able to gallop through the dense woods. He left his horse next to the barn and went on foot to search the surrounding area. He ran across the field, and as he reached the trees, he heard a noise. He stopped, trying to determine the direction the noise was coming from. Then he heard it again. It wasn't close, but he was sure he'd heard a growl. He ran again, but after about hundred yards he realized that the noise, which was much louder now, was moving toward him.

Fray didn't want to be seen, so he got as close as possible and stopped behind a thick trunk. A few seconds later, two pairs of yellow eyes shone in the darkness. A black shadow was running away from them. He knew that it was Joanne, but before he could make a move, he heard Craig's voice.

"Eleanor, go get her. I'll take care of these two," said Craig.

Both werewolves turned at the sound of his voice. Snarling, they leapt at him. But Craig was too quick. He kicked one away and clutched the other one by the throat, slamming it to the ground. Eleanor flashed away, and Fray lost her from view. Following the noise, he realized Joanne was running toward the house. He guessed why. She wanted to get in and then get out through the basement and into the woods.

When he reached the field, he finally saw them. Eleanor was only ten feet away from Joanne. Joanne looked back at her, and in that moment Fray darted forth, stopping in front of Eleanor.

"Fray." Eleanor gazed at him, angry and astonished at the same time. "What are you doing?" she shouted. "I almost had her."

"I got this. Go help Craig," said Fray. Eleanor didn't move, still staring at him. "Go," said Fray firmly. Running after Joanne he glanced back to make sure Eleanor was gone. A few minutes later, he sent her the signal. He pressed his ring once to his coin and twice to Eleanor's, which meant that the job was done.

Later, Joanne told Fray that when she was in the village, she'd heard news of animal attacks in the woods. In the last two months one hunter and two lumberjacks had died and one was injured. The surviving lumberjack had said that he and his friend were attacked by a mysterious animal the previous night, which looked like a wolf but was too big, and his paws looked like hands. *Fear has big eyes*, people said, and not many believed him, but to Joanne it was clear that there was a werewolf in the woods. The Hunters weren't that far away, and if there was a witch nearby, it wouldn't take long for them to show up. Trying to keep her new home safe, and hoping it wasn't too late to prevent the Hunters appearance, Joanne decided to find the wolf and kill it herself.

She found the wolf on the last night of the full moon, but to her surprise it wasn't alone. There were two of them, with the Hunters in tow.

Chapter Twenty-Six

"OH MY GOD," exhaled Eleanor, barely awake, her eyes still closed. "He was there." She opened her eyes and sat up. The dream she just had was almost the same as the previous ones. It had only one difference. She was chasing the same woman in a black dress. When she grabbed the vampire by her shoulder, she vanished, like before, but this time, the moment it happened, Fray appeared in front of Eleanor. Only his face. And he was laughing.

She flung herself from the bed. Now she was sure it wasn't just a dream. She remembered that day, and that place, and everything that had happened there. "That's it. It has to be," she muttered, pulling on her clothes.

When she came downstairs, Lindsey was already in the kitchen.

"Good morning," he said, putting down the newspaper.

"Hi, Dad."

"You're up early. Going somewhere?"

"To Hanna's." She couldn't wait to run to the others and tell them about her discovery, and she was glad to see Lindsey get up and walk to the door.

"The coffee's ready," he said, smiling on his way out.

"Thanks," said Eleanor. She took a cup, but as soon as her father closed the door behind him, she put it down and grabbed her car keys. The moment Lindsey's car left the driveway, she rushed out. After what happened the previous night, Eleanor was sure that Fray and Alec were nowhere around and her father wasn't in any danger at the moment, but she still drove to his work taking roundabout ways, and when he safely entered the building, she sped away.

Eleanor drove into the yard and stopped the car right before the first step of the porch stairs. She dashed into the house and stopped abruptly in the kitchen doorway.

They were having their morning coffee. Eleanor supposed they had been sitting around the table, but it seemed the gnashing of her car brakes had alarmed them. Still holding their cups, they were all on their feet, staring out of the window. Hanna was the first to turn around.

"What's wrong?" she asked, looking startled.

Eleanor looked from her to Ned, then at Ruben and Kimberly, and then stopped, her eyes on Riley. "I think I know where they are," she said, her heart hammering with excitement.

"Who?" Riley raised his eyebrows, looking lost. But when Eleanor rolled her eyes, his face changed. "The bodies?" he asked, astonished. "Where?"

"Really?" asked Ruben, coming forward.

"Wait." Eleanor stuck out her index finger. "I need to check something." She darted upstairs and flew into the study. She pulled rolls of maps from the shelf and began unrolling them one after another. When she found the one she was looking for, she stared at it for a moment, then grabbed it and hurried back.

The others were now waiting for her in the living room. Eleanor picked up the antique vase from the coffee table and tossed it into Hanna's hands, then she squatted in front of the table and put the map down.

"What's the whole hubbub about?" came Kizzy's sleepy voice from the top of the stairs.

"We don't know yet," said Riley.

"Kizzy, come down," said Eleanor. "You need to hear this, too."

"I'm all ears," said Kizzy, climbing down the stairs. Yawning, she went to the kitchen.

Eleanor glanced at the others. "Look," she said, pointing at the map. "You see this field?"

"That's the one where the vampires grabbed Samson," said Ruben.

"Right. This is the field." Eleanor moved her finger to the dots, representing houses. "This is the village, the name of which I don't remember. Those are the woods and this is the way to the Castle. Right?"

"Right," said Riley. "And?"

"Hanna, remember I said it might be the same field? The same one I saw in my dream?"

"Is it?" asked Hanna.

"Yes, I'm sure of it now."

"What dream?" came Kizzy's annoyed voice from the kitchen. "If you want me to understand this," she said, showing up with a large mug in her hands, "you'll have to start from the beginning."

"Since the day I came back, I keep having this same dream. I'm chasing that woman from the picture, but every time I'm about to catch her, she vanishes. Only once did I get to see her face. Last night I had it again, but this time it was a little different. This time, when I was about to catch her, Fray showed up out of nowhere and blocked my way. Then he looked me in the eyes and laughed. When I woke up, I . . . It wasn't just a dream. It really happened." Eleanor looked at Hanna. "I didn't kill her. Fray stopped me. He helped her escape."

"Okay," said Ruben. "This proves one more time that Fray knew her. But what does it have to do with the bodies?"

"You don't understand," said Eleanor. "I remembered everything that happened that night. Samson sent me and Craig to hunt down those werewolves. Fray shouldn't have been there at all. When he suddenly jumped out of the woods, it surprised me, because there wasn't much to do and he never hunted with me and Craig. He said he'd deal with the vampire and told me to go help Craig kill the werewolves. When I was leaving, I looked back. There was a house at the end of the field, and the woman ran to it and went inside."

"You mean, it was her house?" asked Ned.

"Or it was Fray's, and she was invited in." Eleanor looked at Riley. "We need to check that place. That's where the house was, and that's where they grabbed Samson."

"Eleanor, he went back. He checked it and didn't find anything. If there was a house, Samson would've mentioned it."

"He wrote in the journal that something made him stop at that field, and it didn't look like the vampires were there by accident. Samson felt something there."

"Just because you can't see the house doesn't mean it's not there," said Kizzy.

"What are you saying, Kizzy?" asked Ruben.

"I'm saying it might be cloaked."

Everybody stared at her. Then, shaking his head, Riley said, "No. Samson knows what a cloaking spell is, he would—"

"He would guess, yes," said Eleanor, "if he knew there was a house there before." Eleanor jumped to her feet. "Let's go."

"Wait," said Riley. "How big was the house?"

"Not big," said Eleanor, pondering. "It was tall, but it only had one story, I think."

"One story? Could it fit fifty coffins?"

"I don't know," said Eleanor, getting frustrated. "Maybe it has a basement? And maybe the bodies aren't in coffins."

"You mean he just piled them up on the floor?" asked Kimberly.

Eleanor shrugged. "Why not? It's Fray. Anything's possible." She gazed at Riley. "It's not like you have a better clue."

"No, I don't. I just don't want your expectations to be too high," said Riley. "Let's not waste time." He glanced at Kizzy, who was still in her silky night robe. "Go put some clothes on, we're leaving. Ruben, you're coming, too."

"I think we should all go," said Hanna. "What if Eleanor's right?"

"Yeah," said Ned. "What if the bodies are really there? In that case," he shrugged, "it's Fray. You never know what to expect."

"I'm not staying here alone," protested Kimberly.

"Actually," said Kizzy, who was already at the top of the stairs, "we might need Kimberly."

"Me? Really?" Kimberly stared at her, surprised.

Kizzy nodded once and headed to her room.

"What for?" Ruben yelled after her, but in response Kizzy just slammed the door behind her.

Riley said, "Let's say Eleanor's right. If so, then we have to be careful. We can't be seen. It means we have to do this quickly, while the sun is up and shining and vampires can't follow us."

"We have to find the shortest route," said Ruben. "This map is old. I'll print a new and more detailed one."

A few minutes later, they were all ready to leave. Except Kizzy.

"Kizzy," called Eleanor from the bottom of the stairs. There was no answer. Eleanor darted upstairs. When she opened the door to Kizzy's bedroom, she heard the sound of falling water. "Kizzy," called Eleanor again.

"I'm taking a shower," came Kizzy's voice from the bathroom.

Eleanor shook her head. "Seriously?" she muttered under her breath, then said louder, "Everybody is already in the cars. Hurry up."

Riley, Ruben, and Kimberly were in the Jeep. Passing by Hanna's car, Eleanor glanced at Ned, who had already started the engine. "You can turn it off. Her highness is taking a shower."

"Thank God we don't have a bathtub in that room," said Hanna, sitting next to Ned.

Eleanor slid into the backseat of the Jeep. Riley was setting the GPS and Ruben was studying the map, looking for shortcuts.

"How are you doing?" Eleanor asked Kimberly, whose look was fixed at the back of Ruben's seat.

"I'm okay. It's nice to get out of the house. I always liked road trips." She turned her eyes to Eleanor. "What do you think Kizzy needs me for?"

"I don't know. We didn't get a chance to ask, did we?" said Eleanor grumpily. "Don't worry. Whatever it is, we won't let her do it without your permission."

"I'm not worried." Kimberly glanced out of the window. "I want them dead, and I'll do anything to help."

Her joyless voice was so confident, it made Eleanor's chest hurt. For nine years Amanda was Kimberly's best friend, her source of joy and comfort. But after becoming Eleanor, all she brought into her life was fear and death. Kimberly, who'd always called Hanna's tough actions showing off, was now training to fight off a vampire attack. It was Eleanor who was responsible for turning Kimberly's life into a nightmare with monsters who killed her mother and almost killed her. Who knew what would happen next? Whatever it was, she'd do everything in her power to keep Kimberly safe. She would always be there for Kimberly, but Eleanor believed that it would be Ruben, with his love and solace, who would help her get through this grievous time.

Eleanor looked at the front door. They'd been waiting for fifteen minutes now, and Eleanor wanted to go back in and throw Kizzy out. She glared at Ruben in the rear view mirror.

Ruben looked back at her. "Turn your sound on before you choke."

"What the hell is she doing in there?" Eleanor burst out. "We don't have time for this."

"And it's my fault because. . . ?"

Eleanor turned her rage to Riley. "You need to talk to her, explain to her that this isn't a vacation, that we didn't call her here to—"

The front door opened.

The moment Kizzy came out, Ruben started the car, asking, "Kimberly, is your seatbelt on?" as he stepped on the gas.

Now that they were finally moving, Eleanor's thoughts went back to the point of their journey. This time, each thought had a question mark at the end. Was it wise to go all together? What if there was a trap? Or what if there was nothing there at all? Suddenly, all her theories seemed feeble and unfounded. Yes, she'd seen a house at the end of that small field, and it probably belonged to Fray, but there was nothing special about it, and Riley was right; it wasn't big enough to hold fifty coffins.

Eleanor's phone vibrated. It was a message from Alec. "Thank God," she whispered as she read the short text.

"What is it?" asked Kimberly.

"It's Alec. He says he took care of Debra. He got her out of the house before she could hurt anyone. Her family is safe."

"What's going to happen to her?" asked Kimberly. "Does this mean that the next time you see her, you'll have to kill her?"

Eleanor sighed. "I don't know," she said, slowly shaking her head. "I can't think about it right now."

Her phone vibrated again. It was Craig. "Hi," she said quietly.

"Hi. How are you?" asked Craig.

Eleanor closed her eyes, imagining his face. "I'm fine. I'm in your car." She opened her eyes again. "We're driving to Clear Pond."

"Why? What's in Clear Pond?"

"There is a place in the woods we want to check out. I remembered that once, when you and I were hunting there, something happened. It might be important. We'll let you know if we find anything. Where are you?"

"We're in Egypt. Eleanor, the place we're going next," Craig hesitated, "it's the crucial point of our journey. What I'm going to do, it's not just about the mission, it's a big deal for us—I mean, for you and me. I needed to hear your voice." He paused for a second, then said, "To do this, I need to know that you still trust me."

"I do, I trust you," said Eleanor softly. "Whatever it is you're going to do, I'm with you. You have my full support."

"Thank you," said Craig. She heard relief in his voice. "If you don't hear from me for a while, don't worry. We might have no reception for some time. And, Eleanor, when this is all over, nothing will part us again. Nothing."

"You promise?"

"I promise." Eleanor could feel him smile. "I love you," said Craig.

"I love you too."

Eleanor clutched the phone in her hands. Her insides went cold. She didn't even know what she'd given her blessing to. What if it was something dangerous?

Ruben's eyes were looking at her in the rear view mirror. "Tell me I did the right thing," said Eleanor.

"You did the right thing," said Ruben, and he turned his eyes back to the road.

With shortcuts, it took them about an hour and a half to get to Clear Pond. From there, they headed to where the village was supposed to be.

They were driving down the main road when Riley, sitting with the map in his hand, pointed at an unpaved road. "This one," he said to Ruben. As Ruben turned left, Eleanor looked back at Hanna's car. At the same moment, Hanna's hand stuck out the window, thumb up.

The road narrowed and turned into the woods. As the car slid into the shade of the trees, a big red sign rose in front of them: PRIVATE PROPERTY. NO TRESPASSING. Ruben kept driving, and shortly they came upon a large clearing, with a few extremely old, abandoned houses. They stopped the cars and got out.

"I thought this place would be a town by now," said Eleanor.

"He bought the woods around your old house," said Riley. "If he bought this too, then you might be right, there's something here."

"I'll check out the surroundings," said Ned and flashed away.

Hanna headed to one of the houses. She tried the door, but it was locked. She went to the window. To block the sunlight, she cupped her hands around her face and looked in through the dirty glass. "Judging by the utensils, nobody's lived here for at least a hundred years," she said, walking back.

"There are no coffins here," said Kimberly, who was peering into the window of a house on the other side of the road. "Everything is so old," she said with excitement. "Can I go inside?" she asked Ruben, her eyes sparkling.

"No," answered Riley, before Ruben could say anything. "This might be his. We can't leave traces."

"Kimberly." Ruben stepped to her and pulled her away from the window. "After we kick Fray's butt, we'll come here and you can disassemble this place into tiny little parts." He beamed at her. "I'll help you."

Eleanor and Hanna glanced at each other. Since her mother's death, this was Kimberly's first positive emotion. "Can I come, too?" asked Eleanor, grinning.

Kizzy was standing in the middle of the road, her eyes closed.

"Kizzy, do you feel anything?" asked Riley.

Lifting her eyelids, she slowly shook her head. "No. There's no magical energy here."

"Then let's not waste time," said Riley. As he started toward his car, he heard Ned's voice.

"There's no road from here," yelled Ned, coming out from the woods. "We'll have to go on foot."

There was no trail, either.

"How are you doing?" Eleanor asked Kimberly after about ten minutes of wriggling between trees.

"Thanks to Hanna, I'm fine," said Kimberly, and she looked down at her feet. "She lent me a pair of her sneakers." Pressing her lips together, she glanced at Eleanor. "I know, I'm slowing you down. It would be much faster if you used your powers."

"Nah," said Eleanor. "These woods are dense, the powers wouldn't help much. Besides, you aren't the last one in line." Eleanor waved her head backward.

Kimberly looked back at Kizzy, then said with a smile, "You don't like her much, do you?"

"What? No, no," said Eleanor, and threw a quick glance at Ruben, who was just a step away from them and could hear their conversation. Eleanor's dislike toward Kizzy was a protective reaction. Kizzy's undisguised interest in Ruben alarmed her. Kimberly was too vulnerable at the moment, and if she suddenly found out about their past and Kizzy's intentions, it could mess things up between Kimberly and Ruben. Eleanor trusted Ruben, she knew that he'd never do anything to hurt Kimberly, but she couldn't say the same about Kizzy. "It's not that I don't like her," continued Eleanor. "It's just, sometimes she's so . . . you know . . . slow, it pisses me off."

It wasn't a long hike. Nearly forty minutes later, they came out in front of a field.

"Is this the place?" asked Riley, glancing at Eleanor.

"It's not as big as I remember," said Eleanor. "But, yes, this is it."

The field was a bit smaller than a football pitch, and it was empty. There was nothing but tall grass.

Kizzy looked around, her eyes narrowed. "Where was the house?" she asked.

Eleanor pointed at the right end of the field. "There."

They walked closer and stopped, facing the trees.

Kizzy stepped forward and put her hands before her. She held them palms out, her fingers slowly moving like she was feeling the air.

Eleanor's heart hammered. She gazed at the others. They were standing in a row at the edge of the field, and by the looks on their faces, she could tell they felt the same way.

"Anything?" asked Riley as Kizzy lowered her hands a couple minutes later.

Kizzy turned her head and glanced at him with glassy eyes. She didn't answer but took a few steps back into the grass and stopped again. She stood there another minute, this time with her eyes closed, then turned around. "I knew it," she murmured under her breath.

"Knew what?" asked Riley.

She looked at him absently, not seeming to hear him.

"Oh God." Eleanor drew in small, quiet gasp. She moved closer to Kizzy and said a little louder, "They're here, aren't they?"

Barely nodding, Kizzy said, "I think they are. I started feeling it a while ago."

"Feeling what?"

"The power," said Kizzy. "It's enormous." She looked at Riley. "Ten times stronger than all of yours combined."

"So, they're here. It's just that we can't see them," said Ruben, looking stunned. "Kizzy, can you do it? Can you break the spell?"

"Yes. But it's not a simple cloaking spell. This veil is strong, as I thought it would be. A simple cloaking spell wouldn't last long."

"What do you need for that?" asked Hanna. "Kizzy, you didn't bring anything with you," she said with a little panic in her voice. "How are you going to do this?"

"I brought everything I need," said Kizzy confidently. "This is a strong spell and it's sealed with blood, as I supposed it would be if we found it. What I couldn't be sure was what kind of blood they would've used. To undo the spell, I'll need my power and the same kind of blood."

"But if you don't know what kind—" started Eleanor.

"That's why I brought all I had at hand," said Kizzy with a sly smile. She pointed at Riley, "The Hunter's blood," then at herself, "the witch's blood," and then at Kimberly, "and pure, non-supernatural, human blood."

Ruben took Kimberly's hand. "Don't worry. It's just a few drops." He gazed at Kizzy. "Isn't it?"

Kizzy rolled her eyes.

"Can you all stop saying that?" said Kimberly, throwing her hands in the air. "I'm not worried. And I want to help."

"Let's try mine first," said Riley, pulling a jackknife out of his pocket.

Kizzy walked back to the edge of the field. Facing the woods, she closed her eyes and began chanting. It took a long moment before she turned to Riley. As Riley cut his palm, she took his hand and, holding it palm down, said louder:

Et destruam parietem. Revelare tuum secretum.

The air before them rippled. Kizzy must've felt it, as her eyes flew open. Holding her breath, Eleanor took a few steps forward. But that was it, one short moment, like a mirage, and then everything went back to normal.

"Maybe it needs more blood?" asked Riley.

"No. That's not it," said Kizzy, looking puzzled. She took the knife from Riley, then said, "Step back." Riley stepped away. Kizzy deftly ran the blade across her palm and dropped the knife. As the blood from her hand dripped down, she repeated the incantation. The air rippled again. But just like the first time, after a few seconds the waves were gone.

From the back pocket of her jeans, Kizzy pulled out a thin rectangular package. She ripped the plastic, pulled the bandage out of it, and pressed it to her palm. When she looked up, Kimberly was already standing next to her. Kizzy picked up the knife. "Do you want me to help you?" she asked arrogantly.

Eleanor didn't like that idea, and neither did Ruben, she could read it on his frowning face. The fact that Kimberly had to cut herself made Eleanor feel bad enough without seeing Kizzy put extra effort into it.

"No, thanks," said Kimberly. "I think I better do it myself."

"As you wish," said Kizzy, handing over the knife.

Kimberly bit her lip and pressed the blade to her palm. As she pulled the knife, she winced, then she outstretched her hand and turned it palm down. Kizzy closed her eyes and repeated the incantation. But the effect was absolutely the same.

Eleanor heard the sighs of disappointment. Kizzy got another bandage out of her pocket.

"Thanks," said Ruben, taking it out of her hand. He ripped open the package and put the bandage on Kimberly's still bleeding wound.

"So, what do we do now?" asked Hanna, looking from one to another.

"Kizzy, what do you think is wrong?" asked Riley. "Is it the blood? Or a lack of power? I mean, maybe the spell wasn't done by one witch. Maybe there were two of them, or more."

"No," said Kizzy, musing. "It's not the power." She crossed her arms over her chest and began walking back and forth with a concentrated look on her face.

"It might be a different kind of blood," suggested Hanna. "Vampire blood, for example."

Kizzy shook her head. "The blood is working. It's something else," she said, absently staring at Hanna. She stopped, and her eyes came to focus. "Here's a creepy thought. What if there's a witch sitting behind that veil and fighting me?"

Ned, who was sitting under the tree, got up. "You think someone's been sitting there this whole time to guard the bodies?"

"No. Not this whole time. But it's possible Fray took extra precautions after you got your powers back."

"Actually," said Eleanor, "it seems pretty weird that nothing stopped us on our way up here. No spells, no traps. It's not like Fray."

"I don't think it's weird," said Ruben. "I think he's just sure that, if we hadn't managed to find this place in a hundred and sixty-two years, we're incapable of doing it in a couple of weeks. Besides, the place is invisible. Now that we have our powers back, nothing can stop us. Traps and barriers would only attract attention. It would be a hint."

Kimberly cleared her throat. "I know I'm an amateur at all this," she said, fiddling with a piece of grass in her hand, "but I was thinking . . . as Kizzy said, the blood is working. But what if we're using it wrong?"

"What do you mean, *wrong*?" Kizzy glared at her.

Kimberly looked at the others. "If they used only one kind of blood, for example the Hunters', then my blood shouldn't have any effect on it at all. Or Kizzy's. But it does." She looked back at Kizzy. "What I'm saying is, maybe we should do it at the same time. What if the witch, the one who did the spell, used all three kinds of blood together?"

"It makes sense," said Riley, "and, it doesn't hurt to try."

Kimberly squeezed her bandage.

"I'm sorry," said Riley. He put his hand on her shoulder and stretched his lips into a guilty smile. "Is it healing?"

His funny expression made Kimberly laugh. "I'm not a Hunter, you know. But, don't worry, it will at some point."

"Wait," said Kizzy. "If Kimberly's theory is right, then it should have worked already. When she shed her blood, mine and Riley's were already there."

Ruben walked out from the grass and picked the knife up from the ground. "No. Riley's wasn't," he said calmly. "Because a Hunter's blood dries very fast." He looked down at the three blood spots. "By the time Kimberly shed her blood, Riley's was crystallized." He rubbed the dry stain with the tip of his shoe. Ruben pressed the blade to his palm and squeezed it. "Let's try it again." He yanked the knife out of his hand.

Standing next to him, Kizzy began chanting. Once again, the

air rippled, but this time the rippling didn't stop. The waves grew bigger and thinner, and then they were gone. All of them stared at the new view, which the vanished veil left behind—a tall, old, one-story house.

"It worked," shrieked Hanna.

"Here it is," said Riley, looking at beaming Eleanor. "You were right."

"Let's see what's inside," said Ruben.

But as he took a step, Kimberly pulled him back. "Guys," she called faintly, and when they all turned their eyes on her, she said, "Look," and pointed at the field behind them.

Eleanor's blood froze. "Oh my God," she gasped.

"Holy crap," mattered Hanna.

All of them, standing side by side, stared at the field. The grass wasn't there anymore, only earth. On which, in straight rows, stood about fifty stone coffins.

"We did it," said Eleanor, looking at the others. "We found them." But when nobody shared her excitement, she looked back at the coffins, and her teeth clenched.

"Holy shit," muttered Hanna. She moved forward. So did Ruben. Walking between the tombs, Hanna counted, "One, two, three, four . . ."

"Dammit," cursed Riley through gritted teeth.

"Eleven," said Ruben darkly. "There are eleven."

The lids of eleven tombs were open. And they were empty.

∽

"IT'S HERE," said Samson.

"Where?" asked Craig. He stood in the middle of the desert, his boots sunken into the hot sand. Craig pulled his sunglasses up on top of his headdress and looked around. There was nothing.

Samson, who was only a few steps away, said quietly, "Right

here. It took me many years to find this place." Then he touched the air and began speaking words Craig could not understand.

> *Gaara kum,*
> *Gaara cutto,*
> *Met Gaara.*
> *Shahak citto te rumm*
> *De Retto de Hrumma.*
> *Pilla de rok*
> *Pitta de hurach.*

Just like when he touched the veil around the castle, an arch opened in front of them. The view beyond it made Craig's heart throb. Samson walked through the arch, and so did Craig. After a few steps, they stopped before a tall stone door of a big, sand-colored temple. The door was covered with symbols familiar to both, except Samson was the only one who could read them.

"Are you nervous?" asked Samson.

"I can't feel my legs," muttered Craig.

"Yeah," said Samson, "I'm nervous, too."

He drew closer to the door, then pulled the wooden box out of the bag and took the golden disc—the Key—out of it. On the right side of the wide, stone door frame was a horizontal slit. As Samson pushed the disc into the keyhole, a strip of silver light shot out of it, and the disc began rotating. After a short moment, they heard a click. The light was gone and so was the Key. Then there was a rattle, and the heavy stone door moved aside, rasping against the sand. They looked into the darkness ahead, and all they could see was the golden glow of a great pentacle.

"Are you ready?" asked Samson, and when Craig nodded, he smiled. "Good. Let's go meet the Higher Powers."

Also by Lana Melyan

LANA MELYAN

FORGED BY FATE
Trilogy

Book 1 — Wolf Cursed

Book 2 — Hybrid Born

Book 3 — Heir Chosen

THE WEIGHT OF MAGIC series

9 Episodes

1. The First Wave
2. The Legacy
3. The First Spell
4. The Family Tree
5. The First Fight
6. The Last Bell
7. The Sacrifice
8. The Last Secret
9. The Call of Blood

BELLS and SPELLS

Romantic Christmas adventure

Novella

Follow Lana Melyan on Amazon for new release alerts

Visit Lana Melyan's website lanamelyan.com to subscribe to the mailing list and be the first to learn about new releases and discounts.

Printed in Great Britain
by Amazon